Callie possessed a [...]
others' feelings. [...] one
terrible exception, Callie had
found it to be true. She'd learned to
observe people. And saw what
they needed, what she could do
to bring a smile or ease a worry.

As they strolled along the tree-lined walk toward
town, she decided to give that strategy a try.
"You're an excellent carpenter, Mr. Smith."

He took her arm and a jolt of electricity shot
through her. "Watch your step," he said in a calm
voice, but the gaze he shot her said he'd felt that
same wild reaction. "Carpentry comes easy to me,"
he said, "like building a nest comes easy to you."

Once past the hump in the walk, he released his
hold on her, leaving her feeling strangely bereft.
"Building a nest?"

"Yes, making a home, a welcoming place for
friends like Elise, even a stranger like myself.
That's a gift." His eyes warmed. "I've seen my
share of places and the people who live there.
Hospitality like yours isn't something you see
every day."

Everything inside her turned to jelly. Why did this
man have such an effect on her?

Books by Janet Dean

Love Inspired Historical

Courting Miss Adelaide
Courting the Doctor's Daughter
The Substitute Bride
Wanted: A Family

JANET DEAN

grew up in a family that cherished the past and had a strong creative streak. Her father recounted wonderful stories, like his father before him. The tales they told instilled in Janet a love of history and the desire to write. She married her college sweetheart and taught first grade before leaving to rear two daughters. As her daughters grew, they watched *Little House on the Prairie,* reawakening Janet's love of American history and the stories of strong men and women of faith who built this country. Janet eagerly turned to inspirational historical romance, and she loves spinning stories for Love Inspired Historical. When she isn't writing, Janet stamps greeting cards, plays golf and bridge, and is never without a book to read. The Deans love to travel and to spend time with family.

WANTED:
A Family

JANET DEAN

Steeple
Hill®

Published by Steeple Hill Books™

STEEPLE HILL BOOKS

Steeple
Hill®

Recycling programs
for this product may
not exist in your area.

ISBN-13: 978-0-373-82862-3

WANTED: A FAMILY

www.SteepleHill.com

Printed in U.S.A.

And be ye kind to one another, tenderhearted, forgiving one another, even as God for Christ's sake hath forgiven you.
—*Ephesians* 4:32

To Karen Solem, my savvy agent.
Thank you for overseeing the business end
of my career. To Tina James, my gifted editor
and Shirley Jump, dear friend and talented critique
partner these past thirteen years. Thank you both
for your insights that make me a far better writer. To
my readers. A huge thank you for your encouraging
words, a blessing I never take for granted.

Chapter One

Peaceful, Indiana, April 1900

How long before someone got hurt? How long before she couldn't pay the bills? How long—

Lord, help me find a way to keep my house and make it safe. For Elise. For my baby.

Automatically, Callie Mitchell's hand cradled the swell of her unborn child. Martin had been gone a few weeks when she realized that she was pregnant. She wanted this baby with an intensity that stole her breath away. In less than four months she'd hold a tiny infant in her arms. Soon she'd be too clumsy to make repairs herself.

She swiped a strand of hair clinging to her damp skin and let her gaze roam the old Victorian, the house where she and Martin had lived the past two years. Once majestic, now the house's peeling paint demanded another coat, the rickety porch begged for solid boards and rails, the roof pleaded for shingles. The house looked like a princess down on her luck.

Her breath caught. Martin had called her his princess, usually when he sought her forgiveness for some infraction. Those infractions usually involved skipping work or spending money they didn't have. But how could she not forgive that happy-go-lucky charmer almost anything? Her throat tightened. Especially now?

Of their own volition her eyes traveled the steep gabled roofline, to the spot where Martin had lost his footing in November and tumbled to his death.

The words she'd said to him that morning echoed in her mind. *If you don't repair the leak, one night the ceiling's going to fall on us while we sleep.*

Her gaze darted away. She wouldn't think about that now.

She wouldn't remember how he looked lying there.

She wouldn't.

Tightening her grip on the milk pail, she trudged toward the small barn at the back of the property, the prospect of tearing out and replacing each board on the porch slowing her steps. Lady needed oats. Bossy needed milking. The garden needed hoeing. That much she could do.

But the list of chores she couldn't handle grew longer every day. The roof leaked. The window casings on the north side of the house had rotted. The staircase railing wobbled.

Inside the barn, she fed and watered the mare, then moved to the open stall where Bossy waited. Callie pulled up the stool, giving the jersey a pat. Laying her forehead against the cow's wide side for balance, she closed her eyes, taking a minute to inhale the familiar scent of livestock, hay and manure. Across the way, the mare snuffled her ration of oats. As always the serenity of the place soothed her and eased the weight of her responsibilities.

The cow placidly chewed her cud, paying Callie no mind. As the first stream of milk hit the galvanized pail, she prayed for strength and wisdom to handle the needed repairs. To rally around Elise and regain harmony with her father-in-law, a strong-minded man she didn't usually buck.

Callie had grown weary of Commodore fussing about her dilapidated house, yet not lifting a finger to help. Instead he pressured her to move in with him and Dorothy. He blamed the house for his son's death. And though he'd never said as much, he blamed her, too.

Sometimes lying in bed at night, sometimes rising at the dawn of a new day, sometimes at the cemetery standing before Martin's headstone, she blamed herself more.

But nothing would stop her from giving Elise and other unwed and pregnant women refuge. Her home would be a place for them to live, free from judgment.

Not long after she and Martin moved into the house, she'd talked to him about that very thing. He'd rejected the idea, citing the cost as the reason. A valid concern, but Callie suspected his main objection centered on the work involved and the lack of privacy, something she'd understood.

Now she had only her baby to consider and a large, empty house. Once she completed the repairs, she'd seek funds and community support and make her dream of an unwed mothers' home a reality. God would work it out in His time. A blessed sense of peace stole over her, renewing her awareness of God's provision.

Stripes trotted over, tail high, and rubbed against her skirts, purring like a well-oiled engine. "Where are your kittens?" No doubt on the back stoop waiting for breakfast.

Bossy's tail swished Callie's way. A signal the milking was done. "Thanks, girl."

Accompanied by her strutting cat, Callie hauled the pail to the house. In the kitchen, she skimmed cream off the top and poured the rest into two pitchers. She crumbled day-old bread into an iron skillet, soaked it with milk, and then stowed the pitchers in the icebox.

Outside, Stripes and her offspring crowded around the pan, lapping the meal with dainty pink tongues. The male of the litter shoved one of his sisters aside and stuck in his paw.

"Mind your manners. There's plenty for all of you," Callie said.

Finished with her morning chores, Callie gathered tools from the barn and walked around the house to the front porch. The fistful of nails she'd driven into the boards a few days back made no difference.

With one gloved hand clutching Martin's toolbox, the other gripping the crowbar and her dyed-black skirts, she climbed the wobbly steps, careful to avoid the rotten wood. Once she removed the deteriorating planks, she'd replace them with the lumber stacked in the barn.

She forced the tip of the crowbar under a board and pushed down with all her might. Instead of coming up, nails and all, the plank splintered, pitching her forward. Gasping, she staggered, dropped the tool, but remained on her feet.

Heart pounding from her near fall, she knelt and used a hammer to knock off the remaining pieces of wood until she'd removed one board. At this rate, the task would take weeks. Callie wiped a hand across her moist brow and let her gaze roam the neighborhood.

Up the street, a stranger strode up the walk to Mildred's house. He was not a salesman. He carried a sack, not a sample case, and looked strong enough to handle this job. But if he sought work, she couldn't spare a penny to hire him.

She repositioned the crowbar and shoved again. Nails squeaked in protest, then slowly the board lifted. A few more shoves and it pulled free. Smiling, she tossed the plank aside.

The screen door creaked. Elise Langley, just eighteen, her family home a few doors down, stood in the opening, resting an arm on the bulge beneath her apron. "That job's too hard for you. Why not hire someone?"

From a family with money to spare, Elise wouldn't realize that Callie didn't have funds to hire anyone. Nor would Callie tell her, lest her houseguest feel unwelcome.

"It's good exercise." Callie grinned.

"I'll help." Before Callie could stop her, Elise, heavy and awkward with child, stepped onto the porch. The boards sagged and she stumbled, lurching sideways. "Ouch!"

The crowbar clattered to the floor. "Are you hurt?"

Elise hobbled to the door, pushed open the screen and lowered herself to the threshold. "I twisted my ankle is all." She lifted her skirts and rubbed the injured spot.

Callie picked her way to Elise's side and took a look. "It's already swelling."

Wrapping an arm around her middle, Callie helped Elise shuffle inside, settling her on the parlor sofa, then removed Elise's shoe and elevated her foot on pillows. She hurried to the kitchen, returning with chunks of ice wrapped in a dish towel and propped it on Elise's ankle with more pillows.

"I'm sorry, Callie. You warned me about the porch. Why do I always have to learn the hard way?"

"You were only trying to help." She patted Elise's hand. "If you're all right, I'll get back to work."

After Elise's mishap, Callie edged her way across the porch, determined to remove a few more planks before she had to change the ice on Elise's ankle. She reached for the crowbar. A movement out of the corner of her eye stopped her.

The man she'd seen earlier ambled toward her, a jacket

and sack tossed over his shoulder, his sleeves rolled to the elbow, revealing tanned, muscled forearms. He moved with a loose-legged ease, suggesting he'd covered his share of ground on foot.

Strangers were rare in Peaceful.

What did he want?

At the bottom of the steps, he tipped his hat. "Ma'am." His gaze landed on her rounded abdomen then slid to her face. "I'm looking for work. Heard at the Corner Café you'd lost your husband and might need help."

"If I did, I've no money to pay you."

His eyes roamed the house. "Your roof's missing shingles, the wood siding needs scraping and a couple coats of paint."

Hadn't he understood what she'd said? "Lots needs doing, but—"

"Nothing I can't handle." His self-assured tone held no hint of arrogance. He reached into his jacket pocket and removed a paper tucked inside. "This backs my claim."

When had she encountered a pushier man?

When had she been as desperate for a man with push?

Callie picked her way down the steps, took the paper from his hand and read the reference praising Jacob Smith's skill and work ethic, even his character.

What did that prove? He could've written it himself.

Above-average height with a wiry, broad-shouldered build, the man's angular face looked hard, chiseled from stone. The power radiating off him reminded her of a caged tiger pacing its enclosure, ready to spring. A guarded look in his eyes, as if he'd lived under scrutiny and been deemed defective told her this man had been hurt by life as much as she had. But that didn't make him honorable. It could mean exactly the opposite.

"Does anyone know you in this town?"

"No, ma'am."

"I'm sorry. I don't hire strangers." Not after the incident with the last handyman. She gave an apologetic smile, then returned to the porch and began prying up the next board. As she shoved against the lever, a jolt of pain streaked up her arms. She bit back a moan.

Eyes flashing, he bounded up the steps and hauled the crowbar from her hands. "You can't raze this porch in your condition."

Angry tears flooded her eyes. She wanted to slap that disapproving scowl off his face.

As if reading her mind, he took a step back. "I don't mean to criticize, but that much exertion could harm your baby."

Ignoring her refusal to hire him, he bent to the task, removing the board with ease, and then tossed it to the yard. "How do you plan to replace the missing shingles on your roof?"

The mere thought of that roof made Callie queasy. "If I trusted you—which I don't." Her tone should make that perfectly clear. "I can't pay you."

Again his gaze roamed the house. "I'll restore this beauty for a roof over my head and three meals a day, a price most folks appreciate."

She appreciated the price all right. But he was still a stranger. "I've got to wonder why a man with your experience would work without a wage. I'll still have to say no."

"I can't allow a woman to harm herself, even a headstrong woman like you."

Of all the nerve! She glared at him. "I'm perfectly capable of handling whatever task I set my mind to."

His eyes held a flicker of respect. "I'm sure that's true, if setting your mind to a task got it done. But this job requires more brawn than brains." He winked, bold as brass. "That makes me perfect for the job."

Aghast at the rush of attraction that shot through her, Callie folded her arms across her chest, more determined than ever to send this rogue packing.

"One day I want a business of my own. Why not give me a chance to test my mettle by bringing this Victorian back to life?"

Though he'd used that spiel to manipulate her, she couldn't argue with his logic. Fixing up her house would prove his ability and allow her to keep her home.

Besides, she didn't see anyone else lining up to help her.

If the house wasn't safe, Martin's parents would insist that she live with them, putting an end to Callie's dream. What would happen to Elise and her baby then?

As she grappled with the decision, the man returned to the task of ripping up boards. As if enjoying the effort, his sinewy muscles danced, her stomach dancing right along with them. She dropped her gaze to her feet, tamping down the ridiculous reaction. What had gotten into her? Those muscles of his merely proved he could handle the job.

Stranger or not, what choice did she have? Jacob Smith had a reference and the skill. Had offered a price she could afford.

Lord, I've prayed for an answer. Is this drifter Your solution?

The knot between her shoulder blades eased. The final assurance she needed. "I'll risk hiring you."

The corners of his mouth turned up. "Reckon we're both taking a risk."

"How so?"

"I'm taking a chance you're a passable cook."

She couldn't contain a grin. "I'll cook as ably as you work."

"Good enough for me," he said, the rumble of his voice ending on a chuckle.

"Have you had breakfast?"

"No, ma'am."

"I'll prepare a meal to fuel a working man."

He shoved his hat brim up his forehead. "Appreciate it."

The morning sun lit his face. A smile softened the hard edge of stubble on his unshaven jaw and spread to his eyes. Green. They were green as jade.

Callie's mind went blank. "Ah." What was she about to say? "While you're, ah, waiting, you can put your things in the lean-to attached to the barn. The last hired hand had no complaints about the accommodations." At the mention of that scoundrel, her hands fisted. "Thanked me by running off with the money from my sugar bowl. You don't plan on doing the same thing, do you?"

His jaw jutted. "No."

"In that case, settle in. I'll serve your breakfast on the back stoop." She turned then pivoted back. "Oh, I'm Callie Mitchell."

"Folks call me Jake."

"Just so you know, Mr. Smith, there's no money in my sugar bowl or anywhere else in the house."

He met her gaze, his eyes as steely as his muscles. "Just so you know, Mrs. Mitchell, I'm no thief."

Her hand flew to her throat. Giving a brisk nod, she hurried toward the chicken coop, glad to put distance between her and the stony-eyed drifter.

Smith was a common enough name. Her heart tripped in her chest. Too common.

Suspicious name or not, he'd come along when she needed his help. Badly. Still, she'd trust him only as far as her stoop.

Jake removed his hat to get a better look at the spitfire who'd hired him. The snippety woman had all but accused him of being a thief with that prickly tongue of hers. And those probing eyes, suspicious, reproachful, as if he had *burglar* stamped in capital letters across his forehead.

He sucked in a breath of free air and watched her march across the lawn, a woman on a mission. Even dressed in black, with those brown tendrils escaping her pompadour and feathering her neck, she looked beguiling. Taller than most women, she carried her delicate frame with a dignity almost disguising her condition. Surely she was heartier than she looked. Still, no matter how strong-minded, a pregnant widow wouldn't have an easy road. But then who did? No point in getting sappy about it.

What sort of a woman would risk unhitching that baby she was carrying?

A woman with no one to help her.

The haste of his recrimination pricked his conscience. He of all people should know better than to leap to conclusions. Mrs. Mitchell wouldn't have agreed to hire him if she knew he'd spent time behind bars. Framed by Lloyd, his so-called friend, vying for the affections of the woman Jake had thought loved him. He'd experienced firsthand that women were disloyal, even deceitful.

What a fool he'd been. Well, not even a fool made the same mistake twice. Jake might be a lot of things, but stupid wasn't one of them. He had no intention of trusting another woman.

Still, he'd handle Mrs. Mitchell's work for now. See that she didn't get hurt. Or harm her baby.

Perhaps in this town, several counties away from the penitentiary, he could stay a spell. One thing he'd learned— innocent or not, a man who'd done time wasn't free. He'd merely traded jail bars for barriers he couldn't see, but those invisible barriers were equally as solid. Prejudice. Suspicion. Judgment.

Not that he blamed folks, at least those who didn't know him. But those who did—

Well, after his release, except to get a reference from his boss, he didn't linger in Bloomington, the town where he'd been tried and found guilty, railroaded by flimsy evidence and an overeager sheriff. He couldn't face the skepticism, couldn't face being treated like a criminal.

But what he hadn't expected…

No matter where a man traveled, his past dogged his every step. One day, Mrs. Mitchell would look at him with the same doubt he'd seen often enough in the eyes of others. Not that he'd get close to anyone, not even to a woman with a stubborn tilt to her chin and dazzling sea-blue eyes.

He strode to the lean-to and opened the door into a room the size of a cell. A cot sat against the wall, bedding stacked at the foot, even a pillow for his head. Next to the bed a washstand held a kerosene lamp. Beside it, a chair where a man could fold his clothes at night and pull on his boots in the morning. A small window let in fresh air and a slice of the sky. Even under this roof, the moon and stars would keep him company.

He needed lodging. And whether Mrs. Mitchell wanted to admit it or not, she needed his help. He could mend a run-down house even if he couldn't repair the mess of his life.

A mess built by another.

No point harping on the past. The truth had come out. Lloyd was in jail. His treachery had cost Jake a year of his life, but he'd done Jake a favor by saving him from a life sentence with a fickle woman. Still, that year had deprived him of his good name and destroyed the last flimsy thread of his optimism.

Before his record caught up with him, he'd try to set this neglected, regal old house to rights.

More importantly, if she lived in Peaceful, he'd find the woman he sought.

Once he did, he'd leave. Moving from town to town, exposed to the elements. Not the greatest life, but he was free. Not only from the bars of prison, but unencumbered by relationships that had given him nothing but grief. When a man got burned, it didn't take him long to learn that the stove was hot.

A lesson he wouldn't forget.

On the chair, he laid the sack, holding a change of clothes and the Bible the warden gave him upon his release. Jake couldn't fathom why he bothered hauling that tome around. Tossing his jacket on the bed, he tried out the mattress. Not bad. Everything was clean and serviceable. Mrs. Mitchell treated hired hands well—that said plenty about her. He'd give her a full day's work and then some. All he had.

Maybe in a town with the unlikely name of Peaceful, he'd find his roots. Not that the insight would give him a moment of peace, no matter what the town's name was.

He shoved the thought away. Soon he'd sit down to a home-cooked meal. The prospect brought a rumble from his stomach.

Things were looking up.

Chapter Two

In Callie's large kitchen, cabinets ascended from wide baseboards on the plank floor to crown molding bordering the pressed-tin ceiling. At the enormous cookstove, Callie prepared breakfast. Hot grease popped out of the skillet and landed on her hand, bringing a hiss from her lips. That's what she got for frying side meat as if her life depended on it.

Her hands trembled. Maybe it did. She wanted Jacob Smith, if that was his real name, making repairs. Repairs Martin never got around to. Yet, within minutes of meeting her, the rugged stranger had taken charge as if he owned the place. An urge to slap his bossy face battled with an undeniable longing to savor his concern. He'd made her feel protected, cared for, as if he wanted to ease her load. When had Martin ever done that? Still, she didn't fancy relying on an outsider.

Through the window, she watched Mr. Smith haul an extension ladder from the barn. By the time she'd taken the pan of biscuits out of the oven, he'd made another trip, this time carrying an armload of shingles and a small keg of nails. The man didn't waste a minute, which she admired.

He stopped at the pump, splashed his face and neck with water, then scrubbed his hands. For a drifter, the man took responsibility and valued cleanliness. Virtues she respected.

Elise, leaning on an old cane Callie had found in the attic, hobbled to Callie's side. Her auburn hair was pulled into a low knot that failed to corral her mass of curls. "Can I help?"

"You're supposed to keep your weight off that ankle."

"It's stronger today." As she took a seat at the table, Elise glanced out the window. "Who's that?"

Callie set a plate of food in front of her. "His name's Jacob Smith. He's going to fix the roof and the porch." She smiled down at her. "So you won't twist your other ankle."

"I was more concerned about you hurting yourself than my ankle. That man's a blessing."

"I'm reserving judgment, but I hope you're right."

While Elise ate her breakfast, Callie poured a mug of coffee, then scooped onto a plate scrambled eggs, fried potatoes, two slabs of pork and three biscuits hot from the oven.

"Come meet him," Callie said. "Oh, and bring the flat-ware, please."

Under a smattering of freckles, Elise paled as if she wanted to refuse, but took the napkin-wrapped utensils and followed Callie to the door.

On the stoop, Jacob Smith doffed his hat then opened the screen. His hair, black as a moonless night, met his collar. Callie had an urge to grab her scissors, but introduced Elise instead.

"Nice to meet you, Mrs. Langley," he said, taking the utensils she offered.

Color dotted Elise's cheeks. "It's Miss Langley."

Mr. Smith's gaze landed on Elise's stomach then darted away, matching Elise's speed as she left the stoop and ducked into the kitchen.

Callie fixed a disapproving gaze on the newcomer. "Elise may be unwed, but she's a sweet girl. I expect you to treat her accordingly."

The hard set of his jaw gave Jacob Smith the look of a man ready to do battle. "I'm not one to judge."

"Good. Lord knows plenty of folks are." She motioned to the bench. "Have a seat, but watch the cats. They think the stoop's a feline café."

He plopped his hat beside him on the bench. "Breakfast looks mighty fine." He took the plate and mug from her hands then waited, as if expecting her to leave, so she did.

Glancing back, she watched him dive in. The man was hungry. Too hungry to pray? Or the action of a man without faith? Time would tell. Either way, she'd keep her doors locked at night.

As she entered the back door, a wave of light-headedness swept over her. She'd been up since dawn. The bowl of cold cereal she'd eaten was long gone.

In the kitchen, her food untouched, Elise drooped at the table, as limp as a rag doll, tears running down her cheeks.

Callie splayed her fingers over the girl's nape and massaged her muscles. "Are you all right?"

"You saw how he looked at me."

"Don't take it to heart. You know we expectant moms can't trust our perceptions. Why, we're laughing one minute, crying the next."

"I know I'm right, Callie. I've seen that look of censure before."

"Well, if that's the case, he'd better keep his opinions

to himself or I'll send him packing faster than a camel can spit."

"Camels spit?"

"I've heard they do. And I can, too, if I'm riled."

Elise's snuffles ended on a giggle, a rainbow in the stormy ups and downs of expectant motherhood.

Callie headed to the stove, slipped an egg and a slice of pork onto her plate. "I'll see what Jacob Smith has to say for himself."

While Elise finished eating, Callie left the house.

Across from Mr. Smith, she sat on a weathered chair with splayed legs. Her full skirts all but touched the scruffy toe of his boot.

As if uncomfortable with the contact, he yanked his foot back, then lifted the last forkful of food to his mouth. His hand was large, long-fingered. The nails were clean and he had a sprinkling of dark hair between his knuckles.

"Looks like I'm too late to ask if the food needed salt."

"Breakfast was perfect, as is. Every bite."

She'd missed cooking for a man, especially an appreciative man. She smiled. He smiled back. The dimple winked in his left cheek, giving his angular face a boyish look.

Bowing her head, she offered a silent prayer then cut into the pork.

Stripes wove between them, rubbing against Mr. Smith's boot. He gave her ears a gentle scratch and was rewarded with a grateful purr. The way people treated animals said a lot about them. "Where's home?" she asked.

"Nowhere in particular."

Eyeing him, she scooped egg onto her fork. "We're all born somewhere, Mr. Smith."

"Yes, ma'am, but… I don't know exactly where."

Her hand stilled. "Care to explain?"

"I grew up in an orphanage." He'd said the words in a matter-of-fact voice, with no trace of emotion, yet his eyes didn't meet hers.

The bite of egg lodged in Callie's throat. If not for Aunt Hilda, Callie would've met the same fate. Swallowing hard, her gaze darted his way.

He looked tranquil enough, but a twitch in his jaw suggested otherwise. "Not a happy experience?"

He shrugged, but the raw bleakness in his eyes confirmed her opinion.

"You got kin around these parts?" he said, deftly changing the subject and avoiding his past.

"My late husband's parents live a few blocks west."

"I'm sorry about your husband." Green eyes locked with hers. "Must be comforting, having his family nearby."

She nodded. Those searching eyes noticed her lack of enthusiasm. The man missed nothing.

"So what brings you to Peaceful?"

He gave a lopsided grin. "Reckon I'm here to help you."

"Are you saying you came to Peaceful by chance?"

"The town's name drew me." He laid his plate on the bench. Except for a few biscuit crumbs, he'd wiped it clean. "Thank you for the meal." His gaze settled on the lean-to. "And for the lodging." He plopped his hat in place. "I'd say I got the better end of our deal."

"You may think otherwise once you wrangle with the roof."

"I'm part mountain goat." He rose. "If it's all the same to you, I'll repair the roof this morning. Tackle the porch during the heat of the day."

"Do as you think best."

A flicker of surprise skidded across his face. That boss at the construction company must've been a stickler.

"I'll bring your dinner out at noon. Wait a minute." She walked inside, grabbed a fruit jar with a galvanized lid from the kitchen. "It's going to be a scorcher. Fill this or you'll wear yourself out making trips to the pump."

He took the jar and tipped his hat. "Much obliged."

"Take care on that roof. It's steep."

"Yes, ma'am." His eyes sobered. "I will."

He strapped on a pouch of nails and stuck the hammer under his belt, then leaned the ladder against the back of the house, making adjustments until he had it centered to suit him. Before she could steady it, he'd grabbed an armload of shingles and scrambled to the top and out onto the roof. As he clomped up the incline, she held her breath and then slowly released it, noticing his confidence and agility.

And the way his back muscles rippled through his shirt.

At the unwelcome response to the man, her cheeks burned. With her hands full to overflowing and no idea where she'd get the money to take her and Elise through the winter, how could she keep noticing a man's muscles, a *drifter* at that?

Her father-in-law would say only a no-account man chose to work for room and board, instead of settling down with a good-paying job.

Callie shivered. Jacob Smith had been closed-mouthed. Was he running from something? Or to something?

Whatever his motive for coming to Peaceful, she didn't need another complication in her life. How long before he could get the work done and leave?

Couldn't be soon enough to suit her.

Sweat stinging his eyes and blurring his vision, Jake pulled a nail from the pouch and fastened a shingle in place. He yanked a handkerchief from his hip pocket, threaded it under the crown of his wide-brimmed hat, then plunked it on his head.

Laying shingles in this unseasonable heat was hard, dirty work, but he welcomed the exertion, liked being in control. Control he'd lost in jail, but needed badly. A man felt alive when he pushed the limits of his endurance. Afterward, his muscles might ache, but nothing equaled the satisfaction of repairing something broken. If it sometimes ate at him that remodeling houses came as close as he'd get to a home of his own, he forced the thought away. No reason to expect anything more. He had no interest in forming a family.

Every half hour like clockwork, Mrs. Mitchell came out to check on him. No doubt scared he'd break his neck. Not that he blamed her, considering what happened to her husband. If she knew how at ease he felt perched on this roof, she'd worry less.

He liked the expanse, the sense of freedom, the clear view of nearby gardens with slender rows of leaf lettuce and green onions. A few patches overgrown with dead pumpkin vines and cornstalks bordered red barns, white-washed sheds and outhouses, all tucked behind clapboard houses.

Did one of these homes hide the woman who'd given him birth?

Not his mother. A mother took care of her child. Fed him. Tucked him into bed at night.

Or so he understood.

But one thing he knew—a mother didn't toss her baby away like an unwanted trinket. Clenching his jaw, he slammed the hammer into the head of the nail, driving it in place. He wanted that woman to know the price he'd paid for her negligence. The orphanage had provided the basics to sustain life, but no affection, no encouragement, no joy, merely existence.

She sent a yearly birthday greeting to the orphanage addressed to Jacob, not even using his last name, as if Smith was a lie. Those cards didn't diminish her desertion. Merely proved she knew his location yet never bothered to see him. Never bothered to reveal his roots. Never bothered to make sure he survived.

As he pounded shingles into place, his mind drifted back to the winter he was seven. He'd fallen from a tree on the orphanage grounds. With pain searing his broken arm and emptiness branding his heart, he'd lain on the frozen earth staring at the bare branches, silhouetted against a cloudless sky. A boy surrounded by people, yet starving for love, he'd cried out for his mother. No one came.

From that moment, Jake dropped the pretense he'd clung to and faced the truth. He had only those postcards. Postcards couldn't hold him. Postcards couldn't wipe away his tears. Postcards couldn't atone for her abandonment.

At last he'd quieted, then struggled to his feet. Cradling his broken arm against his chest, he'd shuffled toward the orphanage, a vow on his lips.

Never again would he care about that woman. Never again would he deceive himself into believing that one day she'd come for him. Never again would he hold on to hope for a family.

His arm had mended. But in the sixteen years since that day, nothing had proved him wrong.

Even as an adult, when he knew circumstances might've made her coming for him difficult, even impossible, he couldn't find it in his heart to excuse her.

The postcards had been postmarked Indianapolis. Once, just once, a card had come from Peaceful. He'd kept all those postcards. Just to remember the town names. Not that they meant anything to him.

As he hammered another nail home, his stomach

clenched. In truth, he'd studied each stroke of the pen, compared the handwriting to his own, searching those pitifully few words for some connection. Never finding one.

After his exoneration and release from prison, he'd spent a month in Indianapolis, searching birth records, locating every Smith he could find, but he hadn't turned up a clue. For some reason, he had the strong feeling she'd sent the postcards from there to throw him off her trail and he'd find her in Peaceful.

Well, if she'd found peace in this town, perhaps he would, too. Once he'd given her a huge hunk of his opinion. Not charitable of him, but the best he could do with all the bitterness burning inside him.

He didn't wish her harm. He didn't even want to disgrace her. He merely needed her to know the penalty he'd paid when she'd swept him under the rug of her life.

The beat of his heart pounded in his temples with the rhythm of his hammer. If there was a God and He was the Author of Life, as some claimed, He hadn't gone out of His way to lend a hand to Jake's life story.

Not in the circumstances of his birth.

Not in those years in the orphanage.

Not in the injustice exacted in that courtroom.

He sighed. Why not admit it? He wanted to see his mother with a desperation he couldn't fathom, yet couldn't deny. He wanted to meet her. See if they shared a resemblance. Learn the identity of his father. Maybe then he could move on with his life. If only he had a way to make his search easier, a sign with an arrow pointing in the direction to turn. He huffed at such absurdity. What would the sign say? This way leads to Jake Smith's mother?

"How's it going?"

Whirling around, Jake scrambled for footing, scraping his knuckles against the hot shingles.

Mrs. Mitchell looked up at him, eyes wide with alarm. "I'm sorry. I didn't mean to startle you, but dinner's ready."

"My fault, I didn't hear you coming." He forced his lips into a grin that pinched like ill-fitting shoes. "Your timing's perfect. I just replaced the last shingle."

Her eyes lit. "Oh, now I won't have to cringe at the first peal of thunder."

Forcing his gaze away from that sparkle in her eyes, that sweet smile on her lips, he tucked the hammer into his belt. She drew him like a mindless moth to a candle's flame, a lure that would prove as lethal.

"Any damage inside?" he said, barely able to concentrate with her peering up at him.

"My bedroom ceiling's cracked. I moved the bed to ensure that I won't awaken one morning blanketed in plaster."

Knowing the danger of entanglement, yet unable to stop himself, he said, "Can't have a chunk of ceiling marring that pretty face of yours."

The apple of her cheeks colored, but her eyes turned wary. "You men know the words a woman likes to hear."

Why didn't an attractive woman like Callie Mitchell appreciate a compliment? "I'll take a look at the ceiling when I've finished the porch." Jake pivoted out onto the ladder, descending the rungs two at a time, the ladder vibrating with each footfall.

By the time he'd reached the bottom, she'd dashed over and gripped the sides. He all but bumped into her coming off the last step. Wide-eyed and obviously shaken, she quickly moved aside. When had anyone worried about his safety?

"I'm accustomed to ladders and this one's sturdy."

"Even a careful man can meet disaster, Mr. Smith."

No doubt she referred to her husband's fall, but her remark summed up his life. "Your words don't give a man much hope."

Her eyes narrowed, as if trying to see inside of him. "Hope doesn't come from words of mine. Hope comes from God's Word."

A man couldn't manufacture something he didn't believe. "I don't see a point in opening a Bible."

"Without God's Word to point me in the right direction, I'd lose my way." Mrs. Mitchell looked at him with eagerness. "You might give the Bible and church a try."

"From what I've seen, churchgoers aren't likely to offer clemency." The words shot out of his mouth before he could stop them. What about this woman made him bleed his innermost thoughts?

Her gaze bored deeper. "Do you need clemency?"

Jake removed his hat and slipped the handkerchief stuffed inside into his hip pocket then swiped the sweat off his brow in the crook of his elbow. It didn't take a genius to recognize prying. "Reckon we all do."

A flash of remorse traveled her face. Her eyes lifted to the roof, filling with anguish and self-reproach that pushed against his core. If he didn't know better, he'd believe Mrs. Mitchell shoved her husband off the roof. Well, he had no interest in getting involved with her or her problems. Yet she looked so fragile standing there fighting back tears.

An overpowering urge to tug her to him, to tell her everything would be fine, mounted inside him, yet his hands remained at his sides.

Everything had never been fine.

He couldn't promise such a thing.

To her.

To anyone.

"I'll get your dinner." She headed to the house, shoulders bent, as if carrying a heavy burden.

No doubt she did. A burden he could ease by repairing this house. But the rest—unwed mothers, babies, grief over her husband's death—he'd stay clear of all that.

At the pump, Jake stuck his head under the spout. Cold water sluiced down his throat and into his sweat-soaked shirt. Perhaps the dousing would cool his empathy for the young widow.

The woman tried to shove God and church down his throat, a prescription Jake couldn't swallow. She'd indicated that the Bible would point a man in the right direction, as if the road ahead lay with God. He'd more likely find that arrow he wished for earlier than answers in an ancient gilded book.

And as for prayer—

If God existed, He didn't give a fig about Jake. No matter what Callie Mitchell said, God wouldn't be helping him. Jake would need a sensible way to find his mother.

Wielding a crowbar, Jake pried a rotted board from the porch floor, easy to do with the missing or inadequately set nails. He'd make repairs and ignore Mrs. Mitchell's attempt to get him to church. Yet, he could feel himself getting drawn into her life. Worse, drawn to her. That scared him silly.

The faint scent of roses drifted through the air. Mrs. Mitchell stepped onto the porch, a straw boater perched at a jaunty angle on her head, wearing a high-neck white shirtwaist and gored skirt that rustled at the hem as she moved.

Jake sat back on his heels and drank in the sight of her, the gentle arch of her brows, her almond-shaped aquamarine eyes, her thick tresses the shade of rich coffee.

"Hello." He'd sounded like a smitten schoolboy instead of a man who'd been burned.

"Hello." She smiled at him. "Lovely afternoon."

"It is." Especially since she'd appeared, but he wouldn't say that. If he had one speck of control over his addled brain, he wouldn't think it, either.

"I'll try not to get in your way." She edged across the porch to check the flower boxes of pansies.

"You aren't bothering me."

When had he told a bigger lie? He could barely keep his eyes off her as she nipped off some dying blooms.

He clenched his jaw and pried up another board. What had gotten into him? The woman might be pretty, might even have a good heart, at least if her desire to take in an unwed expectant mother meant anything, but she was a woman after all.

If he could read her thoughts, he suspected her motive for helping wasn't as pure as it appeared. Most people had an underlying scheme for everything they did. He'd figure hers out eventually.

"Does Miss Langley have family?" Jake asked.

"Her parents live up the block."

"Then…why is she living with you?"

Mrs. Mitchell hesitated, as if deciding what to say. "Her father insists that she give the baby up."

Jake's stomach tensed. "What would he have her do? Dump it in an orphanage?"

She sighed. "Either that or put the baby up for adoption far from Peaceful."

An urge to tell Elise's father what kind of a life his grandchild would have in such a place gripped Jake, holding him firmly in its clutches, then tightening like a vise. "Nice and tidy for everyone," he said in a voice as rough as sandpaper.

Why was Callie Mitchell getting involved with such ugliness? "If Miss Langley had thought of the consequences, she wouldn't have gotten involved with a no-account man."

Her eyes flashed. "Your censure doesn't solve anything. What's done is done."

"I'm sorry." He swallowed against a sudden lump in his throat. "I'm just…angry."

"I'm sorry you spent your youth in an orphanage." Compassion filling her gaze, she reached a hand toward him.

He'd revealed too much. He took a step back, avoiding her touch. "As you say, what's done is done."

That morning she'd tried to pry into his past, tried to see inside of him. He knew better than to let anyone get close.

Mrs. Mitchell sighed. "If only Mr. Langley could see that an orphanage isn't the solution."

How many kids had Jake seen tossed into that orphanage from every situation or circumstance imaginable? Few thrived. If he tried to tell Elise's father anything, he might resent Jake's interference enough to dig around in his past. Perhaps discover his stint in prison. If word got out, he'd be forced out of town before he had a chance to find the woman who'd given birth to him.

Avoiding her penetrating gaze, he turned to his task. He'd repair this house, look for his mother and avoid more than conversations about the weather.

"Oh!" Mrs. Mitchell's hand darted to her stomach.

Jake leaped to his feet. "Is something wrong?"

Like a rosebud opening, her smile unfurled. "Something's very right," she said, her tone laden with wonder. "I think my baby just moved for the first time."

Of its own volition, Jake's hand moved toward her middle, hovering inches away. Had his mother reacted like this when he'd moved inside her? No, if she had experienced Callie Mitchell's joy, she couldn't have tossed him out like yesterday's garbage.

"In four more months, I'll have a child." Her voice trembled with emotion. "A family of my own."

Behind the emotion, Jake heard Mrs. Mitchell's determination to create a family with her and her baby.

Family.

The word conjured up birthday cakes and bedtime stories, kisses on small hurts and hugs after a nightmare. All the things he'd never had. "Not every woman would want to raise a child alone."

"I have God and my baby. I'm never alone."

Her eyes reflected a faith so bright, so pure, Jake felt filthy in comparison. The idea that he could have such a woman in his life ricocheted through him. He tamped down the ridiculous notion. Callie Mitchell grieved for her husband. He grieved for his past. Not a foundation for second chances.

Chapter Three

Callie cringed, heat blooming in her cheeks. How could she have shared with Jacob Smith, a man, a *stranger,* the first movement of her baby? An intimate detail too personal to share with anyone but her doctor, her friends and the baby's father, but Martin was gone and she hadn't been able to contain her joy.

Worse, Mr. Smith appeared as overcome and delighted by the news as a prospective father. This would never do. Her breath caught. Jacob Smith was turning her world upside down.

Across from her, he took a long drink of water from the fruit jar, his Adam's apple bobbing with each swallow. His sweat-soaked shirt clung to his torso, a surprisingly broad chest on that sinewy frame.

Martin had been soft, pudgy. The unkind comparison of her deceased husband to a drifter knotted in Callie's stomach. "I'm going to town for my mail," she said, eager to be on her way.

"Mind if I join you? I could use a break."

At the thought of walking side by side with this man, a shiver snaked down Callie's spine. Why couldn't he have stuck to the task at hand? She ought to make an excuse and hurry inside, but she heard herself say, "I'd enjoy the company."

He smiled, flashing that fascinating hollow in his cheek. "Give me five minutes."

Looking pleased, as if accompanying her mattered, he vaulted over the railing to the ground with the grace and the quickness of a deer. Callie's belly flopped like one of Martin's landed fish. She tamped down such silliness. Mr. Smith merely needed a breather, exactly as he'd said.

Slow-moving clouds threw shadows on the house, pulling Callie's eyes to the turret rising in the sky. Her family home had resembled this old Victorian, except the upper-story windows had worn stained-glass crowns, throwing splashes of color on the walls, delighting her little-girl heart. From those windows, donned in the cloak her mother had sewed and a beaded cardboard crown, the princess of her domain, she'd surveyed her kingdom—the fertile valley nestled in the foothills of Tennessee.

But the dam had been compromised and rushing water had whipped through the valley, sweeping the house and her family along in the flood.

She'd survived their loss. She'd survived Martin's death. She'd survive whatever life threw her way. Her faith would keep her strong. But the deep ache of loneliness stirring within left her vulnerable. Vulnerable even to a man she knew nothing about.

Hadn't she learned anything from her marriage to Martin?

Alone and adrift after Aunt Hilda died, Callie had soaked up Martin's cheerful disposition and affectionate nature like parched ground and missed his lack of responsibility.

The minute he proposed, Callie had said yes. They set the wedding date for less than a month away. When the

old Victorian came up for auction, Martin coerced his
father into buying it as a wedding gift, insisting that the
large family he wanted wouldn't fit into Aunt Hilda's tiny
house. Once Callie sold the house, they used the proceeds
to purchase furniture and had enough left over to put some
money in the bank.

On her wedding day, Callie had never been happier.
Martin had a secure job at his father's store. They had some
savings. His parents had accepted her with open arms.

It didn't take long for the glow of marital bliss to fade.
With Martin's penchant for guns and fishing gear and the
cost of supplies needed to rebuild the house, they tore
through their savings. The more that Commodore did
to keep them solvent, the more he expected to run their
lives.

Not that anyone could control Martin.

Perhaps with a baby on the way, he would have stepped
up to his new role. She'd never know.

But she'd learned a hard lesson. A man wasn't always
what he appeared.

Mr. Smith strode toward her, his hair damp under his
hat, wearing a clean shirt and a contented smile that set
her pulse racing. She folded her arms across her chest,
vowing that she wouldn't let him have this effect on her.
No matter how much she admired his responsible nature
and impressive accomplishments, she wouldn't care about
another man, especially a drifter.

When he reached her, their gazes locked. The yearning in his eyes lodged in her heart. They were two people
cramming their days with meeting the needs of others, yet
hungering for closeness. Every single bit of logic and mis-
giving vanished like dew on a summer day. Replaced by a
pull towing her to him with a power she couldn't explain.

A pull she wouldn't heed.

Yet, her feet took her toward him. His eyes flared. Something meaningful and disturbing passed between them. Callie quickly looked away, breaking the hold this man had over her.

As she strolled beside him along the tree-lined walk toward town, she was all too aware of his height, the firmness of his stride, the power and energy he barely contained.

That first day she'd suspected he wasn't a believer. How could she be drawn to such a man?

Martin had possessed faith, well, faith of sorts. Not much for combing Scripture, he'd left his edifying to the preacher at those times he didn't snooze in the pew. In the two years they'd been married, they'd never shared a spiritual discussion.

Yet within hours of meeting, she and Mr. Smith had touched on their faith. From what he'd said, the man needed God. She would not get emotionally involved with a faithless man, but with God's help, she could try to fill more than his stomach. She could nourish his soul. Help him find the answer to the pain she sensed lurking beneath the surface.

Callie gulped. As long as that answer wasn't her.

Aunt Hilda had said Callie possessed a keen intuition about others' feelings. Except for that one terrible exception with Nell, Callie had found her assessment true. She'd learned to observe people. Saw what they needed, how she could bring a smile or ease a worry. Perhaps she could give that strategy a try with Jacob Smith.

As they approached a hump in the walk, he took her arm. "Watch your step."

A jolt shot through her. The startled look in Mr. Smith's eyes said he'd felt that same wild reaction. She quickly released her hold on his arm, yet felt strangely bereft. She groped for a safe topic. "You're an excellent carpenter."

"Carpentry comes easy to me," he said in a husky voice, "like building a nest comes easy to you."

"Building a nest?"

"Yes, making a home, a welcoming place for friends like Elise, even an outsider like me." His eyes warmed. "That's a gift. I've seen my share of places and the people who live there. Your hospitality isn't something I encounter often."

Everything inside her turned to jelly. Why did he have such an effect on her? The answer came. He understood what she valued, the importance of home and family.

"My house is a gift from God and way bigger than I need. I want to share it with others."

As if he doubted that God gave gifts, he didn't respond. She'd do what she could to share her faith. And leave the outcome to the One who controlled the universe. In the meantime, she'd focus on the arrival of her baby, on giving refuge to unwed mothers and ignore this transient man at her side.

As they passed Elise's family home, Callie's steps slowed. In the shadows of her porch Sarah Langley sat on the swing. She was a good Christian woman and Callie always thought the same way about Mr. Langley, but Elise's decision to keep her baby called for strong support from her father, not opposition.

Sarah waved. "Callie, can you spare a minute?"

Callie glanced at Jacob Smith. "Elise's mother may have something important to say."

"I'll walk on ahead." He strode off, his lanky, easy gait eating up the distance to town, leaving a baffling void. A void she would ignore.

Sarah left her porch, motioning Callie toward the shelter

of her lilac bushes. Did she think neighbors would report the conversation to her husband? "I hoped I might catch you on your walk to the post office." She fingered the collar of her dress. "When the baby decides to come, get word to me. If I can sneak away…" Her voice trailed off.

New lines of worry etched Sarah's plump face. Shots of gray Callie didn't remember seeing before streaked her auburn hair. "I understand."

"I talked to Doc Wellman. He'll let me make payments on his fee. Get him to help Elise when it's her time." She dug into the pocket of her apron, then thrust a stack of bills at Callie. "This is for diapers, a dress."

Callie put the money in her purse. "This will mean the world to Elise. After our doctor's appointments tomorrow afternoon, we'll go shopping for the baby."

"I know that girl can eat." Sarah gave a shaky smile. "Wish I could help more, but…"

Obviously, Elise's father wouldn't let go of a dime to help his daughter. "I have shelves of canned food in the cellar and soon we'll have produce from the garden. We'll manage fine."

Eyes filling with misery, Sarah stared off into the distance. "We had such plans for Elise. You know, for schooling, a good marriage." Her voice faltered. "Now that's gone."

Callie laid a hand on Sarah's sleeve. "Elise can still have those things, Sarah. Maybe not right away, but her life isn't over. God will bring something good from this."

A spark of hope lit Sarah's eyes. "You're right. God will work it out. I know it. I do."

"You and Mr. Langley are in my prayers."

"God bless you, Callie. I don't understand why you're doing this for my girl, but I thank you."

But Callie knew. And if Sarah weren't wrapped up in her own worries, she'd know, too.

With a hug goodbye, Callie walked up Serenity Avenue, her eyes on the uneven brick, her mind filling with the image of Nell. Callie swallowed around a lump in her throat. Redheaded Nell—upturned nose with a dusting of freckles, blue eyes sparkling with innocence. They were only sixteen, sheltered from the facts of life. Nell had trusted a man, fallen hard. A lesson Callie ought to remember.

At the corner, she turned left on Liberty. Jacob Smith lounged against a tree. At his thoughtfulness something inside her twisted. "You waited." But then she remembered how fooled Nell had been by a man.

"I'm in no rush," he said as they continued up Liberty. "Life must be more complicated with Miss Langley in your house."

"Elise is a help and I enjoy her company."

"I know you don't like me saying so but no man should leave a woman in her circumstances."

"Perhaps he did Elise a favor."

"How do you figure that?"

"Marriage to some men would be intolerable."

"Why would a woman involve herself with such a man?"

No one could be that naive. "What's hidden can't be seen, Mr. Smith."

He studied her, his eyes filling with compassion, as if he suspected that she referred to her late husband. Well, he could keep his ill-placed sympathy to himself. She'd never met anyone more secretive.

Up ahead, the street bustled with activity by Peaceful standards. Carriages and wagons clattered over the brick. Shoppers stopped to chat on the walk. The one family in town with a newfangled automobile rounded the corner, honking its horn, frightening horses and young children.

"What do you know? Someone in Peaceful owns a Waverley Runabout."

"That's Mr. Burch, president of the bank."

"I visited the Waverley factory in Indianapolis," Jake said. "Can't think battery-powered carriages will come to anything. Now those gasoline motor automobiles Haynes-Apperson is turning out in Kokomo interest me."

"Really? You'd want one? My mare is a lot more reliable."

"If they can get the kinks ironed out and a way to lower the cost, it wouldn't surprise me if one day the streets were teeming with automobiles."

"Sounds dangerous."

"Danger is a sign of progress, I reckon."

An odd thought. One she'd examine later.

Callie greeted passersby as they strolled by the variety of shops dotting the main street: Langley's Barber Shop, Lily's Millinery and Gloves, Harrington's Grocery, Cunningham's Pharmacy. Up ahead the Mitchell Mercantile. A dog sniffed his way along the walk beside her, and then trotted across the street, successfully dodging horses' hooves and buggy wheels.

Outside the post office, Jacob turned toward her. "I think I'll look into getting a haircut."

"Your hair *is* a bit shaggy," she said with a smile.

He doffed his hat and plowed his fingers through his ebony hair. "We mutts aren't groomed as often as those fancy lapdogs."

"Nothing about you suggests mutt, Mr. Smith."

His lips tilted up into a soft smile that climbed into his eyes and settled on her with such intensity that her mouth went dry as dust. She glanced away. "The barber is Elise's father."

"Thanks for the warning." He plopped his hat on his head, flashed his dimple, then strode off, turning more than one woman's head in his direction.

Jacob Smith was all male, more cowboy than any man she'd met. Unable to take her eyes off his lanky figure, she watched until he entered the barbershop. Chiding herself for such foolishness, she pivoted toward the post office and stepped inside, letting her eyes adjust to the dim interior.

Marlene Thompson, the postmistress, looked up from sorting the mail and punched her wire-rimmed glasses up her nose with her index finger. "Afternoon, Callie. How are you feeling?"

"The fatigue and nausea are long gone." She smiled. "I just felt the baby move." So much for telling only her friends such personal news, but she couldn't seem to keep it to herself.

"What do you want? Boy? Or girl?"

"I want whatever I'm having."

"With that attitude, you won't be disappointed. Mr. Thompson was determined to have a girl. Five boys later, he decided I was girl enough for him." She chuckled. "I could've told him that a whole lot sooner."

Callie giggled. "Do I have any mail?"

"Nothing today. Nothing that is, except a question." She motioned her closer. "I heard Elise Langley's staying with you."

"She is."

"Good." Mrs. Thompson's brown eyes warmed with interest. "My nephew Albert and his wife, Sally, would love to have that baby if Elise is looking for a good home for it."

"I believe Elise plans to keep her baby."

Marlene's shoulders sagged. "Well, if she changes her mind, ask her to talk to Sally."

"I will."

Callie knew the Thompsons and their desperate desire for a child. They would make wonderful parents. Callie doubted that Elise would consider such an arrangement. Yet her heart ached for the Thompsons. Why did some women long to have a child, yet remained barren, while others conceived babies with no interest in or means of caring for them?

What circumstances had led Jacob Smith's mother to put her son in an orphanage? Or perhaps she had been forced to give up her child, as Elise's father was trying to do.

If Callie had questions, she could only imagine Mr. Smith's desire for answers. Could that be the reason he'd come to Peaceful? She sighed. Why was she getting involved with this man's life? He'd only bring her grief.

A block down, Callie entered Mitchell's Mercantile. The cavernous room held every utensil, tool, canned good, fresh-baked good and ready-made article of clothing imaginable. She dreaded running into her father-in-law. Yet, if she shopped elsewhere, the news would get back to him. She glanced around. No Commodore. No customers. Callie breathed a sigh of relief.

Since Martin's death, her father-in-law had badgered her to move in with him and Dorothy, and Callie suspected he wanted her and her baby to fill the void in their lives after losing Martin. She understood that, but the vehemence of his insistence unnerved her. Did something beside grief motivate him?

At a table piled with an assortment of tiny garments and fabric for making blankets and diapers, Callie plucked a white gown from the stack. Silky ribbons closed the neckline, cuffs and hemline, every detail precious. She couldn't imagine caring for an infant small enough to wear this. But in four months, she would. Would she even know how to be a good mother? What if the baby got sick? Or—

No, she refused to worry. Just because her parents and Martin had died tragically didn't mean disaster lurked around every corner. Countless women had children and managed fine.

But alone?

She knew very few who'd handled that responsibility without a husband. She laid a hand on her abdomen. *Please, God, keep my baby safe. Help me be a good mother.*

If only she could talk to her mother, to ask advice, to share the specifics of motherhood. Her throat clogged. She didn't have her mother, but she did have a mother-in-law and the ladies at church to advise her. She'd have support.

As she fingered the soft blanket, visualizing cuddling her baby swathed in its folds, filling her arms and her heart with a family of her own, tension drained out of her.

"Small, aren't they?" Commodore's gentle, almost reverent voice startled her. "Takes me back to Martin's arrival."

Surprised by this sentimental side of Commodore, Callie met his moist gaze and smiled. "From the pictures I've seen, Martin was a beautiful baby."

"Sure was. And strong. Why, he held up his head that first week." His voice sounded gruff, thick with emotion. "If you want material to make our grandbaby anything, I'll, ah, wrap it up." He shifted. "No charge. Get some dresses, too."

"Thank you. That's most generous." Callie had no idea

how she'd manage it, but somehow she'd find a way. "I'll work here on Saturdays to repay you."

"Nonsense. We want to help. We still have Martin's crib, high chair, baby carriage. Dorothy saved everything he touched."

Commodore's effort to build a bridge between them softened Callie's wariness. "I could put the crib in the small bedroom."

His gaze hardened. "If you'd move in with us, we'd see to your and the baby's every need."

At the familiar argument, a constant sting between them, Callie sighed. Could she make Commodore understand? She had to try. She took a fortifying breath. "I need a place of my own to raise my child and make a life. Not to shut you and Dorothy out, but to have my own traditions, my own routines."

"You can do all that at our place. Why are you being stubborn? You used to be reasonable, someone we could talk to." He exhaled impatiently. "Why not be honest? All you can think about is housing that Langley girl."

"That's part of it, but not all. I wish you could understand."

"I understand, all right." He folded his arms across his barrel chest. "You'd rather remain in a house that caused Martin's death than move in with us. My son would want you and his baby with us."

As if Commodore had known Martin's mind. They'd been at odds for years. Fighting to control her emotions, Callie inspected several baby things.

"Commodore, I appreciate your concern about the house, but I want to assure you I'll be fine." She forced a smile. "I know the house's every flaw and will be careful."

"I can't stomach the sight of it." Commodore's tone was harsh, condemning. "If not for that eyesore, my son would be alive today, not laid out in Walnut Grove Cemetery. But no, *you* had to have this house. Nothing but that monstrosity would do."

Callie wrapped her arms around herself. Did he blame the house for Martin's death? Or was he dancing around the fact that he blamed her? "I'm heartsick about Martin's fall, his death." A sob tore from her throat. "But leaving my house won't bring him back. Nothing we do will bring him back."

Her nagging had cost Martin his life. If only Callie had asked someone with experience to replace the shingles, instead of fussing about the cost, about yet another bill they couldn't pay.

Perhaps living with Martin's parents would be her penance. But she couldn't cope under Commodore's accusing eyes. Decrepit or not, she had to keep the house, the one place where she felt at home. The one place she could re-create the family she'd lost.

And fulfill the promise she'd made to Nell. The promise she'd made to God to provide for unwed mothers.

"Commodore, please. Martin saw our home as a perfect place to raise our children."

"It hardly makes sense for Dorothy and me to rattle around in that big house of ours, while your place drains you dry. From where I stand, you're going to lose it anyway."

His words tore through Callie and ricocheted in her chest. How would she provide for Elise and two babies, once they arrived? "I've got to go." She whirled toward the door.

If God wanted her to give Elise a home and others like

her, He'd show her a way to handle the expense, just as He'd brought her a carpenter to make the repairs.

It would all work out.

She was sure of it.

Chapter Four

Sporting a new haircut and a surly attitude toward the barber who'd shorn him like a spring lamb, Jake returned to demolishing the porch. Elise's father had bombarded him with questions. No doubt suspicious of a newcomer. Or, if Jake chose to think the best of people, perhaps Langley merely was making conversation.

In any case, Jake admitted that he was renovating the Mitchell place and had met the barber's daughter. Neither spoke of Elise's condition, though obviously her father had her on his mind. He'd had the gall to suggest that Callie Mitchell had persuaded his daughter to move in with her. Jake had leaped to her defense, raising Langley's ire. The man used his scissors to emphasize his points. Jake was fortunate to still be in possession of his ears.

Mrs. Mitchell opened the screen door. "Do you need the fruit jar refilled?"

Did this woman never stop thinking of others? "I'd appreciate it." He carried the jar to her, promptly getting lost in the depths of her dazzling blue-green eyes.

"Did Mr. Langley say anything about Elise?"

"He's not happy she's living here."

Her eyes dimmed. "I know."

An urge to teach Langley a thing or two for upsetting Mrs. Mitchell this way gripped Jake. But what did he know about being a father? About dealing with an unwed daughter in a family way?

"Yoo-hoo! Callie!" A twig of a woman, white hair frizzing around her face like a windblown cloud, lurched up the walk pulling a loaded wagon, impressive for someone surely approaching eighty.

"Mildred, whatever are you toting in that wagon?"

"Memories, dear. Births, deaths and everything in between." The lady's hand swept the stacks of newspapers and scrapbooks crammed to overflowing. "Some of this memorabilia dates back to the town's beginnings."

"That's nice but...I don't understand why you're bringing all that here."

"You will as soon as I explain." She tilted her head toward Jake. "You're that fellow who stopped at my place looking for work. I'd have hired you, but I'm not sure of my plans for the house."

Jake nodded.

"It's about time you got help, Callie, before this house falls down around your ears. Not an easy way to get them pierced." She gave an unladylike snort.

"Mr. Smith's already replaced the roof shingles."

"Ah, a hard worker *and* easy on the eyes." The woman winked. "I may be old as dirt, but I can still appreciate a good-looking man. Not why I wed my dear husband, but I enjoyed that handsome face of his more than dessert after a meal."

At Mrs. Uland's perusal, Jake's neck heated. The feisty older woman merely grinned, as if enjoying his discomfort.

"This old Victorian sat empty too long. All it needs is someone who cares like Callie here and someone with the know-how to give it life." Her approving gaze rested on Jake. "Appears that's you, Mr. Smith."

"Sitting empty isn't good for a house," he said.

"Sitting in an empty house isn't good for a person, either." Mrs. Uland laughed. "I'm not in mine, more than I have to be."

He motioned to the wagon. "Let me help with that."

"Oh, a knight in shining armor." She wagged a knobby finger. "Just keep your nose out of them. Took me hours to get those issues in order of publication."

"They're safe with me." His mind raced like a hound dog after a fox. The information in this wagon could possibly unlock his birth mother's identity. If he examined these newspapers, he might find his birth announcement.

"I'm not following you," Mrs. Mitchell said, looking slightly dazed.

"Of course, you're not, dear. If you have time for tea, I'll explain."

"I do."

Jake scooped up an armload of newspapers. "Where do you want these?"

From the flicker of dismay in Callie Mitchell's eyes, she didn't want them anywhere, but she didn't let on. "Follow me," she said, gathering the scrapbooks, then taking the older woman's arm. "Watch your step, Mildred."

They picked their way across the dilapidated porch. "A strong man around the place comes in mighty handy." She lowered her voice, but not so low that Jake couldn't hear. "Maybe you can find a way to keep him around permanently."

For a moment, Mrs. Mitchell hesitated, and then hurried her elderly neighbor along, as if fearing what would come out of her mouth next.

The women entered the house and led him down a

wide hallway, the wooden floor gleaming, past a magnifi-
cent staircase nestled into the curve of the outside wall.
The house was an extraordinary example of Victorian
architecture.

At the back of the house, they stopped at a door opening into a small library, the book-laden shelves rising from
floor to ceiling. He stacked the newspapers on the large
desk, a desire to look at them building inside him. As soon
as he finished the porch, he'd ask permission. He suspected
both ladies would question his interest. But he wouldn't
open that Pandora's box.

With the contents of the wagon stowed in the library
and the wagon back in Mrs. Uland's yard, Jake returned
to the porch.

Inside, Callie Mitchell sat across the table from her
neighbor, a pot of tea and some kind of secret between
them.

Callie poured Mildred's cup of tea. "What's this about?"

"I've spent days rummaging through every nook and
cranny in my house searching for that memorabilia, then
getting it in order."

Callie's usually dapper neighbor looked like she'd gotten
into a brawl and lost. Her hair appeared uncombed. The
lapels on her dress tipped like a bird in flight. Her stockings were drooping around her ankles. Finding and putting
those newspapers in order had taken its toil.

"I'll tell you it wore me out. I'm not what I used to be.
Why, last week I had to rest while weeding the garden."
She smiled. "Isn't the early lettuce yummy? I love wilt-
ing it, though it's tender enough to eat straight out of the
garden."

Though she had a sharp mind, upon occasion Mildred went off on some tangent and forgot the point of the conversation.

Her eyes met Callie's. "Oh, sorry, dear. You asked about the newspapers."

"Why did you bring them here?"

"Those newspapers and scrapbooks are records you'll need." Her voice had a slightly impatient tone, as if unable to understand Callie's dim-wittedness.

"Why would I need them?" Callie asked gently.

"So you can write our town's history."

"Why me?"

"Your wonderful essays and poems used to make me cry. You love history. Told me that yourself. I wouldn't trust anyone else with the job."

"That's nice of you to say, but why do you want a history written?"

"I've lived in Peaceful all my life. One look at the obituary column makes it clear we oldsters are dying off. Soon no one will be left to answer questions about the town. Down the road, young people will want to know." She rolled her eyes. "They don't realize that now, of course, but it's true. Most of us never think to ask our elders anything until it's too late. I know my ancestors came over from England. But I have no idea what part and…"

As Mildred went on about her heritage, Callie thought about the countless times she'd wished she could've asked her parents some detail about their lives. Like when and where her father and mother first met. Either Aunt Hilda couldn't remember or never knew. Her pulse tripped. These articles might reveal something new about her mother or her mother's parents. The prospect of learning even one fact to fill the blanks on her family tree was reason enough to take the job.

"You've got the talent. And I've got the facts." Mildred sat back, looking pleased.

Callie hated to refuse her friend, especially since she'd enjoy delving into the town's past, but could she squeeze in another task? "It'll require a lot of time to organize the information and write it up."

"I know. That's the reason I will pay you and pay you well."

Was this God's answer? Not only for her longing for information about her family, but also for her financial predicament? As certainty filled her heart, a smile curved her lips. This put the lie to Commodore's prediction that she'd lose the house. God had provided a way to handle expenses, not with a miracle but through Callie's hard work.

She'd need other sources of revenue to increase the number of women she could help. As soon as the house was safe, she'd seek community support. If her plan were God's will, He'd provide. Her eyes misted. She'd been unsure, even discouraged about how she'd manage. God cared about every detail of her life. She'd lean on Him, the one constant in her ever-changing circumstances.

"I have the money," Mildred was saying, "and I'm running out of time to spend it." She grinned. Every line in her face stood at attention like a squad of eager recruits. "Mr. Uland, God rest his soul, always said I could squeeze a penny until Mr. Lincoln hollered."

Knowing the truth of that statement, Callie bit back a grin.

"All my life, I fought letting go of a dollar. Last I looked, those dollars were breeding. Why, I've got more than enough money to last me and then some. And you…" She paused. "With Commodore's attitude toward this house, I doubt he's helping with your bills. You need income, especially with Elise living here."

Who would've thought Mildred Uland, a tight-fisted friend, and Jacob Smith, a closed-mouth drifter, would be the keys to launching her dream? "Thank you, Mildred, for the opportunity. I'll work on the town's story in the evenings."

"I'll help all I can. It'll be good to have a new purpose, since that husband of mine up and died on me. Why, I'm as adrift as a rudderless sailboat."

Though her husband had been gone for more than twenty years, Mildred often groused about his passing, as if the poor man had died just to annoy her. Perhaps her way of handling grief was better than holding everything inside, as Callie often did. "I'm sure Elise would help, too."

"If she does, tell her to keep quiet about the book. It'll be my gift to the town at Peaceful's seventy-fifth anniversary two years from now. I don't want it blabbed about until it's in print." Mildred reached a blue-veined hand. "I'm paying for your talent and your reticence. Agreed?"

"Agreed." Callie gave her neighbor's hand a squeeze. "You're an answer to a prayer."

"Not surprised. God's been nudging me to get moving on this." She sighed. "Lately it's been more of a shove. I don't hanker to wrestle with God and end up with an out-of-kilter hip. Got me enough aches and pains as it is." She smiled. "I'm late learning the lesson, but when God says, 'Do it,' I do it."

Callie rose and came around the table, wrapping her arms around Mildred's shoulders. "Remember the spring after I came to live with Aunt Hilda? I picked your tulips." She kissed her cheek. "I still can't believe you forgave me for ruining your front flowerbed."

"You were only seven and meant well, wanted to give them to Hilda on her birthday. You weren't the brightest vandal I've come across." Mildred grinned up at her. "You left a trail of petals clear to her house."

"You followed that trail. Carrying a bouquet of tulips you'd picked from your flowerbed out back, claiming I'd missed a few. Then you helped me put together a bouquet, though you surely wanted to paddle my behind."

Tears flooded Mildred's eyes. "No, dear girl. You'd lost your brother and your parents. I lost only petals."

A sudden spasm seized Callie's throat. Her baby brother, Ronnie, just starting to walk. Mama and Papa going about their routine with no warning that the dam was about to give way. All gone.

When she could finally speak, Callie said, "Where would I be if not for Aunt Hilda and people like you, who took a frightened little girl into your hearts?"

"You'd be fine. You were born with all the strength you needed, just like your mother. She's up in Heaven chatting with that inconsiderate husband of mine." She patted Callie's cheek. "That faith of yours will see you through. I'm proud of you, Callie Marie Mitchell."

Callie's smile trembled. "You've been my rock. I'm happy I can do something for you now. Writing this history will be fun. Imagine, Peaceful's past at my fingertips."

Mildred removed some bills from her pocket. "This'll get you started."

At the generous sum, Callie shook her head. "I can't accept this."

"You'll soon have four mouths to feed." Mildred said, then left through the back door and disappeared between the shrubs separating their houses.

In Callie's hands was enough money to meet their needs for months, maybe more. As she tucked the bills into her purse, the weight of obligations she'd had no idea how she'd pay fell from her shoulders. And she knew—

A naughty little girl's petal trail had brought Mildred Uland into her life, a very special friend. God had seen Callie through her troubles every step of the way. He'd given her this home. He'd sent Jacob Smith to make repairs. And Mildred with an offer of much-needed funds. Ensuring that she'd be able to take care of her baby and keep the promise she'd made to Nell, a desperate young girl who'd believed she had nowhere to turn.

With her heart filled to overflowing for the good fortune God had brought into her life, Callie could barely contain the unfettered joy pounding through her. A walk would help expend some of that energy.

She opened the screen door and jerked her foot back. Most of the porch floor was missing. The boards had been stripped away, revealing support timbers underneath. Thankfully, they appeared solid and wouldn't need to be replaced.

Jacob Smith turned from tossing another plank to the lawn.

Callie smiled. "I'm amazed at the progress you've made while Mildred and I have been visiting."

"I don't believe in wasting time."

Truer words had never been spoken. Jacob might not be an open book but he could be trusted to do a good job in a timely manner.

"If all those newspapers your neighbor brought get in your way, I could haul them to the barn."

"They're fine where they are."

"I'm curious why Mrs. Uland dumped them on you."

"Mildred's—" She wouldn't spoil her neighbor's surprise. "Asked me to handle a project for her. I have plenty of room."

"Might make interesting reading. I like looking into the

history of old houses. When you're finished, I'd like to take a look, see what I can find."

"I won't be done anytime soon." She cocked her head at him. "Are you planning on staying in town that long?"

"Only long enough to…repair your house. Then I'll move on."

Exactly as she'd thought. She wouldn't get involved with Jacob Smith or the problems she felt lurking beneath his polite, standoffish exterior. Why, he could walk out of her life as quickly as he'd walked in and never finish the job. She straightened her spine. Another reason to steel herself against this strange attraction she had for him.

"You might want to lock the screen so you and Elise don't use that door and fall through the floor joists."

Nodding, Callie closed the screen, hooked it, closed and locked the wooden door, and then found a red ribbon and tied it around the knob. Satisfied that Elise wouldn't miss the warning to avoid the porch, she left for her walk by the back door.

A warning she'd take to heart. The truth was Jacob Smith could hurt her. Not physically. She'd never think that. But hurt her nevertheless. She'd lock her heart against this drifter. And focus on making a family with her baby, with Elise and her child and focus on her dream. She'd have a full life.

The excitement bubbling within her like an effervescent underground spring sputtered and died. In truth, she'd been lonely for years—most of her life. Marriage to Martin hadn't filled that aching void.

Hadn't she learned anything? Attraction meant nothing.

Jacob Smith was the last man on earth she wanted in her life.

* * *

In a matter of hours, Jake had torn the planks off the porch. He'd found ample lumber in the barn to replace them, the boards covered with a layer of dust and mice droppings, evidence that the intent to make repairs exceeded Martin Mitchell's follow-through.

As Jake pounded in another nail, he cringed at his rush to judgment. If he'd been married when he'd ended up in jail, he'd have no doubt left some things undone. Not everyone was suited for restoration. The poor guy lost his life trying.

Still, Martin's widow lived in a house all but unfit for human habitation. Jake couldn't let a woman endure such conditions. Not that he blamed the house. Time and effort would bring this place back to its former grandeur. Though enough work was here to tether a man indefinitely, a sentence without parole.

Yet to walk away, when he'd witnessed Mrs. Mitchell's relief and joy at the house's revival would be cruel. In the time he remained, if possible, he'd see the task to completion.

His heart lurched. Was the pull more the woman than the work? Either way, he doubted he'd get the job done. Someone was sure to discover his jailbird past.

The aroma of something sugary drifted on the air. Jake pulled the tantalizing scent of home into his lungs then released it in a gust.

Who was he fooling? This wasn't home—at least not his.

He grabbed the length of lumber he'd cut. Grasping another large nail between thumb and forefinger, he pounded it into the pungent pine, the perfume of Jake's life. Far better than the stench of prison, but nothing like the aromas floating out of Mrs. Mitchell's kitchen.

A shadow fell across the porch floor.

He turned to face a man and woman standing on the flagstone walkway. Offering a tentative smile, a round-faced, sturdy woman wore a feather-adorned hat atop her salt-and-pepper hair.

The burly man's brow furrowed beneath the brim of his hat. "Who are you?"

Jake laid the hammer down and rose. "Jake Smith," he said offering a hand.

The visitor didn't take it. "The name means nothing to me."

"Doubt it would. I'm new in town."

"What are you doing to our daughter-in-law's porch?"

So these people were Callie Mitchell's in-laws.

The screen door opened and Mrs. Mitchell stepped out on the solid boards he'd laid, looking fresh as a summer morning after a rain. She glanced at Jake, then at her in-laws. Her bright smile slipped. "I see you've met Mr. Smith, the carpenter who's fixing up the place. I'm sure you're pleased to see I'm taking action to ensure our safety."

Square jaw set in a stubborn line, Mitchell folded beefy arms across his chest. "The best thing you could do is torch this place."

Callie sighed, obviously not the first time she'd heard such nonsense. Father-in-law or not, Mitchell had no right to badger his dead son's wife, a gentle woman with a heavy load.

He turned his gaze on her, ready to toss the idiot off the property if she showed the slightest inclination, but she continued to wear that calm expression of hers. How did she keep her patience, when Jake would like nothing better than to punch the guy?

"We aren't here to argue, Commodore." Dorothy Mitchell laid a hand on her husband's sleeve. "Tell Callie why we've come."

Mitchell shifted on his feet. "I, ah, we brought the fabric and some of those baby things you were looking at before we, ah, got off on the wrong foot."

"Thank you." Smiling, Callie Mitchell motioned to the house. "Would you care for tea? I just took an angel food cake out of the oven."

Ignoring his daughter-in-law's peace offering, Mitchell swept a hand toward Jake. "Can't see how you can afford a handyman."

"Mr. Smith agreed to do the work for a roof over his head and meals."

He turned narrowed eyes on Jake. "Why? When you could get a good-paying job at the grain elevator or lumberyard?"

"I don't plan on staying long."

"That so? Then why did you come?"

Jake kept his expression blank, a skill that had held him in good stead in prison. "Peaceful sounded like a nice town."

"Peaceful is the way we aim to keep it. Most folks around here distrust drifters."

"I appreciate your concern, Commodore, but I've already arranged for Mr. Smith to do the work." Callie Mitchell tapped the toe of her serviceable shoe on the newly laid porch floor. "His work speaks for him."

"Let's have that tea," Callie's mother-in-law said. "Please."

Ignoring his wife, Mitchell frowned. "You're hardly a good judge of character, Callie. The last man you hired ransacked the place and took every cent in the house."

Jake took a step forward. "Where I come from, a man speaks kindly to a lady."

Mitchell turned suspicious eyes on Jake. "And where is that, Smith?"

"Does it matter? I believe good manners are the same everywhere."

"I'll tell you what I believe. A drifter has something to hide." He smirked. "As soon as someone gets close to his secret, that's when he leaves." He turned to Callie. "Reckon I'll stop at the sheriff's office. See what he knows about 'Smith' here."

He thrust the bundle at his daughter-in-law, then took his wife's arm and stomped down the walk.

The threat tore through Jake, heating his veins. Even if the sheriff didn't find out anything about him, that didn't mean he wouldn't come around asking questions. It wouldn't be long until his past caught up with him and forced him out of town.

Jake didn't know where to pin his gaze, but he couldn't look at Callie Mitchell. He couldn't risk the suspicion he'd see in her guileless eyes. He couldn't risk her seeing the alarm surely hovering in his.

"I'm sorry about that. About him," she whispered, then stepped inside.

Something frozen inside him knotted tighter. Callie Mitchell had lost her husband. She managed this run-down house and her daily chores while giving refuge to a young unwed mother—all that responsibility rested on her slender shoulders.

Yet without a moment's hesitation, a member of her family had piled on more burdens. No doubt Commodore Mitchell would call himself a Christian. The man was a hypocrite. The world was full of them, further evidence that if God existed, he had little impact on anyone's conduct.

Anyone that is, except Callie Mitchell. From what he'd seen, people in this town either harassed or leaned on her.

The woman needed someone to look after her. Someone who'd help carry her burdens. Someone like…

Not him.

Anyone but him.

Jake knelt on the porch, then grabbed a nail and swung the hammer. This time, he found his thumb, not the nail's head. Through gritted teeth, he bit back the cry of pain and cradled his throbbing thumb in his palm.

No point in getting all riled up about Mrs. Mitchell's load. He wouldn't—couldn't—get involved with her. He'd never known a woman he could trust.

He was in Peaceful for one reason and one reason only. He had a woman to find. Soon as he finished for the day, he'd visit the Corner Café.

If the waitress proved as informative as she'd been on his way into town, she might lead him to the woman who'd discarded him like a broken tool. Then he could finish what he came for—and get out of town. Before he got tied to things he couldn't have.

Chapter Five

Callie found Elise in the parlor, her feet propped on a footstool, a ball of yellow yarn spinning with each knit-purl. "How's your ankle?"

"Good as new." Elise raised her needles, her face glowing. "I'm making a blanket for my baby."

The joy Callie read in Elise's face matched her own. Sometimes Callie thought she'd burst with the wonder of her impending motherhood. Still, considering Elise's circumstances, she might have had a far different attitude.

She sat beside her and ran a palm over the softness. "It's going to be beautiful and warm."

Elise's lips curved in a smile. "As soon as I'm finished, I'll make one for your baby. What color would you like?"

Precious babies—each one pure as the first dusting of snow. "White. I'd like white."

"That's not as practical as I'd expect from you, but white it shall be."

"I'll use it for church and special occasions. I'll get the yarn on my next trip to town."

"I have enough money to pay for it. It'll be my gift." Her eyes flashed. "No arguing."

"You win," Callie said with a grin then sobered. "I've been asked to tell you something."

Elise laid her needles down, met Callie's gaze then looked away. "From your expression, I'm not sure I want to hear it."

"Hearing what I have to say doesn't mean you have to agree to anything, but I thought you should know." She took Elise's hands. "Sally and Albert Thompson are interested in adopting your baby."

Elise sucked in a gulp of air. "They've wanted a baby forever."

"They have. But what they want isn't important. You need to make the decision that's right for you and your baby."

"Sally would be a wonderful mother, but— Oh, Callie, I know I'm young and don't have a way to earn a living, but I want this baby." She sighed. "Is that selfish?"

"If it is, then I'm selfish, too. We're both facing some of the same issues. I'm not sure how I'll handle all the expenses of raising a child, but with God's help, I'll find a way."

"Mama said a child means fevers, defiance and turmoil. But hugs and jelly kisses compensate for every worry and sacrifice." Her eyes glistened. "Taking the bad with the good—that's love. I love my baby. I can't let it go."

"Then that's settled."

Tears brimmed in Elise's eyes. "I don't know what I would've done if you hadn't taken me in, but I won't live on your charity forever."

"I'm sorry for the trouble between you and your father, but I enjoy your company."

"I've been thinking. Do you think my knitted baby things, shawls, caps and mittens would sell? I want to help with expenses."

"What a great idea! You're a wonderful person, Elise."

Elise's face fell, as if she saw nothing good in herself. A husband would simplify her life. "We've never talked about this and I haven't wanted to pry, but would you consider marrying the baby's father? Or isn't that an option?"

"He's not from around here." She withdrew her hands from Callie's and knotted them in her lap. "Remember the trip I took to North Carolina to see my cousin Carol Ann?"

"Yes, you were excited about taking the train and getting away from the cold for a couple months."

"I met Gaston at a square dance. I fell hard." She sighed. "I sneaked out of the house to meet him several times. I got caught up in his kisses…one thing led to another." Her cheeks flushed. "I was devastated when I had to leave him. We corresponded. I lived for those letters…" A sob tore from Elise's lips and she hung her head. "I was such a fool."

Callie laid a hand on Elise's arm.

"Once I told Gaston about the baby, he…stopped writing. Aunt Audra said he must've left town the day he got the news." Elise swiped at her tears. "My aunt blames herself. No one's to blame but him. And me." She met Callie's eyes. "He said I was pretty and he loved me."

"You *are* pretty." Callie pulled a handkerchief from her sleeve and handed it to Elise.

She blew her nose. "I'm not using his sweet talk as an excuse for breaking God's commandment. Papa wasn't much for praise. Gaston's words…were so different from what I was used to hearing from Papa. I believed every thing he said."

The baby's father wasn't an answer, but would Elise's dad relent and allow Elise to return home? "Can the rift between you and your father be mended?"

Fresh tears filled Elise's eyes. "Papa doesn't love me. How could he love me and say the things he's said to me? Mama says he's hurt and he'll get over it." Her lower lip trembled. "When?"

God gives His forgiveness quickly, at the speed of lightning. But mankind often took longer. "Have you asked your parents to forgive you?"

"More times than I can count. Mama's forgiven me, but I've disappointed her." She gave a strangled laugh. "I've disappointed myself. But Papa…"

"Give him time. Once the baby is here, he'll come around."

Elise fingered the yellow blanket in her lap. "I've asked God to pardon me, but I don't feel forgiven."

A lump formed in Callie's throat. She understood. Too well. Hadn't she asked for forgiveness for her part in bringing about Martin's death? Yet as much as she knew Scripture, as easily as she could quote the Psalm—"As far as the east is from the west, so far hath He removed our transgressions from us"—sometimes she didn't feel absolved. "The Bible makes it clear we're free from sin when we repent. But sometimes it's hard to feel pardoned. Perhaps clemency seems too easy, like we got off scot-free."

Elise snorted. "Memories are longer than Methuselah's beard. From what I've seen, folks expect forgiveness for their mistakes but aren't quick to offer it. I don't mind so much for myself, but I won't be able to bear it if anyone looked down on my baby," she said, her hand hovered over the movement of a little foot or hand.

How could anyone begrudge a kind word to an innocent child? Callie tilted up Elise's chin. "When things look dark and you and I can't see what lies ahead, we'll have to rely on God to light the way. Will you try that with me? One step at a time?"

Elise offered a wobbly smile and nodded. "This unmarried forgiven expectant mother is on the march."

Grinning, Callie glanced at the clock. "We'd better get on the march. We're due to see Doc Wellman in less than an hour. After our appointment, we'll stop at the Mercantile." She pulled the money Sarah gave her from her pocket. "Your mother wants you to use this to buy things for your baby. She cares about you and your child."

"I know she does, but she won't go against her wedding vows and defy Papa."

"Those vows are important."

Vows. Callie had taken them and from that first week wondered—

She refused to finish the thought. Even if Martin had never matured, even if she'd had to carry the load for both of them her entire life, even if sometimes that load wearied her, she'd always be grateful for the baby she carried.

She forced her thoughts back to Elise. "Even if your father never changes his mind, you'll have a home here with me."

Elise burrowed into Callie's open arms. "What would I do without you?"

"We're in this together. We'll be fine," Callie spoke softly against Elise's copper curls, "if we seek God's guidance at the start of each new day."

Elise straightened and met Callie's eyes, the misery in their depths banged against Callie's heart. "If I'd done that last summer, I…I wouldn't be in this mess. I'm a fool for falling for a footloose man."

Through the lace curtains in the parlor window, Callie watched Mr. Smith climb the porch steps. A strong, handsome…drifter. Her breath caught. *Footloose* described Jacob Smith. She'd remember that. Both she and Elise had learned they could be fooled by a man.

Elise rose and tugged Callie to her feet, hugging her or trying to, but her round belly got in the way. They both laughed, easing the tension.

A half hour later, they headed out the door with Elise showing no sign of a limp. Elise looked pretty with her auburn hair swept into a French twist, her shawl pinned in place with a lovely old broach, a keepsake from Callie's Aunt Hilda. Nothing would disguise the girl's advanced pregnancy, but the shawl softened her silhouette.

Jacob Smith rounded the back of the house, tools dangling from his belt and slapping against his denims. He might be a drifter, but she appreciated his help. Goodness, the man never stopped. How long could he keep up the hectic pace?

He tipped his hat. "Afternoon, ladies."

His eyes locked with Callie's, his eyes pools of jade she felt she'd drown in. When had green become her favorite color? Even though she didn't trust him, her feet had a life all their own and brought her closer.

At the sound of Elise's giggle, Callie gathered her wits about her. "Tomorrow's the Lord's Day. You've earned your rest, Jacob," she said unable to look away from the intensity of his gaze. "If you're looking for a place to worship, church service begins at ten o'clock."

His full lips thinned, turned mulish. "Thanks, but I plan on sleeping late tomorrow."

"If God changes your mind about that, we're having a potluck after service. It's your chance to eat food prepared by the best cooks in town."

"Can't see how anyone could improve on your cooking."

The warmth of Jacob's regard spilled into the empty places inside her. "If you're aiming for larger portions, you're succeeding."

Chuckling, he bounded onto the porch and got back to work. He'd accomplished a great deal. Only a few boards needed replacing. Strange how quickly she'd gotten used to having him around the place. His long strides, the noise of saw and hammer, the scent of soap on his skin after washing up at the pump. An image of damp hair curling at Jacob's nape filled her traitorous mind. She shivered and quickly said goodbye.

As Callie and Elise strolled along at a snail's pace, Mildred Uland's cocker spaniel trotted over for a pat until a squirrel captured his attention. He sped after it, chasing it up a tree. "Sandy's feeling feisty this afternoon. Maybe we could use him to round up Mr. Smith for services."

Her attempt at humor fell on deaf ears. Apparently, Elise had her mind elsewhere, probably missing her parents. For all her bravado, Elise loved her father.

Lord, Elise and her father are hurting. Please heal their wounds.

God controlled the outcome. He loved them all and in time would bring them peace. With that assurance, Callie filled her lungs with the soft afternoon air, listening to the chirping birds.

"Only three weeks until the baby comes," Elise said in a wobbly voice. "Oh, Callie, I'm scared."

"I am, too, a little." Callie smiled with as much assurance as she could muster. "Just think, by the time my baby arrives you'll be giving me advice."

"I can't imagine that." Elise laid a hand on her abdomen. "The way this baby's doing somersaults, it has to be a boy."

"So what do girls do while waiting to be born? Read?"

"Silly." Elise giggled. "They knit."

Laughing, they turned onto Liberty toward Doctor Wellman's office, a couple blocks down.

Up ahead, Lowell and Naomi Burch stepped outside the door of the First National Bank. As the bank's president, Mr. Burch had power and influence in town. His wife always wore the latest fashions. Naomi adjusted the skirts of her gown, the jet beads catching the light, then raised her lace-trimmed parasol and took her husband's arm. As the couple ambled toward them, Callie knew the moment they spied Elise by the hitch in their stride.

Elise's steps slowed. "Turn around."

"We'll do no such thing. You're neither a criminal nor contagious." As the couple approached, Callie smiled. "Good afternoon, Mrs. Burch, Mr. Burch."

"Hello, Mrs. Mitchell," Mr. Burch said. "Fine day."

Mrs. Burch gave a nod. "Hello, Callie."

The couple passed by, not uttering a word to Elise. Behind her, Callie could hear Mrs. Burch whispering. The word *disgrace* and *shameful* reached her ears. No doubt Elise's, too.

Did these people believe they'd never done anything wrong? Mrs. Burch was known to gossip. Mr. Burch had an affair with his secretary a few years back. The woman left town and the marriage survived. Still, what right did they have to treat Elise like an outcast?

Elise clenched a shaking hand over her shawl. "If I keep my baby, it'll never be accepted in this town." She turned sorrowful eyes on Callie. "I want to talk to Sally and Albert Thompson."

As much as seeing Elise snubbed hurt, Callie knew sin had consequences. But those consequences shouldn't spill over onto an innocent baby.

A lump rose in her throat. For all intents and purposes, Callie was an unwed mother herself. Not with the social stigma Elise faced, but with the same realities. "Talk to Doc Wellman. Talk to Pastor Steele. If you still want to give up your baby after that, I'll arrange a meeting with the Thompsons."

But inside Callie wanted to scream—don't let anyone force you into that decision. She remembered the loving arms of her mother. Arms she still missed. If Elise wanted her child in her arms, then that's where her baby should be, but Callie had no right to interfere.

She hoped Elise understood that once she gave up her baby to the Thompsons, she couldn't change her mind, no matter how much that decision broke her heart.

Lord, give Elise wisdom to make the right choice.

Here she'd been advising Elise and praying for the girl's wisdom, but what about her own decisions? Could she be both mother and father to her baby? Could she provide for her baby's needs? How long could she take care of her child and still provide support for the unwed mothers' shelter? The money she made writing the town history wouldn't last forever. Callie swallowed against the lump in her throat.

What would she do then?

What she would not do is worry. The tightness in her chest eased. If God gave an assignment, he enabled its success. She'd find a way to care for these girls and her precious child.

Unbidden, the image of Jacob Smith popped into her mind. She forced it away. Nothing good would come from her attraction to that man.

After securing the last board on the porch, Jake stowed the tools, his work done for the day. The idea of examining those newspapers and scrapbooks for information about his birth crept into his thoughts. If he asked to see them, Mrs. Mitchell would want an explanation. An explanation he couldn't give.

The temptation to enter her house uninvited lurched

in his stomach. Unlocked or not, such an action would be deceitful. Time in jail didn't mean he'd lost his standards. Perhaps she'd give him an opportunity. But for now he'd visit the café, talk to that chatty waitress and see what he could learn. Nothing to stop him now that he'd finished the porch.

Not so long ago he'd lived behind bars, confined to a space the size of the lean-to. Now he could move about the Mitchell property, the town of Peaceful, why, the State of Indiana, even the whole country if he got the itch to roam. Grinning, he gave a whoop, then headed out.

On Liberty, he entered the Corner Café, a nondescript colorless place, but spotless as a shiny penny. All eyes turned to him, the stranger in town. Some filled with curiosity. Most appeared welcoming. Not the reaction he'd come to expect. He removed his hat and gave a friendly nod.

Small-town scrutiny was a far cry from what he'd experienced in prison. The warden, guards, convicts serving time appraised each new inmate. All formed judgments, putting a man into one of two slots—troublemaker or target. Troublemakers got respect. Targets got contempt. That first day, Jake learned he'd have to wear a tough-guy persona to survive.

Better remember that welcoming smiles didn't mean these folks wouldn't probe into his past. A past he wanted to forget. But couldn't. No, shouldn't. That past taught him a valuable lesson. Never trust anyone. Even those he felt close to.

Especially those he felt close to.

"Hiya, handsome." The waitress, a crisp apron tied around her waist, approached the counter.

"Hi, Jessie."

A dazzling smile lit her pixie face. "A gal likes to be remembered. What can I get ya?"

He laid his hat on the stool beside him. "Coffee, black."

She grabbed a cup with one hand, the pot with the other and poured mid air, never spilling a drop. "Heard you're working at Callie's."

"Word travels fast." Jake took a sip, strong and hot. Not as pungent as Mrs. Mitchell's, but good. "Thanks for the suggestion."

"Plenty wrong with that old mansion to keep a man busy for months." She poured a cup for herself then sidled closer. "I hope this means you're staying."

"My plans are indefinite."

She chortled. "Isn't that always the way with you good-looking types?"

Jessie's interest was obvious, even to him, a man who avoided connections. She was cute, but lacked the gentle refinement of Mrs. Mitchell.

Why was he thinking about either of them? He had no intention of getting entangled with anyone. No right to consider it, especially with the attractive young widow. He had no idea about what made a family. No idea how to create one. Even if he trusted a woman enough to consider settling down.

Conversation resumed in the café, permitting Jake to pursue his objective. "You get lots of people passing through?"

"No such luck. Life would be more exciting if we did." She leaned a hip against the counter. "You're the first stranger to come into town in ages."

"Have you lived here long?"

"All my life." She leaned toward him. "So tell me, is it true that Elise Langley's staying with Callie?"

Here was the opening he needed. Surely Jessie had heard

the local gossip, even back twenty-four years. "Yes. I reckon a young lady in her fix is a rare occurrence in Peaceful."

"Not as rare as you'd think. Most get married before word gets out, but folks can count." She smirked. "And usually do, if you get my drift."

"Yes, ma'am, I do." He took a sip of coffee. "You keep up with the news."

"I hear things. Most folks have a skeleton or two in their cupboard."

Jake would choose his words with care. Anything he said to this woman wouldn't stop there. "A distant relative of mine may have lived here once, years ago. I don't know exactly where."

She stirred sugar into her coffee. "What's the name?"

"That's the catch. I don't recall. Just remember someone saying the woman lived here. The town name stuck."

She chuckled. "Reckon it would. Well, if you remember her name, ask that neighbor of Callie's, Mildred Uland. She's the town's oldest resident and never forgets a thing." She fiddled with her hair. "Or even better, come in and talk to me."

Ignoring the not-so-subtle message, Jake took another sip of coffee. Jessie sighed and took a step back.

The waitress made a good point. Mrs. Mitchell's neighbor would know all the secrets in this town. "I've met Mrs. Uland. She appears to be a good friend of Mrs. Mitchell."

"Callie attracts friends like pollen does bees. And she needs every one. Can't imagine your husband dying then discovering you're expecting." Jessie picked up the pot. "Reckon what don't kill you makes you strong." She patted his arm, then made the rounds, pouring coffee.

Jake drained his cup. On top of the heavy load she carried, Mrs. Mitchell would cope with motherhood alone.

Why did that trouble him? Wasn't that what he thought his mother should've done? And hadn't?

He paid his bill, adding a generous tip. He'd come, hoping Jessie would rattle off a list of other unwed mothers in town, but he'd gotten nowhere. From what she'd said, unwed mothers weren't as rare as he'd thought. One thing for sure, the waitress had a soft spot in her heart for Callie Mitchell.

Much like the feelings he had for the woman.

Jake's stomach plunged as it had when he'd heard the jury pronounce the guilty verdict. He wouldn't care about Callie Mitchell. Caring carried a stiff penalty. He wasn't here to get involved with anyone. Not even with a woman whose heart appeared to be the size of Texas.

Jake knew better than to pin his happiness on how someone appeared. Both Lloyd and Susan had taught him that even a loving demeanor could hide a devious heart.

Chapter Six

As she sat on one of the two chairs in the examining room, the scent of antiseptic tingled in Callie's nostrils. Across the way, Doctor Wellman, a thatch of blond hair falling across his forehead, moved his stethoscope along Elise's stomach. Doc looked like he could use a wife, to see he got a haircut and his suit pressed, but the life of a small-town doctor probably didn't give a man much time to court.

Doc straightened and removed the earpieces of the stethoscope. "Everything's fine. From the baby's heart rate, I'm guessing you're having a girl."

Elise beamed. "If it is, I'm naming her Kathryn Marie. Marie is Callie's middle name."

Callie grinned. "I'd be honored."

If she had a girl, Callie would give the baby her mother's name. If a boy… She probably should name him after Martin, but she thought of her father and brother and knew she wouldn't.

"If you're wrong, Doc," Elise said, "and this baby's a boy, I'm naming him David."

"Thank you."

"David's your name?"

"Joseph David Wellman. My folks call me Joe David."

"King David was God's man, a perfect name for my baby if it's a boy." Elise's smile drooped. "Oh, David sinned with Bathsheba. Maybe I should select another name—"

"Nonsense." Doc tapped her on the hand. "God used David in a mighty way, sin and all. None of us are perfect."

"Obviously, I'm not." Laying a hand on her abdomen, she flushed. "My sin is out there for everyone to see."

"That baby was knit in your womb by God Himself. That makes her special." He waggled his brows. "No more of that harsh talk, you hear?"

Callie wanted to hug Doc for reassuring Elise.

"Some people make sure I don't forget what I've done." She sighed. "Not that I should."

Doc helped Elise to a sitting position. "If I thought it would do any good, I'd crack a few hard heads together." He lifted Elise's chin. "But it's folks' hearts that need softening. Only the good Lord's got a cure for that."

Something close to adoration filled Elise's eyes. Did Doctor Wellman realize how much he meant to Elise? Perhaps she saw him as a father figure, a substitute of sorts.

"Your baby's healthy and hardy, Miss Langley. Most likely, she'll make an appearance around May Day."

"I like the name David."

"You can use David for the next baby," Doc said with a laugh. "This one's a girl."

Elise smiled up at Doc as he leaned over her, a teasing look on his lean face. Why hadn't she noticed the magnetism between them at other appointments? Doc always joked with Elise, tried to ease the guilt she wore like her personal scarlet *A*.

Up until now, Callie had thought Doc's kindness toward

Elise stemmed from a physician's concern for his patient, but now she wondered if it could mean more.

Just as she'd decided that Elise and Doc had forgotten her presence in the room, Doc motioned to Callie. "You're next."

Callie traded places with Elise and stretched out on the narrow table. Doc Wellman leaned over her. "Have you felt movement, Mrs. Mitchell?"

"I've felt fluttering sensations of late."

"Good, exactly what you should be feeling at five months. That's your baby waving hello. Enjoy it." He grinned. "It won't be long before he'll wallop you awake at night."

Elise giggled. "And send you racing to the chamber pot."

Doc chuckled. "Ah, the inconveniences of motherhood."

After he'd finished his examination, Doc helped Callie upright. "Your lives are about to change, ladies. Don't get me wrong. I grew up in a big family, oldest of seven. I've seen babies bring great joy…and a heap of responsibility." He ran a hand through his hair. "Not easy for either of you, since you'll most likely raise your children alone, at least, in the beginning. That first week or two, enlist the help of others."

"Doc, I'd like to enlist your help, if I may," Callie said then went on to explain her plans for housing unwed mothers and concerns for their care.

"You can count on me, Mrs. Mitchell."

"You've relieved my mind. I'm not sure I could deliver babies alone."

"I'll be glad to take care of delivering their babies. If they can pay, fine. If not, I won't allow them to go without medical care." He sighed. "Too many women die in childb—" He closed his eyes then opened them. "I'm sorry. I'm not much of a doctor to voice that in front of two expectant mothers."

"A walk through Walnut Grove Cemetery makes it clear." Callie glanced at Elise. Hoping the talk didn't scare her.

"Most women do fine. These days, doctors know the importance of hygiene. Not that many years ago, doctors performed surgeries wearing street clothes and without washing their hands. We've come a long way." He smiled. "I like the idea of your unwed mothers' home. I can see that Elise has flourished since she's moved in with you." Doc looked at Elise. "Miss Langley, your mother told me she'd pay for your care."

Elise smiled. "She did?"

"Others may be able to do the same," Callie said, "but it's a huge blessing to know a young woman without money will have the care she needs."

"That's why I'm a doctor." He looked at Elise. "See you next week—same time, Miss Langley. Mrs. Mitchell, schedule for next month. Enjoy this pretty afternoon, ladies."

After making their appointments, Callie and Elise left the office, heading to the Mitchell Mercantile, a smile suffusing Elise's face. Perhaps the prospect of shopping for her baby had put it there, but more likely Doctor Wellman was responsible.

Perhaps it would lead to something. That was fine for Elise, but not what Callie wanted. She'd live her life taking care of her child, giving unwed mothers a home. If a smidgeon of loneliness chaffed on occasion as it did now, she'd follow the advice she'd given Elise and take it one day at a time.

Up the street, Jacob Smith emerged from the Corner

Café and strode toward them, his long legs eating up the distance. Mere steps away, his gaze connected with hers. He gave her a brilliant smile, putting a sudden hitch in her breathing and a wobble in her knees and confirming her worst fear.

No matter how much she told herself she shouldn't, she was attracted to this stranger. His smile might make her feel special, but meant nothing more than a passing interest. These unwanted feelings came from her gratitude to the carpenter for shouldering some of the weight of responsibility on her shoulders.

How could she let a drifter throw her off balance this way? Clearly, the uncertainty of her circumstances and a handsome face had overruled her common sense. When it came to Jacob Smith, Callie questioned if she could trust her judgment.

One look at Callie Mitchell, her face glowing in the afternoon sun, and Jake's heart galloped like a racehorse nearing the finish line. The strangest longing twisted inside him, pressing against his lungs. Callie's eyes reflected goodness, warmth, a gentle spirit, everything he admired. What would it be like to have someone like Callie sitting across the breakfast table from him? What would it be like to have someone like Callie to come home to after a hard day's work? What would it be like to have someone like Callie to inquire about the details of his day?

He had no idea. But, oh, how he wanted to find out.

"I, ah, finished the porch." Like a tongue-tied toddler, he could barely get the words out of his mouth. "Got a hankering for coffee and walked to the café."

"I'd have made you an entire pot for finishing that porch. But I can't blame you. The café's coffee's the best in town."

He knew better. "Your brew has the Corner Café beat."

At his words, her cheeks took on the hue of a summer peach. "Jessie should've made a fresh pot for you. I would have. I'm sorry I wasn't home."

As the colorless cloak of dusk settled around them, streetlamps flared to life. The clamor of the afternoon had softened to a sigh, leaving a sense of serenity that whispered the town's name. Peaceful. If only it could be for him. But he knew how quickly life could change. He had to be on guard and resist believing in what looked like an idyllic life.

He'd had a reason for coming here, though with that sweet smile on Callie's lips and the lemony scent of her hair, his motive fled his mind.

"Hi, Mr. Smith."

Jake jerked toward Elise. "I'm sorry, I didn't see you there, Miss Langley."

Elise giggled, heating Jake's neck like a branding iron.

"Few people miss me these days. I think I know the reason for your poor eyesight," she said, then glanced at Mrs. Mitchell.

What did a man say to that?

Jake heard footfalls behind him. A man, tall, burly, appearing forged of steel, tipped his hat to the ladies. "Callie, Elise, good to see you."

"Hello, Hal." Mrs. Mitchell smiled. "How's Loretta?"

"Strong-minded as usual. If my wife says jump, I jump."

Mrs. Mitchell's eyes lit with humor. "Better keep that to yourself in an election year. No man's going to cast his vote for a coward."

"Loretta's the best shot in these parts. That makes me

a mighty brave fellow. Not a man in Peaceful would dare disagree."

Elise giggled.

He chucked Elise under the chin, and then swung his gaze to Jake, appraising him with one long look. He stuck out a hand. "I'm Hal Frederick, town sheriff."

The news thudded in Jake's stomach, squelching every thought of Callie from his mind and filling him with foreboding, the familiar tightening in every muscle. "Jake Smith, Sheriff."

"I've heard the name. Appears you've got some folks fired up, Smith."

That could only mean one thing. Commodore Mitchell hadn't wasted a minute getting to the law.

Mrs. Mitchell let out a gust. "If you mean my father-in-law—"

"Commodore paid me a visit. As I told him, a town by the name of Peaceful treats our visitors accordingly. That's assuming visitors are the peaceful sort." The smile never left his face. "How long you planning on staying?"

"Long enough to repair Mrs. Mitchell's house."

The sheriff nodded. "Glad you're giving Callie a hand."

Mrs. Mitchell tapped the sheriff on the arm. "Don't forget that you and Loretta are coming to dinner at my house Tuesday evening at six o'clock."

"Not likely to forget, especially if you're serving pie for dessert. Now that Loretta's bagging rabbit and quail, she's got no interest in rolling dough."

Callie laughed. "How's apple sound?"

"Like music to my ears."

"The boys are invited, if they'd like to come."

"A delicious meal would tempt them but they practice baseball on Tuesdays."

With the conversation off him, Jake felt his muscles ease and made a mental note to be scarce Tuesday evening.

"Jacob and Elise will join us, I hope." Callie turned to Jake, her azure eyes full of entreaty, as if his attendance mattered.

He bit back a refusal. Trying to get out of the dinner invitation would look suspicious. He wanted to have as much time with Callie as he could. Not smart but how could he say no to a woman with eyes that blue? "Thanks, I'll be there."

Mrs. Mitchell's eyes fairly danced with pleasure at the prospect. "It'll be fun."

The woman loved cooking and helping others. She'd made him feel at home, had cared about his safety. When had anyone ever done that much for him?

The sheriff turned to Jake. "That'll give us a chance to get acquainted."

How long before the sheriff learned about his past?

Sharing a meal with the law was the last thing Jake wanted to do. But he supposed moving from the stoop to the table proved that Callie Mitchell had begun to trust him. One thing he knew—any pie of hers would be worth the hassle of spending the evening with the sheriff.

"I'll look forward to it, Mrs. Mitchell," Jake said.

Frederick gave Jake and Callie a speculative glance then strolled on, stopping to chat with the few folks lingering on the street.

"Mrs. Mitchell's too formal for a dinner guest. Please, call me Callie." She smiled. "Would you mind if I called you Jacob? I love biblical names."

No one had ever called him Jacob before, but the gentle, dignified sound of it coming off Callie's lips coiled within him. "That's fine, ma'am."

"My, you make me feel old. Callie, remember?"

"Callie."

The prospect of spending time with her rippled through him. They'd share a meal around the dining-room table he'd glimpsed from the hall. All the mealtimes in his entire life had been eaten at a row of long tables. Or alone. What would it be like to stick his feet under Callie's table? And pretend for a while that he was part of a family?

Jake glanced up the street. The sheriff stood watching him, dousing his mood faster than a rainstorm quenching a campfire.

Hal Frederick tried to throw a man off with humor, but Jake never doubted the sheriff's competence.

A lawman would have questions.

They always did.

Callie awakened at dawn with a knot in her stomach and a prayer on her lips. *Please, God, help people to treat Elise kindly today in church.*

Lying in bed expecting trouble wouldn't solve anything. God was in control. She grabbed her robe and headed for the kitchen to prepare food for the basket dinner following service.

By the time Elise plodded into the kitchen, Callie had chicken frying, green beans with ham bubbling on the stove, slaw made and a pie cooling on the counter alongside the stove.

Elise yawned. "Smells good in here. You should've awakened me so I could help."

"You needed your rest. I made oatmeal." Callie pointed at the sink. "I'd appreciate your cleaning up the dishes after breakfast."

"It's the least I can do." Elise took a bowl and filled it, then sat at the table and added sugar and milk. "I've been thinking," she said between bites, "I could stay home today and do the morning chores."

"I've milked. The rest can wait until we're back." She smiled. "You're not fooling me, Elise Langley. You're scared."

"Papa locked me in. And you're shoving me out." She jutted her lower lip. "Not sure I like either one."

Callie moved to Elise's side and laid a hand on her shoulder. "You won't be alone."

"Speaking of alone—what's going on between you and Jake?"

"What do you mean?"

"In town yesterday Jake behaved as if you two were the only people on earth."

"He did not."

"He didn't even know I was there—me, as big as a barn door." She giggled. "You had this goofy grin on your face. You're falling for him."

"Why wouldn't I grin? Do you know how long it would've taken me to replace those rotten boards?"

Elise snorted. "You were grinning about the porch? I don't believe that for a second."

"You're imagining things." Callie plopped her hands on her hips. "Probably because Doc couldn't take his eyes off you."

Color climbed Elise's cheeks. She ducked her head and concentrated on her oatmeal.

"You don't have much to say now."

"Mama taught me never to talk with my mouth full." Eyes twinkling, Elise popped the spoon in her mouth.

Callie laughed, relieved that Elise wasn't fussing about going to church.

A knock at the back door summoned Callie.

Jacob stood on the stoop holding a basket of eggs. At the sight of him, Callie's traitorous heart stuttered in her chest.

"I thought you might need these."

"Thank you." She reached for the basket. "I thought you were sleeping in."

He rubbed a hand along the back of his neck, avoiding her gaze. "Woke before the sun was up."

"I told you God might change your mind."

He harrumphed. "I figured you ladies could use help with chores this morning."

"That's thoughtful of you."

Obviously, Jacob refused to credit God for anything. Perhaps she could still get him to attend church.

She thumbed toward the kitchen. "I've made oatmeal for breakfast, but I could fry a couple of these eggs."

"Oatmeal's fine." Though his tone wasn't convincing.

"You sure?"

"Positive." He took off his hat and dropped to the stoop.

Jacob worked like a dog around the place, but that didn't mean he should be treated like one and continue taking his meals on the stoop. Callie still knew next to nothing about him, but one thing she did know—he wouldn't do them harm.

"Don't be silly. Come in and eat at the table." Callie stepped aside to let him enter. "I won't apologize for being leery at first. But you've proven that you're trustworthy."

His eyes leapt to hers then looked away.

As Jacob stepped inside the back hall, Callie realized that, with the exception of her father-in-law, Jacob Smith was the first man she'd had in her home since Martin died. The first man she'd had in her life. In any way.

Could Elise be right? Could he have an interest in her? No, he was a drifter. Drifters didn't stay.

Roused by the puzzled expression in Callie's eyes, Jake kept his mouth shut and crossed the threshold before he blurted out that he didn't belong there, even though that was the barefaced truth.

At the arched doorway leading from the hall into the kitchen, he removed his hat and held it in both hands, spinning it between his fingers. Tantalizing aromas drifted toward him. The serenity of the room, reflecting Callie's gentle spirit, wrapped around Jake, tugging him in.

He felt jumpier than a freshly broke bronco. When had he ever been invited inside a home, a real home, where folks shared their meals, their lives, their hopes and dreams? Never. Well, except for hauling in those newspapers for Callie.

He'd slept in the back room at the construction company where he worked, took his meals at a nearby café or carried food in from the neighborhood grocer. Not so different from others he knew. Someday he'd buy a home of his own and put down roots, so why didn't that prospect hold the appeal of this kitchen?

"Hi, Jake." Elise's eyes twinkled as if she found something funny, but he had no idea what.

Callie moved to the stove. "Come to church with us this morning and stay for the potluck. I've made plenty of food."

"Smells great." He was certain he'd do no such thing.

His gaze roamed the kitchen, took in the cupboards, their patina mellow with age, then the checked green-and-white curtains framing the windows, the soft green walls, the vase of bleeding hearts in the center of the table. Everywhere he looked he saw Callie's penchant for making a nest. "This is cozy."

"My aunt always said the kitchen's the heart of a home." She motioned to the sink. "Feel free to wash up while I pour your coffee."

Jake eased past her, keeping his distance. At the washbasin, he scrubbed his hands and dried them on a towel. Not the rough, threadbare towels he'd used in the orphanage and in prison. When had he felt anything softer?

Turning from the sink, unsure where to sit, he glanced at the three empty chairs. Callie handed him a mug. As he took it, his hand brushed hers, sending a jolt to his spine and his feet toward the table. "Thanks for the coffee. Uh, which seat is yours?"

"I sit here." She pointed to the head of the rectangular table. "Now."

Had that been Martin's place at the table? Did she fill it to avoid seeing the seat empty? If so, that proved Callie Mitchell grieved for her husband. As if those widow's weeds she wore weren't enough of a reminder.

"I've already eaten. Sit wherever you like," she said.

He dropped to the middle seat. Callie put a bowl of oatmeal in front of him. Nothing about this cooked cereal resembled the winter fare he ate every day in the orphanage, either runny as gruel or solid as cement.

Jake added sugar and cream then scooped a spoonful of oatmeal and took his first bite. "Delicious."

Callie gifted him with a smile. "I'm glad you like it. From your expression earlier, I thought you didn't."

"I've never had oatmeal that tasted like this."

Elise rose and took her bowl to the sink. "Please come to church with us, Jake. You'll be doing me a favor."

Did she believe his presence would take the focus off her?

"Nothing like a visitor to get folks excited." Callie met his gaze. "This will be Elise's first time to attend…in months."

Jake would prefer taking a thrashing than to darken a church door, but one glance at Elise's drawn face and he understood. Walking into this home had made him uncomfortable, as if he didn't belong and had no right to be here. But it was nothing compared to the stares, the whispers, the muttered comments at his trial and upon his release from jail.

No doubt Elise would experience the same thing at church with her pregnancy in full bloom. He'd go if for no other reason than to shield her from that nightmare. And to please Callie. "I suppose you could use reinforcements."

"We're all going," Callie said in a contented tone, then turned to Elise. "If anyone is impolite to you, they'll answer to me."

Elise grinned and winked at Jake.

Callie folded her arms across her chest. "Do you doubt I'm a formidable opponent?" She attempted a glower and failed.

"No." Elise was laughing now.

Jake chuckled. "I wouldn't want to go up against you, Callie." Then he thought better of it. Going up against the young widow might just be fun.

Callie grinned. "I'm glad you both see I'm a force to be reckoned with." The grin faded as she tucked the dishes she'd prepared into a large woven basket. "Some people believe they're pure as driven snow, but pew sitters are sinners, too. Saved, but not by their goodness."

From what Jake had seen, people who ranked sin were quick to judge. Innocent or not, he'd been in prison. To most, prison spelled guilty. Callie would probably feel the same way if she knew he'd served time.

"If your father-in-law's reaction means anything, Callie, my presence at church might make things worse."

A flash of disquiet crossed Callie's face. She quickly controlled her expression. "As long as the house is unsafe, Commodore assumes I'll have to move in with him and Dorothy. He's upset that you're thwarting his plan."

Elise's brow furrowed. "Can he take your house away?"

"No, it's mine. I'm staying and you are, too, for as long as you want." She glanced at Jake. "Once Commodore sees you in church, he'll have to admit that you're not the scoundrel he makes you out to be."

Jake suspected that Mitchell didn't change his opinions that easily. Still, he'd go. What choice did he have with Elise looking at him with those soulful eyes of hers? With Callie's gaze issuing a challenge?

This cozy kitchen and its occupants enveloped him in the warmth of home and family—all the things he'd missed and yearned to have. He wouldn't let Commodore run him off.

But Jake suspected that his and Elise's presence in church today would stir up trouble. For years he'd avoided trouble. Now it appeared he'd go looking for it.

Chapter Seven

Callie jabbed a hatpin in the crown of her Sunday best, facing the mirror in the elaborately carved hall tree with more appendages than an octopus—hooks for coats, slots for umbrellas and canes, a shelf for men's hats or ladies' gloves and a bench to ease off one's boots. She'd get far more accomplished if she could handle that many tasks at once. Though, at times like this morning, she felt more octopus than human.

With all she had going on, she'd had little time to consider Jacob's baffling demeanor in her kitchen earlier. She'd entertained a host of friends and family, but had never witnessed the kind of discomfort he'd exhibited.

In his realm, making repairs to the house, he appeared totally at ease. So why would a take-charge man who handled one chore after another with confidence become hesitant, look as if he didn't know whether to sit or stand or run?

Tucking a wisp of hair in place, her hand stilled, as an idea took hold in her mind. That first day, Jacob told her he'd grown up in an orphanage. Was it possible he'd always lived in an institution or rented a room somewhere, taken his meals in cafés and never stepped foot inside a private residence?

That didn't make sense. Perhaps the reason for his uneasiness had more to do with attending church. No doubt the reason his lack of faith. Yet, he'd agreed for Elise's sake, almost as if he felt a kinship with her, and then gulped his breakfast and left, supposedly to change for services.

Would he reconsider? No, he'd said he would attend. One thing Callie believed—Jacob kept his word.

The grandfather clock chimed the half hour. While the clock ticked away, she'd been dillydallying, trying to decipher Jacob Smith, a puzzle she couldn't solve. "Elise, are you ready?" she called up the stairs, tugging on her gloves.

Her young charge appeared on the landing, her hair corralled in a tight bun, her cheeks pale, her gaze tethered to Callie's like a lifeline. "Ready as I'll ever be," she said, but her voice wobbled.

Smiling to impart courage to Elise, even as a lump rose in Callie's throat, she motioned her down. "We don't want to be late."

As Callie stepped onto the porch, the odor of pine wafted from the newly laid boards. Her mind flew to long ago Christmases. Freshly cut tabletop trees, the branches adorned with strings of popcorn and her paper ornaments. Ornaments, pictures, keepsakes, all swept away in the churning water. Along with her parents, baby brother and three others who drowned that tragic day. With trembling hands, she took Elise's elbow and they descended the sturdy steps.

"Is Jake planning to paint the porch boards?"

The odor of pine couldn't be obscured fast enough to suit Callie. "Yes, once he gets the railings fixed." Callie's gaze roamed the yard, but she saw no sign of the carpenter. "I hope Jacob didn't change his mind about going."

The words had no more left her mouth than he appeared, his raven hair damp and glistening, his jaw clean-shaven, his rangy frame sporting creased pants and a starched white shirt.

Callie's breath caught and held as she drank him in. Not his usual denims, but no matter what he wore, clothes draped on his lean muscular build with an elegance that made him stand out in a crowd. Something told Callie he'd prefer to blend in.

He greeted Elise, then turned to her. "I bought these clothes in town yesterday for that dinner you invited me to. Didn't expect to need them this soon."

"You look very handsome," she said, pleased that he'd wanted to make a good appearance for her.

His gaze traveled her purple dress, the snowy-white high neck and wide lapels covering her shoulders, then slid down her length to the hem. "You look beautiful. Like violets in bloom."

Their eyes locked and something significant passed between them, deepening the connection Callie didn't want but couldn't resist. "Thank you," she managed, trying not to let him know his compliment had melted her insides into a puddle.

"You look pretty, Elise."

With downcast eyes, Elise gathered her shawl more tightly around her bulging middle. "Your mother raised a polite son."

The light in Jacob's eyes dimmed. Elise had forgotten he'd never had the comforting presence of a mother. Callie had a crazy notion to pull him into a hug, to try to make amends for the years he'd spent in an orphanage. But, of course, she wouldn't.

"Where's your basket?" he asked.

Callie motioned to the porch, trying to turn her way-ward thoughts to the task at hand. Jacob bounded up the steps, lifting the heavy load with ease. He was considerate. Considerate and reliable, a combination Callie respected. Yet without a family, life had left him wounded. Some-thing Callie understood all too well. Her heart went out to this loner, yet his lack of openness warned her to keep their relationship impersonal. Or was it already too late for that?

Returning to their sides, he swept a hand up the walk. "After you, ladies."

With Elise all but dragging her feet, the four-block walk to Peaceful Christian Church took far longer than it should have. At the entrance, Elise froze.

"Be brave," Callie whispered. "We're marching, remember?"

Biting her lip, Elise straightened her spine. Jacob held the door and they walked into the vestibule, Elise with her head held high. Callie had never felt prouder of anyone. Once her eyes adjusted to the dim light, Callie got her bearings. Most folks sat in the pews or were moving in that direction.

"Jacob, would you please put the basket over there with the others?" She pointed to a bounty-filled bench.

He did as she asked, jaw rigid, eyes straight ahead. The look of a man prepared for trouble. When he returned to her side, Callie, her heels clacking on the wooden floor, led the troop toward the last pew on the right. Every head turned in their direction, eyes focusing on Elise. From some of the startled, then stern expressions, not everyone rejoiced that Elise had returned to services.

Behind the altar the stained-glass window sparkled, radiating the joy and peace of the Lord. Or so Callie saw it. How she loved this beautiful church with its dark wood-work and whitewashed walls. She hoped nothing would happen to bring ugliness to this house of worship.

"Please stand. Open your hymnals to page 37, 'What a Friend We Have in Jesus.'"

Sandwiched between Jacob and Elise, Callie flipped to the hymn and held the book for her companions as the song leader signaled the organist, then led the singing.

Callie glanced to the right, to Elise's trembling lips and wondered what thoughts filled her mind—guilt, humiliation or elation to worship once again in God's house? She put an arm around her and squeezed. Elise's lips turned up in weak smile.

To her left, Jacob's tight-lipped profile looked rigid, as if chiseled from marble. Was he angry at their reception or merely loath to be in church? Perhaps years in an orphanage had erected stumbling blocks between him and God. Stumbling blocks he needed to demolish, as he had the rotten boards of her porch, before he could find peace.

As she turned the pages to the next song, Callie prayed that after the service, congregation members would welcome Elise and Jacob. Whether they intended it or not, their behavior would send a message—censure refuted a loving God. Mercy revealed God's love.

Jacob had said the church wanted their pew sitters clean. She'd argued the point then, but now…

Now she wondered if he'd been right.

Callie took a shaky breath. She'd come this morning to worship and worship she would. And perhaps, just perhaps, God would soften hearts and transform what looked like trouble into harmony.

Please, Lord, help everything that's done and said this morning be in accordance with Your will.

Having laid it before the throne, Callie released the

weight of her concerns and sang with abandon, filled with expectation that God would bless Elise and Jacob for setting aside their qualms and attending church.

Just as He'd blessed her when she'd come to Peaceful, a frightened little girl. This church family had opened their arms to her, giving her guidance, love and support.

Surely two hurting people would be welcomed with the same love as a grieving child.

Wouldn't they?

Jake half listened to the sermon on harvesting the sheaves, guessing that most folks sitting in the pews didn't care to save every soul, and considered some not worth saving.

After the sermon, a ruddy-faced gentleman read a list of the sick and announced the potluck to follow. The preacher gave the benediction and the congregation spilled into the aisles, hauled by their noses toward the tantalizing aroma of food.

Jake rose from the pew and stepped aside, letting Callie and Elise lead the way. As in jail and the towns he'd stopped in since his release, he felt eyes on his back. A stranger would naturally arouse curiosity. How long before those stares turned hostile? And curiosity became judgment?

Why he'd agreed to stay for the meal baffled him. With an instinct that rarely failed him, Jake sensed that few would welcome Elise or him into the fold. Fine. He'd never seen anyone until Callie do more than mouth their faith anyway.

When Gerald Swartz had picked him out from the lineup of orphans, right after Jake's sixteenth birthday and taken him home, Jake had believed he'd attained his childhood dream. As long as he could remember, his fantasies had centered on having a family, a home, perhaps sharing a room with a brother or two. At last, someone wanted him.

They'd wanted him all right.

To work from sunup to sunset, handling every imaginable chore they threw at him. Eager to please, he'd slept in the barn, bathed in the creek, worn hand-me-down clothes, done exactly as he was told without complaint, certain he'd earn their trust and prove he wouldn't be a burden.

Soon they'd include him in the tight circle of family.

Soon never came.

Not that the Swartzes were cruel. They'd filled his belly. Had taken him to church and sent him to school, exactly as the rules required. But he'd never been welcomed in. He'd never spent a single night under their roof. He'd never received an affectionate hug or a kind word.

Each Sunday, they'd sat in their church pew, nodding at the message of love, but never showed him a speck of it by word or deed. The night of his seventeenth birthday, he'd run away. Better to expect nothing than to live with unfulfilled hope. Better to learn a trade and earn a wage than depend on scraps of a family that shut him out. Better to go through life a loner than count on anyone.

Hadn't Susan given him further proof of that?

One church visit brought it all back. If these folks resembled the people he'd spent that year with, they were welcome to their songs. Welcome to their sermons. Welcome to their God.

Hypocrisy. All of it.

He couldn't wait to leave, to reject the stifling pretense of piety, but he couldn't desert Elise and Callie in case they needed him.

In the vestibule, parishioners flowed around the three of them, as if steering clear of an uncharted island, an obstacle on the way to their baskets.

"Good morning, Callie," a woman said, then she turned to Elise. "How are you feeling, dear?"

"Fine, Mrs. Thompson."

"You've got that glow about you. It won't be long now."

"Marlene, I'd like you to meet Jacob Smith, who's doing some work around my place. Mrs. Thompson is Peaceful's postmistress."

The woman shook his hand like a long-lost friend. "I hope you're staying for the meal, Mr. Smith." She glanced toward the door. "Speaking of which, I'd better get going. I'm in charge of setting up the tables." She darted off.

Mrs. Thompson appeared nice enough, but that didn't ease the tension knotting inside Jake. Like a greenhorn on a cattle drive, Jake trailed the women toward Callie's basket, meeting a few friendly parishioners along the way. For a man who'd been misjudged, he'd been quick to do the same. Perhaps he'd been wrong about these folks.

Carrying Callie's basket in one hand, Jake ushered the ladies toward the door where the pastor stood shaking hands. Callie introduced Jake.

Pastor Steele greeted him and Elise with warmth, then took Elise's hand. "Good to have you back."

"Thank you," she said softly then hurried to Callie's side.

"I'm looking forward to a slice of your pie, Callie," Pastor Steele said. "What did you make this time?"

"Cherry with a lattice-top crust."

The pastor all but smacked his lips. He turned to Jake. "Lots of benefits to this calling. Eating the ladies' fine cooking is one of the best. Now don't go tattling to my wife." He winked, then shook Jake's hand. "Good to have a new face in the pew, Jacob. I hope you'll come back."

Jake merely nodded. No point in telling the preacher

he wouldn't. They descended the steps, turning toward the tables set up in the side yard already loaded with food, and into the path of a couple blocking their way.

Jake recognized Elise's father and was immediately struck by their resemblance. Except Mark Langley's eyes reminded Jake of thunderclouds before a storm.

Callie laid a hand on Jake's arm. "Would you mind putting the basket on one of the tables?"

Obviously, she wanted to protect Elise from the embarrassment of facing her father in front of him. Jake didn't like leaving them alone with this angry man. He shot Langley a scathing look, then did Callie's bidding. Wishing he could punch the good barber in the nose. The man was another example of a Christian's lack of clemency.

As Mr. Langley glowered at Jacob's retreating back, Sarah put a protective arm around her daughter.

"That guy was in my shop yesterday. Is he the father?"

"No! He just arrived in town. You know who the father…"

"Who's to say that scum didn't come here?" He leaned toward Elise. "How could you shame us by flaunting your condition at church?"

Elise's eyes glistened. "I'm shaming myself. Not you."

"Elise came for the same reason we all do, Mr. Langley. To hear God's Word, worship and have the support of the church family."

"God's Word is clear. Honor your father and mother. By insisting on keeping your child, Elise, you're defying my authority." He pointed a finger at Callie. "You've made that possible, Mrs. Mitchell, by inviting her in. I don't know how you live with yourself."

Callie reached a hand, then pulled it back. "What's

happened can't be changed, but that baby you're disgraced by is your grandchild."

Color drained from Mr. Langley's face, as if she'd struck him. "We're not staying," he said. "I'll fetch your basket, Sarah."

Eyes brimming with tears, Sarah wrapped Elise in a hug. "I've missed you, sweetheart. How are you? What does the doctor say?"

Elise's father pivoted back. "Are you coming?"

Mrs. Langley didn't answer, didn't move. Her silence lengthened—a mutiny of sorts. Then she heaved a sigh and followed her husband.

"It's almost time to eat." Callie ushered Elise toward the tables. "You can help set out our food."

Elise went through the motions of helping, but Callie could see that her heart was breaking. Callie longed to smack some sense into Mr. Langley's mulish head. He was hurting, but he needed to think of his daughter. She needed his forgiveness.

Why couldn't her father count his blessings? He had a family, a grandchild on the way, an innocent baby needing his love and protection. Callie would give anything if her parents could see her baby.

Signaling the group to silence, Pastor Steele bowed his head. "Lord, thank You for this food and time of fellowship. Open our hearts to visitors and members alike that our actions might be a pleasing offering to You. Surround us with awareness of Your love and the gift of Your grace. Amen."

The unseasonable high temperatures of the past few days had eased, bringing a gentle breeze—a perfect day for a picnic. Even with the run-in with her father earlier, Elise relaxed and managed to eat. Parishioners came by to say hello and wish her well. The pastor's pointed prayer a possible reason.

Several men stopped to talk to Jacob about the work at Callie's, a few asked his opinion on projects of their own. Jacob joined them in a game of horseshoes, tossing ringers almost every time. From the serene, even happy expression on his face, Jacob was having fun.

With her heart overflowing with peace, Callie walked to the dessert table. A piece of Mrs. Uland's chocolate cake would be a delicious finish to a lovely day.

Mrs. Sunderland, the corners of her mouth drooping like the bedraggled flowers on her hat, cornered Callie under an elm. "How could you bring a fallen girl to church? What kind of an example does that give our young people, to rub elbows with a sinner?"

"We're all sinners, Mrs. Sunderland."

The woman sniffed. "Next thing you'll have a party for her and ask for baby gifts. Invite the whole church or some such nonsense."

"Elise made a mistake. She's remorseful—"

"I didn't see her come forward at the altar call. No decent girl would grace this sacred building carrying a baby out of wedlock without begging forgiveness. She should've done that in front of the entire church."

Callie couldn't believe her ears. "You and I are allowed to repent in private. Shouldn't we offer that same grace to Elise?"

"Her sin isn't some little white lie or a bad word voiced in anger. Her sin is fornication. *And* out there for all to see."

Callie's hands balled into fists. "Would an altar call have made a difference to you? You're ranking sin, as if some deserve forgiveness and others don't. Elise needs our love, not condemnation."

The woman smirked. "I'd say she's had all the love she can handle."

"That's just cruel." Unable to bear the presence of this judgmental woman a moment longer, Callie pivoted, tears flooding her eyes until she could barely see and hurried around the church where she'd have privacy.

"Callie?"

She turned, colliding with Jacob. He grabbed her by the shoulders to steady her. With a callused thumb, he brushed away the tears sliding down her cheeks. "Don't pay attention to that battle-axe."

At his caring touch, Callie's breath caught. She longed to step into his arms and accept the comfort of being held.

"I overheard," he said. "I'd regret making a spectacle for your and Elise's sakes, but give the word and I'll deposit that woman's judgmental carcass on the lawn."

At the image popping into her mind, Callie gave a shaky smile. "She probably deserves it, but she's just one person. Everyone else, well, except for Elise's father, has been kind."

"I've noticed. Several men welcomed me to the community. All and all, this is a nice little town."

The exact words Callie hoped to hear. Perhaps that welcome he'd felt would bring Jacob to church. And in time, he'd find his way to God.

"Now that you've seen that most Christians are compassionate and loving, maybe you'll like Peaceful enough to settle here."

The smile on Jacob's face ebbed. A guarded, unreadable expression clouded his eyes. She took a step back.

What made a man look ready to run?

What secret was Jacob Smith hiding?

Chapter Eight

The fishing poles were a ruse. Not that Jake would admit it to Callie. Standing on her stoop, holding the two rods he'd borrowed from the large stash in the barn, he waited for her to answer his knock with the impatience of a kid waiting his turn in a candy store.

The door opened. In Callie's eyes, he saw weariness he hadn't seen before. As if something with the weight of an anvil were perched on her shoulders, sapping her of the energy to take a step. He'd been right. Callie needed to unwind, to dangle a line. Take time for her. And him.

He smiled. "Nice afternoon for fishing."

A spark of interest lit up her eyes. "Yes, it is. You'll find plenty of earthworms in the garden if you're looking for live bait."

"Got them right here." He pointed to the bait box.

"Good, hope they're biting." She turned to step back inside. Away from him.

"Why not find out for yourself?"

She cocked her head, looking as puzzled as if he'd spoken in a foreign tongue.

"I'm asking you to go with me."

"Fishing? With you?"

"Yep, why else would I have two poles?"

"Martin always propped a number of poles along the bank."

"Keeping all those lines straight must've made casting complicated for you."

She fiddled with her collar, averting her gaze. "He never... Well, he never asked me to go along."

"Why's that?"

"I asked him once. He said...he just said he needed time away."

Her words banged against his heart, penetrating his defenses as if they were made of putty, instead of bricks and mortar. "With that patience of yours, I'm guessing you're an excellent fisherman," he said, struggling to keep his tone even.

A sudden smile came to her lips. "I used to be. When I was little, my dad took me fishing. And a friend and I went as kids, every chance we got."

Callie's deceased husband knew she liked to fish and never once took her. The man hadn't appreciated what he had. All the more reason Jake wouldn't take no for an answer. He intended to erase that exhaustion from her face and give her some fun, especially after that biddy's attack at the church picnic.

He could do that much for her.

"I'd like to spend time with you, Callie, doing something besides work. Fishing will be fun."

A sparkle lit her eyes. She glanced inside. "I should probably stay with Elise."

Jake bit back a sigh. "Elise is welcome to come along."

A lie.

He wanted Callie to himself. He wanted to hear her soft laughter again. He wanted to see the delight in her face when a nibble jerked her line. Most of all, he wanted to be an ordinary man out with an ordinary woman.

"I'll ask her." Callie whirled away. "Be right back."

Kneeling, Jake opened the tackle box at his feet to an impressive array of floats, hooks and manmade bait and flies. Mitchell hadn't spared any expense with his fishing gear. Jake had always done fine with a worm dangling from a hook.

A moment later, wearing a straw bonnet and a dazzling smile, Callie appeared with a basket. "Elise dislikes worms and fish, alive or dead, and wants no part of our adventure. She's curled up in the parlor reading a book."

The news that he'd have Callie to himself exploded in his chest and pumped through his veins. "Guess we'll have to manage without her." He'd tried to sound disappointed but from the way Callie's cheeks turned rosy, he'd failed.

"Would you like me to make sandwiches? I always did for Martin. He said fishing made a man hungry."

The only hunger Jake had was for time with Callie. This woman captivated him like no other, made him want to please her, to protect her, to—

He told himself to pull back. This was a fishing trip, not a lifetime commitment. No one's getting hooked here, except a bluegill.

"I'm still stuffed from the church picnic."

"Me, too." She indicated the basket. "Just in case, I've brought cookies."

"What kind?"

"Snickerdoodles."

"Mmm, sugar and spice."

"And all that's nice."

He tapped her chin. "That's what little girls are made of."

"I hope I have a girl." Her mouth formed a circle of surprise. "Oh, what if it's a boy and he heard that?"

"If he did, he'll no doubt make you regret saying it by living up to his reputation." He grinned. "Let's see, frogs and snails and puppy-dog tails, that's what little boys are made of." Unable to take his eyes off her, he offered the crook of his elbow. "Girls are wonderful, especially the grown-up variety."

"Thank you, kind sir." She took his arm as they started down the walk. "Boys are special, too."

"Not according to the girls at the orphanage. They never let us forget our less than impressive makings."

She giggled, looking young, carefree and beautiful.

As they strolled along, the distance between the Victorians lengthened until they reached the edge of town. Across the way, between the trees, Jake spotted a strip of flowing water glinting in the afternoon sun. The scent of loamy soil mingled with the hum of gurgling water. Birds chirped, leaves whispered in the breeze. A sense of peace settled over Jake, as pleasant as the scent of Callie's fragrance.

He helped Callie descend the bank, guiding her toward a large rock at the water's edge. At their approach, a frog, nose barely above water, leaped out of reach. Down the way, the deep drone of a bullfrog geared up for his nightly serenade. Everywhere Jake looked, creatures took part in the mating dance of spring, building homes, re-creating their kind. A deep ache of loneliness throbbed anew inside him.

He dusted the rock off with his hand. "Have a seat, fair lady."

Then he joined her, sitting on the edge, barely on the rock at all, and baited the hooks.

Callie watched, smiling. "You've done this before."

"The orphanage wasn't too far from a pond. We'd sneak off to fish whenever we could. If we cleaned what we caught, the cook would fry them. Nothing's better than a mess of fresh-caught bluegills."

"Bluegill is my favorite. Catfish was Martin's."

How often had Martin considered Callie's likes and dislikes? If at all? If Jake were married to Callie, he'd bring home a bucket of bluegills every week. But he wasn't. He needed to remember that.

Jake handed Callie a pole. "You know how this is done."

"Well, it's been a while."

"Watch the float. If it goes under, yank the pole up to set the hook. Then reel it in. Simple unless the fish aren't biting and all you catch is a twig or an old shoe."

Callie laughed, the melodious sound mingling with the serenity of their secluded surroundings, charming Jake down to his toes.

"To cast, just whip the tip of the pole back, then forward toward the river. As you do, put your finger on the spring to release the line."

Fingers posed hesitantly over the mechanism, she gave him a quizzical look.

"Would you like me to cast for you?"

"Let me try." She rose, swung the rod back, the line shot out…and snared on the undergrowth behind them. Jake untangled the line and asked her to reel it in. Absorption in the task easy to read on her face, she tried again. Again, the line caught in the bushes.

As he worked to free the line, she shook with laughter. "Maybe you'd better show me."

He came around behind her and laid his hands over hers, wrapping her in the circle of his arms. Aware of the proximity of her body, the warmth of her skin, Jake longed to pull her against him, to nuzzle her soft nape, kiss her.

Callie glanced over her shoulder at him, bringing her face mere inches from his and dropped her gaze to his mouth. Just one step and he'd feel those soft lips beneath his. His grip tightened and he lowered his head.

She spun away, facing the river. "How, uh, how do you do this again?"

With yearning mounting within him, he guided her hands through the motions. The line sailed through the air. As soon as it hit the water, Callie moved out of his arms.

He watched the float drift in the current, aching to pull Callie back in his arms. But she held herself apart, her grip tight on her pole, as if her life depended on it, avoiding the attraction sizzling between them.

How could he blame her? He had nothing to offer her and her baby except a past that would surface one day and suck them into a maelstrom of trouble.

"This is fun," she said, keeping her gaze glued on the float and off him.

The float dipped under the water, Callie yelped with surprise, then whipped up the tip of the rod, cranking with all her might, the line growing tauter with every spin of the reel.

A fish emerged, skimming through the water toward her. "I got one!"

Jake grabbed the net, skidded along the bank and scooped up her catch, a bluegill. "It's a beauty," he said, smiling.

As he strode the bank to show her, she laughed again, her face alight with delight. She was having a good time, exactly what he wanted to give her.

After they'd estimated its length, he removed the hook from the bluegill's mouth, put it on the stringer he'd tied to a sapling and eased it into the water. With his stomach flopping like that bluegill had in the net, Jake fought the truth. He was falling for Callie. And he couldn't. But he'd enjoy this day. Wrap it in his memory to take out again and again.

As they fished, he and Callie munched cookies, swatting at an occasional mosquito, exchanging fishing stories and talking about their love of nature.

"Imagine how much fun God must've had making all this." She swept her hand. "And Adam, too, when he got to name all the creatures God created." She laughed. "I can't even decide what to name one little baby."

Looking at her face, aglow with enthusiasm for life, for her God, for her baby, Jake wanted what she had.

"Keep seeking God, Jacob. If you do, you'll find Him."

She must've seen that longing on his face. But she hadn't seen him reading Scripture every night. Nothing had changed. He switched the subject and they moved on to other topics. The time passed quickly, with each of them pulling in several bluegills. Jake even caught a good-sized bass.

"I'll fry them, if you'll filet them," Callie offered.

"It's a deal."

Callie gathered the basket as Jake corralled their catch and fishing gear. "Thanks for bringing me, Jake. I couldn't have a better friend than you."

The smile on his face faltered. She didn't want a romantic relationship. Wasn't that what he wanted, too? So why did her words hook his heart with a painful sting?

On the walk home, the sounds of approaching night enveloped them. Birds called to one another in the trees. Insects hummed, joining the bullfrog chorus, a cheerless chatter that to Jake spoke of endings, not beginnings.

No matter how much he pretended otherwise, he'd been

fooling himself about wanting to give Callie only a fun afternoon. Or that he cared one whit about fishing. He cared about this woman. She charmed him, like no other. Yet he had no hope of reeling her in.

She needed a husband, a father for her child. A jailbird wouldn't do.

He'd seek information about his birth mother and forget this foolishness. He was meant to walk through life alone.

As he always had.

Callie stood as far back from the stove as she could and still keep an eye on the fish sizzling in the large iron skillet. Another skillet of fried potatoes and onions was set to the side. Once Jacob finished stowing the gear and washed up at the pump, he'd be in. He'd sit at her table and eat with the gusto of a man who loved home cooking. And fill the emptiness in her heart.

Across the way, Elise set the table for three. "You actually had fun?"

Her incredulous tone made Callie chuckle. "I did. Catching fish is fun. The river was peaceful. Jake ate a slew of cookies. The man has a hollow leg."

"Did you bait your own hook?" Elise wrinkled her nose with displeasure.

"He insisted on doing it for me, though I could've."

"I feel sorry for the worms. Fish, too." She gave a wry grin. "Guess that makes no sense, since I'm looking forward to supper."

"Me, too."

"So what was it like to spend time alone with Jake?"

Fishing might have been the goal. And they'd caught quite a few, but nothing had prepared Callie for her reaction to the man. Perhaps it had been the solitude, the two of them alone surrounded by the beauty of God's creation and an ever-deepening awareness of each other.

God created man and woman, planting within them a yearning for intimacy, a desire to walk through life two by two. Surely that was the reason, the only reason, she'd had that response to him.

"He's attentive, thoughtful."

Elise grinned. "And a hard worker. He's perfect for you."

But Callie knew Jacob Smith wasn't the right man. God knew that, too. Jacob didn't have faith. He was a mystery. She wouldn't allow herself to get entangled with a man who kept his past and his future hidden.

She sighed. His future wasn't hidden. From the moment he'd arrived, he'd spoken of leaving. For her baby's sake, she would not get wrapped up in this man. She'd keep it impersonal. Avoid being alone with him. Surely with Elise in the house, that would be easy enough to do.

The back door banged shut and Jacob stood in the kitchen, his hair wet from a dousing at the pump. Her treacherous heart leaped at the sight of him. He shot her a smile, his gaze meeting hers with an absorption that suggested he had eyes only for her. Some compulsion lured her closer.

What was wrong with her? Where would this attraction lead?

To yet another loss.

Loss had permeated her life, each one leaving her battered, clinging to God.

She whirled to the stove and checked the fish, crispy on the outside, flaky within. "I'm sorry. I need to lie down. Would you serve, Elise?"

"Don't you want to eat first?" Elise's brow furrowed. "I thought you were hungry for fish."

"Are you sick?" Jacob took a step toward her, his tone laced with concern.

"No, just tired. Too tired to eat." Unable to meet his gaze for fear he'd see the panic in her eyes, she hurried out of the kitchen.

In her bedroom, she wilted onto the bed and hugged a pillow to her chest, aching to hold Jacob in her arms.

Jacob. A man without faith.

A man without a past.

A man without permanence.

Even with all his shortcomings, Martin had given her that much.

She'd protect her child from a broken heart by holding Jacob at arm's length. She released the pillow and laid her palms over her unborn child. A flutter of movement, as if her baby leaped within her, wrapped around her heart. All she needed was this precious little one, God's gift and her future.

Jake knelt on the staircase, tightening the screws in the banister, eliminating the wobble. Steadying the railing with both hands, Callie stood looking up at him with those startling blue eyes. He could've managed without her help, but it gave him an opportunity to ask questions that might lead to information about the woman who'd given birth to him.

"Once I'm finished, this railing should be solid enough to support my weight with two mules on my back."

As he'd intended, she grinned, looking happy.

Unlike the expression she'd worn last night, when she'd raced out of the kitchen with the excuse that she was too tired to eat fresh-caught fish. But she hadn't been able to look him in the eyes when she said it. No, she'd been unsettled by the intimacy sizzling between them at the river.

Well, she wasn't alone.

What he hadn't counted on was his overwhelming reaction to having her near this morning, aware of her scent, her sea-blue eyes and slender, toil-toughened hands. A woman like Callie shouldn't have to work that hard. She ought to find a reliable man, a God-fearing man, and remarry. Yet the notion of Callie attached to another man tightened his jaw until his teeth hurt.

He sat back on his heels and absorbed the tendrils of her hair curling around her neck, the delicate arch of her brows, her full, kissable lips. What would it be like to have that sweet mouth against his? To feel her soft curves pressed against him?

With every ounce of his strength, he concentrated on his objective. "How long have you lived in Peaceful?"

She hesitated, a troubled look filling her eyes. "I moved here when I was seven to live with my aunt after…" she took a deep breath "…after my parents and baby brother drowned."

That Callie had been orphaned twisted in Jake's stomach.

She cleared her throat. "Our farm sat in a valley, the school on high ground." She laid trembling fingers over her lips as if trying to hold back the words. "I wasn't the only child to lose my family that day."

"You were a little kid." He touched her jaw, wanting to take her into his arms, but didn't. "That had to be terrifying."

"You understand better than most," she said softly. "It happened because a disgruntled husband sought to punish his wife's lover and blew a hole in the dam. The whole thing gave way. He claimed he was innocent but the evidence was overwhelming and he finally confessed."

The news crashed into Jake with the force of an avalanche. He couldn't imagine the horror of losing her family, especially that way. A lawbreaker had destroyed Callie's world and now sat in jail, as he should. If she learned of Jake's sentence, how could she not question his innocence?

"I'm so sorry." Knowing the words weren't enough, not nearly enough, for all Callie had missed.

"I was luckier than you. My mother's sister took me in and helped me adjust."

Jake ached to somehow erase all she'd suffered. "Not luckier. You knew what you had. What you lost. I could only guess what it meant to have a family."

Avoiding her eyes, he rotated the handle of the screwdriver, twisting the screw tighter and tighter into the wood. Something despicable must live inside him that prevented others from stomaching his presence. "Even when I lived with one for a little while, I was never part of their circle."

She laid a gentle hand on his arm. "It's better to have had a family and lost it than never to have had a family at all."

That delicate hand burned through his sleeve. He wanted to cover it with his own, to show her he cared, but even a fine woman like Callie, with all she'd experienced would be suspicious of his stint in jail.

"Losing my parents and Ronnie was…" She shivered. "Terrible. But I have memories, happy memories to remember them by. Aunt Hilda had a few pictures of us, pictures I cherish. Pictures I can pore over, hold, touch. They don't replace my family, but they keep them alive in my heart." Her eyes glistened. "I wish you had that."

Jake wanted that, too. Some sense of where he came from and who his parents were. That lack of connection twisted inside him. A constant ache he'd learned to live with, so much a part of him he barely noticed. If only he could share his search for his mother. But if he found her and she rejected him... He couldn't bear for Callie to witness his humiliation.

He forced his thoughts to Callie's aunt. She'd know all the scandals in town, might know the identity of his mother. "The day I arrived, when I asked about your family, you didn't mention an aunt."

"Aunt Hilda had a stroke and died."

The news thudded in Jake's stomach. "You've endured the loss of your family, your aunt and your husband. I've never heard you utter one word of complaint or resentment. You're strong, Callie Mitchell."

"I'm weak, Jacob. God is strong. I lean on Him."

Callie didn't realize what a rare creature she was, an uncommon woman, but Jake knew. And his admiration for her grew. Her baby was fortunate to have such a mother.

A desire to know the woman who'd given him birth gripped him. Perhaps she was a woman of strength with an inner beauty like Callie. He'd judged her, condemned her. But he didn't know her circumstances.

"Even with everything you've been through, you've made friends, gotten involved, put down roots. Probably not much happens in town that escapes you."

"Are you implying that I'm a gossip?"

"I'd never believe that of you. I thought people in small towns generally knew everyone's business."

She sighed. "That can be a problem, like with Elise on Sunday. Some folks poke their noses in more than they should."

Here was an opening. "Elise can't be the first young

woman to find herself in those circumstances. Your aunt probably saw young women in the same fix in her day."

"If she did, she kept it from me."

Callie had lived with a woman who'd protected her from the harsher side of life. "Losing your aunt must've hurt."

"Aunt Hilda was a wonderful, giving woman. I miss her. I married Martin soon after she died. Now he's gone, too," she said softly.

Suddenly her mouth contorted as if she might cry.

Jake brushed her cheek, then stood helplessly, unable to break away. In Callie, he recognized the signs of bone-deep loneliness. Loneliness he lived with every day. Or he had until he came to Peaceful.

He lifted her chin, bringing her face within inches of his. Almost losing his composure at their closeness, he wanted to comfort her, to hold her, to make her pain vanish. But the widow's weeds she wore served as a vivid reminder that she mourned her husband.

"What can I do? Should I call Elise?"

"I'm fine," she said, though her voice trembled. "Once in a while it hits me anew that all the family I had in the world is gone."

"You have Martin's parents."

She nodded but remained mute. No wonder. Commodore Mitchell could've made things easier for Callie. Been the supportive father figure she needed badly. But he badgered her and criticized her. Losing an opportunity Jake would give anything to have. Callie appeared to cope with loneliness by re-creating that family with Elise.

Callie looked away, letting her gaze meander toward the railing. "Martin meant to get around to fixing up the place. But something always interfered." A hint of a smile appeared on her lips. "The fish were biting or his buddies would invite him hunting."

Jake couldn't imagine a go-getter like Callie married to a slacker, even a slacker with good intentions. What had been wrong with the guy? Martin Mitchell had possessed everything of importance. A beautiful wife, a great old house, parents. Why hadn't he put them first, before his amusement?

"Don't judge my husband and find him wanting," Callie said, as if reading his thoughts. "You might see Martin as lazy, but he had many good qualities." She raised her eyes to his.

Jake met her moist, forlorn gaze, all but tearing a hole in his self-control, his eyes stinging and swallowed hard. "I know he did, Callie. You wouldn't have loved him otherwise."

"He liked to have fun, to tease. I never had a dull moment with Martin around." She smiled. "He appreciated nature. He'd call me to watch a pretty sunset or see a rainbow." Her voice faltered. "He died so young. I'm glad he got to enjoy those things as much as he did."

Her forceful tone and the intensity of her gaze dared him to disagree. He craved that loyalty. Loyalty he'd never had. But if Callie discovered his past, she'd never talk about him the way she talked about Martin, with that sweet acceptance, with that tolerance.

Still, what would it be like to have a woman like Callie stick up for him? What would it be like to have a woman like Callie to watch a sunset with? What would it be like to have a woman like Callie to call his?

No point in speculating. He might be a hard worker, his one edge over Martin Mitchell, but Callie could never care about a taciturn jailbird the way she'd cared about her happy-go-lucky husband.

Today had proved that Callie knew nothing about unwed mothers in the town all those years ago. He'd have to find a way to look at the newspapers cluttering her library. Surely somewhere in that pile was the information he sought.

Once he found the woman who'd given birth to him, he'd be on his way, though the prospect of leaving sank inside him with the weight of an anchor. But what was the point of staying? He had no hope of forging a family with Callie.

Chapter Nine

Callie put the finishing touches on the tulip centerpiece. As she rearranged the height of one flower, her hands trembled. Silly to be this shaken by her first dinner party since Martin died. Some would see entertaining this soon as unseemly, but too many deaths, too many funerals had taught Callie to live in the moment. She believed God's Word supported that lesson. As much as she could, she wouldn't let past losses or future uncertainties cast a shadow on her today.

The dinner party gave her a chance to offer Jacob a taste of hospitality, of the pleasure of gathering around a table, sharing a meal and conversation with friends. His edgy demeanor in her kitchen implied that this wouldn't come easily for him. But once he got acquainted with her friends, he'd relax.

She heard a rap on the door. Jacob stood on the other side, clean-shaven, wearing his church clothes and a wary look in his green eyes. She wanted to assure him that which fork he used didn't matter one whit, but a man raised in an institution wouldn't have confidence in social situations.

"Thought I'd fill screw holes then polish the banister. I wouldn't want your guests to think I'd left a project incomplete."

"How thoughtful." Smiling, Callie stepped aside to let him enter.

"I'll try not to get in your way."

Just his presence in the house chased every task from her head. "You won't bother me." When had she spoken a bigger lie?

As he set to work, Callie returned to the dining room, reliving their conversation yesterday. She'd opened up about her past. He'd cared about her losses, understood her loneliness. What would it be like to lean into those strong arms of his?

The prospect of counting on another man skittered along her spine. Caring brought heartache. And she'd had all the heartache she could handle. She'd focus on her baby and refuse to get involved with Jacob, except to help him repair the house.

Through the archway, she had a view of the foyer. Jacob bent over the banister, his black hair catching the light. His haircut gave him a refined appearance, but she missed the rugged masculinity of his collar-length hair.

A loner, Jacob shunned the limelight. She appreciated the care he took with the house, not only to make it safe and functional, but also attractive. He had a patient touch.

Aunt Hilda had possessed that same unhurried way about her. She'd devoted her life to teaching Peaceful's children, first in a one-room schoolhouse, then in the new larger building in town. She hadn't earned much money but with the little left over, her aunt had bought everything on this table.

Callie smoothed a slight wrinkle in the white linen tablecloth, letting her gaze sweep over her aunt's candlesticks, flatware, lovely china. The mahogany table and chairs had

come from her aunt, handed down from Callie's grandmother, a link to her mother's childhood home, something
she cherished.

When Callie arrived with nothing but the clothes on
her back, Aunt Hilda's income went toward providing for
a growing child, but she never complained about the sacrifice. Her example taught Callie the importance of giving,
of helping others. She couldn't repay her aunt, but she'd
taken in Elise, as her aunt had taken her in. She hoped to
make a difference for Elise, for any woman in her situation,
by opening her home and her heart.

Even to her lonely neighbor. Mildred had accepted the
invitation to dinner before Callie had gotten the words out
of her mouth. Knowing the effort it took to prepare food,
only to eat alone, she should ask Mildred to join her more
often.

To ensure that she hadn't forgotten anything, Callie let
her eyes meander over the six place settings. Satisfied that
nothing was amiss, she stepped back, took in the room's
high ceilings, deep moldings, crystal chandelier and gleaming wooden floor. Mere days after she and Martin had
moved in, she'd painted the wainscoting white and hung
above it the striped navy, pink and white wallpaper. She'd
delighted in bringing even this small part of the house back
to life.

Strides in the hall announced Jacob's approach. He stood
under the archway, his stance wide, as if maintaining his
balance on the deck of a wind-tossed boat. His gaze swept
the table, then lifted to her, the expression in his eyes as
skittish as a seasick landlubber heading to open water.

"We can't all fit around the kitchen table," she said by
way of explanation, though he hadn't asked.

"You have the right to eat where you want." His tone

mild, unconcerned, yet he glanced toward the front door as if he were ready to make a run for it.

She chuckled. "Eating in a dining room isn't a jail sentence."

His gaze swiveled to hers. A flash of alarm traveled his face then vanished so quickly she wondered if she'd imagined it.

"It'll be fun. You know Mildred. You've met Hal Frederick."

"I remember."

"I've known Hal's wife, Loretta, for years. She's more big sister than friend. We're exact opposites. She loves to hunt, while I have to work up my courage to kill a chicken for the pot."

The warm depth of his gaze enfolded her. "I'll be glad to handle that chore for you."

Jacob's kindness rippled through her. Martin had known about her squeamishness, yet rarely was around to handle unpleasant tasks. Jacob made her feel cared for. Protected. Cherished.

Inside her chest her heart rat-a-tat to a wayward beat. All because Jacob Smith looked at her with those burnished jade eyes, suggesting that he cared, suggesting they had a future, suggesting—

She wouldn't finish the thought.

"I'm sure Loretta's a fine person," he said. "That all your guests are. Otherwise, you wouldn't care about them."

"Then why look like you've been given a life sentence?"

His smile faltered. "You're imagining that."

"Am I?" Not waiting for his answer, she moved toward the kitchen and tossed over her shoulder, "Want to help put the finishing touches on the meal?"

He followed her in, the staccato of his footfalls discordant with hers. Nothing about the two of them fit.

She enjoyed people. He avoided them.

She loved God. He denied God.

She cherished family. He cherished solitude.

Even so, Jacob's tough beginnings and his commitment to her house connected them, along with a huge dose of attraction she didn't trust. Whenever he was near, that attraction pulled her into a swirling eddy of conflicting emotions. Jacob Smith had a past he avoided and he wasn't staying. She wouldn't let feelings rule her head.

Not this time.

In the kitchen, she handed Jacob a knife. "Please slice the pie. I promised Hal apple, but decided on cherry."

"He'd be a dunce not to appreciate any pie made by your hands."

"Thank you." Callie checked the roast, releasing an aroma bringing a growl from her belly. Across the way, Jacob divided the pie into wedges with the precision of someone accustomed to measuring every cut he made.

She bit back a smile. "The vegetables are almost tender. Everything's ready…except me. I'd better change."

"That'll give me time to polish the banister."

Side by side, they walked to the foyer, Callie aware of the man, towing her to him with a strength that left her shaken.

He looked around him. "Where's Elise?"

"Upstairs taking a nap. I'll awaken her so she can get ready."

When they reached the staircase, Jacob took a jar and a rag out of the sack she hadn't noticed him carry in. "Beeswax and linseed oil should give it a nice finish." He set to work.

"If you don't need anything else, I'll go upstairs."

"I'm all set," he said. "Take your time."

As Callie climbed the steps, she planned what she'd wear. Perhaps the gray silk dress she'd altered to give more ease in the midriff and Aunt Hilda's lavaliere. Normally, she saved the pendant for special occasions, but the ruby would sparkle in the candlelight. Her breath caught. Here she was a widow, trying to look pretty for a Godless drifter.

Forgive me, Lord, for such foolishness. Protect my heart from a man who can destroy it.

Jake watched Callie climb the stairs. Gripped by a desire for her to turn back, he waited. Waited for a brief glimpse of her face.

Another step.

A third.

He kept watching, hoping she'd look at him as she ascended the broad staircase, her hand gliding along the banister, totally unaware of his presence below. No doubt she had her mind on last-minute details.

With the rag poised to wipe down the banister, the mixture in the jar at his feet, the tools of his trade—tangible things he could count on, unlike relationships with others, he took one last look.

She pivoted and smiled down at him.

Joy exploded in his chest and spread through every muscle and tendon, holding him transfixed, captured by her beauty—inside and out. He drank in her warmth and goodness the way sun-bleached boards absorbed the first coat of varnish.

Then, in a blink of an eye, she moved out of view.

Every feature and contour of her lovely face was fixed in his memory. The prospect of an entire evening with Callie burned within him. To watch her slim, expressive brows rise and fall. To watch her full lips turn up in a smile. To watch every nuance of her expression transform her face. What a privilege.

But then he remembered that the sheriff would share that table. How long before Frederick discovered the truth? Truth had not set Jacob free. Truth had imprisoned him.

With the sheriff at the table, Jake would have to watch every word he said. But the invitation gave him an excuse for finishing the railing, the little job a convenient ploy to get into the house early.

On silent feet, Jake moved down the hall toward the library. The knowledge that Callie trusted him alone in her house tweaked his conscience, but seeking the woman who gave birth to him wouldn't bring Callie harm.

At the last door on the right, he turned the knob. Inside the library, he strode to the desk. He'd leave the door open, listen for Callie's return.

The first stack of newspapers looked recent, but over to the side a pile, brittle and yellowed with age, looked promising. He'd start there. Rummaging through the stack, he discovered the newspapers dated decades before his birth.

His hand moved to another stack, yellowed but in better condition. His throat clogged. This stack might hold the information he sought. Flipping through the dates, he located the year 1877. With shaking hands, he looked for May 21, 1877. His birthday.

Or so he'd been told.

A squeak of the floorboards overhead. Jake jerked to his feet. One of the women would soon arrive downstairs. He straightened the newspapers and eased the door closed after him.

He made it to the foyer, grabbed the cloth and polished

the banister, revealing the soft glow of the wood's patina just as Callie made it to the landing.

"Oh, that looks much nicer," Callie said, descending the final flight of stairs. "Lovely."

The description fit her perfectly.

As she reached the foyer, Jake got a whiff of roses, the delicate scent she wore. Her dress accentuated her soft curves and the swell of her baby, and then swirled to the hem. The lower neckline revealed the jewelry she wore, the pale skin of her throat, the pulse hammering in its hollows in rhythm with his.

"You look…stunning."

A smile curving her lips, she laid a palm on his cheek and he covered it with his, looking into her eyes. He yearned to cup her jaw, to lift her face to his. To kiss her.

Elise appeared at the head of the stairs. Their hands fell away.

Callie took a step back. "Doesn't Elise look pretty?"

"Very pretty."

Elise blushed, appeared ready to deny it, but Callie took her arm. "Help me pour water in the glasses."

Once the ladies had entered the kitchen, Jake returned to his work. If the woman who'd given birth to him lived in this town, she'd had twenty-three years to claim him as her son and hadn't. Jake saw no reason why she'd welcome him now. Still, he needed more time to search those newspapers.

His jaw clenched. He couldn't bear the idea of Callie learning of the woman's existence, only to see him rejected and humiliated. Nor could he allow his birth mother to be disgraced.

After spending time with Elise, he cared about his mother's reputation. Getting others involved would stir up a hornet's nest. Someone would get stung.

Chapter Ten

The candles were lit, the food served, the prayer given. At Callie's side, Jacob sat stiff in his chair. Even inexperience in social situations didn't explain his obvious uneasiness.

Talk ceased while everyone tasted the first bites, then resumed as they declared the food delicious. Callie released the breath she'd been holding and thanked her guests.

"I'm glad you've stopped wearing black, Callie. It's never been your color." Loretta gestured across the table to Jacob. "I'm also glad to have the opportunity to meet you."

"The pleasure is mine, Mrs. Frederick."

"Please, call me Loretta. And whatever Hal has said about me, take it with a grain of pepper."

Hal chuckled. "Salt is too bland for my wife."

Winking at her husband, Loretta took a bite of potatoes. "I'm impressed with your skill, Jake. That new porch floor is as solid as Marlene Thompson's fruitcake."

Callie snickered. "You're terrible."

"You know I'm speaking the truth. Marlene carries that fruitcake of hers to church suppers and carries it home untouched. Wouldn't you think after all these years, she'd get the message?" She smiled. "Course if she did, folks would probably miss it. Grumbling about Marlene's fruitcake is as much a Christmas tradition in Peaceful as caroling on Christmas Eve."

At Loretta's assertion, Elise choked on her sip of water. "That's like Papa fussing about Mama's dime novels. If he stopped, he'd take away half the fun of Mama's reading them."

Eyes on Jacob, Hal cut a slice of beef. "Smith, tell us about yourself. Where did you learn carpentry?"

"I apprenticed at a construction company. The owner took me under his wing and saw that I learned more than the basics."

Though Jacob sounded at ease, the tight look around his mouth verified that he didn't relish being the center of attention. His discomfort touched a spot deep inside her.

She glanced at Mildred, wearing a beribboned gown, the round neck edged in lace and trimmed with seed pearls. "You look lovely this evening, Mildred."

"You're sweet, dear, but truth is I look as overdone as a dried out turkey at Thanksgiving." She smiled. "But I'm here. At my age, every day I wake up is a good day."

Elise giggled and the others joined in. Callie could see the tension ease in Jacob's shoulders. "From what I've been reading in the papers," she said, keeping the conversation off him, "President McKinley should win reelection in the fall."

"McKinley and Roosevelt make a good ticket," Jacob said.

"Papa reads the newspapers from front to back," Elise groaned. "At supper he dishes up the news like stew, chunks of politics, dash of the gold standard, pinch of Spain, on and on until Mama and I have indigestion."

Callie chuckled. "I take it you'd appreciate a change of topics."

"I could use some work done on our house, Smith." Hal buttered his roll, apparently determined to return the conversation to Jacob. "Once you're finished here, I'd appreciate it if you'd take a look. Maybe you could teach me and those sons of mine to handle some carpentry."

Jacob shifted in his seat. "Not sure how long that'll be. Most likely I'll move on after I'm finished here."

Not news, but still Jacob's words banged against her heart. As soon as Jacob repaired her house, he would leave.

"Too bad you're moving on. Lots of buildings in town could use repairs, new roofs. There's enough work here to keep an honest man busy for years."

Mildred patted Jacob's hand. "Maybe Jake will change his mind. The Granger place over on Harmony could use some attention. The roof leaks like a slotted spoon. After Elmer died, Louise took in boarders for a while, but didn't earn enough to keep the place up."

"I arrested one of her boarders for forgery, a man from out of town." Hal leaned back in his chair and gave a smug grin. "Found his face on a wanted poster."

Jacob's mouth flattened. He quickly wiped it with his napkin, averting his gaze.

"A squirrel got in there once. The poor thing tore the parlor curtains and upholstery to shreds," Elise said. "That squirrel was the talk of the town."

Loretta grinned. "Louise asked me to trap the varmint. I suggested she just open the door, but she was afraid that the squirrel's pals might see it as an invitation."

"Houses in Peaceful have more stories than floors." Mildred grinned. "Just imagine what we could learn if lumber and plaster could talk."

The sheriff nodded. "The McGuire place at the edge of town has this big old tree, once used to hang a man."

Loretta wagged a finger at her husband. "That's hardly dinner-table conversation, Hal. There's a difference between trapping squirrels and stringing up a man."

"I apologize, ladies. Such talk is routine in my line of work. I forget the sensibilities of the womenfolk."

"No need to apologize on my account," Mildred reassured him. "It's only natural you'd remember houses involved in crime."

Loretta glanced at Jacob. "Any houses with tales to tell where you grew up, Jake?"

"I wasn't interested in houses until I got into construction."

Hal glanced at Jacob. "Where's the construction company where you worked located?"

Lifting a forkful of potatoes toward his mouth, Jacob's hand stilled. "Bloomington."

Elise gasped. "Indiana? Callie, isn't that the hometown of the unwed pregnant girl you said would be arriving soon?"

"Yes, someone in Bloomington knows someone, who knows someone who knows me." She grinned. "I'm expecting a letter any day now with the date of her arrival."

Under his tan, Jacob paled. Callie frowned. If the arrival of someone from where he'd lived upset him, he must have something to hide. His skittish behavior suggested that he'd felt more on trial than carefree, as if he had something to fear from the law.

As Callie walked to the kitchen for dessert, she knew her attempt to give Jacob a nice evening had failed. And worse, all the evening had accomplished was to put a large knot of mistrust of Jacob Smith twisting inside her.

Dinner churning in his stomach, Jake all but applauded when he saw the pie heading his way. Dessert meant the meal would soon end and he could leave. During dinner, Frederick had quizzed him several times, real friendlylike, as if his answers didn't matter. Jake knew better.

Worse, an unwed mother would soon arrive in Peaceful from the town where he'd been arrested and found guilty. She might recognize his name, even his face, since the story had hit the papers. He had to get out of town before she arrived.

A knock sent Callie to answer the door. "Commodore, come in," she said, her voice carrying to the dining room.

"You've got company. I don't want to interrupt. Dorothy asked me to drop off this sack of Martin's baby things. Said to tell you that she aired and washed them."

"Thank Dorothy for me. I'm glad my baby will get to wear his father's things. Join us for a piece of cherry pie." Callie tugged Commodore into view. "You know everyone."

Mildred smiled a welcome. "Commodore, settle a quarrel for us. Who owned the Adams place when you were a boy?"

Frederick pulled a chair up to the table and gestured to Commodore. "Have a seat."

As Callie hurried to get his pie, her father-in-law looked like he'd rather be anywhere else, but he sat. Everyone greeted him, followed by an awkward pause.

"Reckon that would be the Prendergast family," Commodore said. "John Prendergast was one of the town's first settlers."

"That's what I thought," Mildred said. "What a relief to get something right for a change."

Callie sighed. "You don't forget as much as I do."

"That happens to expectant mothers," Loretta said. "I remember my brain turning to mush with our two." Loretta leaned toward Jake. "All evening, I've had the feeling I know you from somewhere."

The bite of pie Jake had swallowed caught in his throat. He gulped it down. "Can't imagine where."

"Your face looks so familiar."

"I've never been to Peaceful before. I probably remind you of someone."

"You do, but I can't think who." A puzzled frown furrowed Loretta's brow.

"Good to know I'm not the only one with a lagging memory, though I rarely forget a face, especially a handsome face." Mildred patted Jake's hand. "If I'd seen Jake before, I would've remembered. Now names...don't always stick."

"This house sat empty all my life," Elise said. "Who owned it before you, Callie?"

"I'm not sure."

Mildred smiled. "Wesley Squier, an Indiana state senator built this house, one of the finest in these parts, even in the state. Strangest thing—the family moved out in the middle of the night."

"Why would someone do that?" Elise asked.

Frederick scooped a bite of pie onto his fork. "No *good* reason I can think of. Did they leave a pile of debts?"

"No, nothing like that. They were upstanding citizens." Mildred frowned. "A fancy Realtor over in Indianapolis tried to sell the house for years, but big-city folks didn't hanker living in what they saw as a Podunk town. And the price was bigger than Peaceful's purses. So it sat empty."

"Until it got into such terrible shape that the house was sold at auction for next to nothing." Callie smiled. "I'm grateful. Otherwise Commodore and Dorothy couldn't have bought it for our wedding present."

"I heard gossip about why the Squier family left but that's all it was—gossip," Mildred said.

Commodore snorted. "People like to talk. What they don't know, they make up."

Elise's gaze dropped to her lap. "Gossip's a terrible thing."

"Yes, it is," Mildred said. "I make a point not to repeat it. I'm glad Callie's giving this beautiful old house new life. And Jake here is handling the renovation."

Why had the Squier family moved out of the house? Did they have a daughter? Perhaps Jake should talk to Mildred, see if she'd open up about the gossip she'd heard. No matter what she said, most people couldn't resist wagging their tongues. He'd offer to do some chore. See what she knew.

Commodore rose. "This house should've been left to rot. You all enjoy your pie." Though he hadn't taken a bite of his, he left the dining room.

The front door slammed. No one said a word.

Jake supposed he could understand Commodore Mitchell's resenting the house he blamed for his son's death. But each time he condemned it, he stomped on his daughter-in-law's heart.

As the tension of Commodore's remark ebbed, conversation resumed. Yet, for some reason Jake couldn't decipher, a whisper of questions hung in the air.

Callie and Elise hugged Loretta and Mildred goodbye. Jacob shook hands with Hal, then headed to the kitchen to start the dishes, a generous offer, but one Callie wished she'd refused. She wanted Jacob gone. Too much about him raised questions.

Callie closed the door after her departing guests and glanced at Elise. In her last weeks of pregnancy, the poor thing looked limp as a wrung-out dishrag. Callie gave her a gentle push toward the stairs, sending her up to bed, then walked to the dining room.

As she loaded glasses onto a tray, she reconsidered Jacob's behavior. Perhaps she was unfairly suspicious, a fault of hers, when he might just be a private man who didn't open up easily. Most people had painful circumstances in their pasts they'd rather not dwell on. Like Martin's fall. Like Nell's tragedy. Like her family's destruction.

Still, she didn't trust a man who kept to himself. If she had any sense, she'd ask him to leave and handle the dishes alone. Yet, the prospect of spending time with him sent her pulse skittering and her aching feet to the kitchen.

Jacob stood at the sink, the sleeves of his shirt rolled up to the elbow, his hands submerged wrist-high in suds. The shadow of a beard defined his rugged jaw.

As he scrubbed a plate, muscles in his back rippled beneath the shirt tucked into his trim waist. Her gaze moved lower to slim hips and long legs. Gulping, she quickly looked away, determined not to give in to these wild feelings of attraction to a man she didn't trust. Hands shaking, she planted the tray of glasses on the counter with a clunk.

"Nice party," he said, glancing over at her with a smile.

"You didn't look like you were having a good time."

"Formal meals aren't normal in my world. But I enjoyed the evening. I've never had better food."

Pleased that he'd at least enjoyed her cooking, she wouldn't argue the point. "You appear to know your way around a kitchen."

"Washing dishes was one of my chores at the orphanage."

"I'm sorry there are so many." She gave a nervous laugh.

"Aunt Hilda complained that I could dirty every pan in the kitchen just making toast."

Grinning, he lifted a hand dripping suds, indicating the waiting stack. "This little batch will be a cinch."

Martin would never have helped with what he'd called woman's work. He never put himself in another's shoes—especially a woman's shoes. To have Jacob's assistance in the kitchen left her rattled, as if her world had tilted and she couldn't get her bearings.

Taking a deep breath, she focused on what needed doing, then proceeded to cover bowls of leftovers with plates and put them in the icebox. Then she grabbed a towel to dry the plates draining on the counter.

He turned toward her, letting his gaze roam her face. "You look tired. But pretty," he added as if afraid he'd hurt her feelings.

"I hadn't thought about it, but I suppose I am." Inside her shoes she wiggled her toes and winced. "My feet hurt."

"We can't have that."

He dried his palms, then took the towel from her hands, ushered her to the table and pulled out a chair, gently guiding her into it. Then he knelt and cupped her foot. Before she could protest, he removed one of her shoes, then the other.

Callie's heart galloped like a runaway horse. "I, uh, my shoes aren't as comfortable now that my feet have started to swell."

Why had she said such a personal thing?

"I can see that."

The concern she heard in his voice and the gentle, caring expression on his face heated hers. What was this man doing to her with just a look?

Moonlight filtered through the window, highlighting his features. His woodsy scent drifted closer.

"Though from what I've seen, ladies worry about fashion more than comfort."

"I, uh, won't make that mistake again. Well, at least until after my baby's born," she finished, not sure if she made sense.

With still-damp hands, he encircled her right foot and massaged her toes through her stockings, something far too intimate for a man who wasn't her husband to do. She tried to retract her foot from his grasp, but his nimble fingers continued kneading her toes, sending waves of pleasure crashing through her until she almost groaned.

She should stop him. She would. "Jacob."

"Hmm?"

"You shouldn't."

But her eyelids drifted closed under his gentle, yet firm touch. His hands slid down her foot to her arch. He rubbed the curve, his fingers easing her aching bones. It was all she could do not to purr like Stripes. His hands moved to the heel, then back to her toes.

When he set her foot on his knee, her eyelids flew open. The intimacy heated her cheeks and she yanked her foot out of his grasp. "I… My feet are fine. Let's finish the dishes."

"Let me do something for you for a change."

He lifted her other foot, ministering to that one as he had the first. Each stroke of his fingers eased the throbbing in her feet and fulfilled her need to be cared for. A need she hadn't known she possessed. Since adulthood, she'd been the one to take care of others. Until now.

She reminded herself that Jacob Smith couldn't be trusted. He might be kind, considerate and hardworking, but he kept his past secret. Why? Had he been harmed by others? Had he done something evil? No, she couldn't believe him capable of harm. Was he simply a lonely man?

Whatever his past, something had brought him to town.

Jacob lowered her foot to the floor. At the loss of his touch, disappointment slid through her. A silly reaction.

He tugged her to her feet then handed her shoes to her. "Go on up to bed. I'll finish here and lock up."

His no-nonsense tone kept her from expressing her gratitude that for once, someone had eased her burden. That someone took care of Callie Mitchell, instead of the other way around.

"Are you sure, Jacob?"

"Very." His tender gaze collided with hers, and then he cupped her jaw. His touch made her wobbly on her feet. "You work too hard. It's the least I can do."

He stepped closer and closer still, until he stood mere inches away. Tiny gold flecks bordered the dark mesmerizing pupils of his eyes glittering in the lamplight, and then settling on her lips. And stayed.

"I see you every day. Every day your beauty socks me in the gut. Not just outside, but inside too, the heart of who you are. And I wonder what it would be like to hold you in my arms." His Adam's apple rose and fell. "Do you wonder that, too?"

She couldn't look away. Couldn't speak. Could only nod.

"May I kiss you?"

Every rational thought fled her mind as she looked into those clear pools of jade. And saw nothing to harm her. What if… What if Jacob Smith was the caring man he appeared to be? What if she could trust and lean on him? What if God had brought Jacob here to mend more than her house? To mend her aching heart? Knowing Jacob would turn to Him in God's time?

With all those questions burning in her mind, Callie looked at his lips—soft, full, slightly parted—waiting for her answer. The slight pressure of his hand under her jaw felt right, as no touch ever had.

She wanted his kiss. Wanted it badly. Refusing to heed the warnings churning inside her, she rose on tiptoe, the only answer she could give. As she slid her arms around his neck, her shoes clattered to the floor.

His lips captured hers. Gentle, teasing, sending shivers up her spine and curling her toes inside her stockings. He pulled her closer and she clung to him, then she raised her palms to caress the sandpaper of his jaw. The pressure of his lips grew stronger, bolder. She returned the pressure, her response to the man left her weak-kneed and wobbly.

Jacob's breathing grew rapid, matching hers. Oh, when had she ever felt like this? His fingers splayed in her hair, sending pins to the floor, unleashing her hair—and triggering her faltering common sense.

Chest heaving, gasping for breath, she pulled away from his arms. Like a starving man, his eyes devoured her. Something passed between them, something unspoken yet powerful. So powerful it frightened her.

She took a hurried step back. "Good night," she said, then fled the kitchen, leaving her shoes and the last remnant of her composure behind.

Struggling to control his breathing, his need for Callie, Jake planted his palms on the counter, hunched forward, the memory of Callie's sweet lips beneath his searing his mind. Sheer torture. Nothing had prepared him for his strong reaction to their kiss.

With shaky hands, he washed and rinsed the tumblers, almost dropping the last one as he set it on the counter, then loaded the dishpan with the pots and pans. While they soaked, he dried the tumblers, peering though the kitchen window at the patch of night sky and the stars twinkling overhead, and relived that kiss. Beneath his tense fingers, the glass squeaked.

One kiss wasn't enough. He wanted more. He wanted Callie.

He released a shuddering breath and laid the towel aside, tackling the roasting pan. Nothing in his relationship with Susan prepared him for his powerful feelings for Callie.

After sharing that kiss, a kiss that bonded him to Callie in a way he couldn't understand, he knew he would do anything for her. He'd go to the ends of the earth to protect her. To comfort her. To take care of her.

Yet, he'd read the panic in her eyes, the resolve to keep him at arm's length immediately before she stepped away and fled from him. The truth slammed against his lungs. She knew what he just now recognized. Callie was a strong, independent woman who didn't need his protection or comfort. What she needed from him, he couldn't give. Or fix. Or build.

She needed his heart.

His heart wasn't worth having.

Shriveled from years of neglect. Frozen at the hands of Susan and Lloyd's betrayal. Etched with the filth of prison.

Callie deserved more. So much more.

Why had he, even for a moment, believed they had a future together?

He hadn't robbed that store. He hadn't deserved that year in jail. What did it matter? Those who learned about his time behind bars didn't believe in his innocence. Didn't trust him.

If only he could tell Callie, be honest with her, but he didn't dare take the risk. If she reacted as others had, he would be destroyed.

But hadn't he also seen her response, that undeniable

pull between them? A pull that would disappear the moment Callie knew about his past. He'd witnessed the lowest depths of man's depravity. Freed months ago, he still felt dirty. Unclean. No matter how often he scrubbed his skin.

As he finished drying the last pot, he glanced around the tidy kitchen. Nothing more to do here.

He locked Callie's house, about to return to the lean-to out back, then hesitated on the stoop. He should leave. Tonight.

That's what a smart man would do. Get out of town before the ugliness of his past touched Callie. But he couldn't leave her in the lurch. Not with all the work that still needed to be done.

Not only did the past stand between them. The future did, too. The baby Callie carried would need a strong, wise father. A Godly man. He didn't know how to create a family. He had never experienced such a thing. Didn't have that faith in God she prized. His past had taught him to run, to keep moving on before staying brought pain.

Better to remember why he came.

He entered the lean-to and dropped onto the cot, staring at the drawer that held those postcards. If he hoped to find his mother, he didn't have much time. Any day now, the unwed mother from Bloomington could arrive and expose his past.

Tomorrow, he'd look at the newspapers. See what he could find. And move on.

He released a gust of air, together with the pent-up desire to get close to Callie Mitchell.

He didn't dare. Some things were better left alone.

Chapter Eleven

Callie handed the tray loaded with plaster up to Jacob as he stood on the ladder, repairing the ceiling.

In her *bedroom*.

After the kiss they'd shared last night, she couldn't look at Jacob without her stomach fluttering like it held a bevy of butterflies. Every word, every glance and movement, multiplied her awareness of the man and their location.

The bed seemed to have doubled in size, her personal items scattered around the room—her hairbrush, robe and slippers—left her feeling edgier than chickens facing a dog in the henhouse.

As Jacob packed the crack with plaster, smoothing the edges as he worked, each stroke bunched the muscles in his arm and back. Callie's mouth went dry, yet she couldn't look away.

After last night, nothing would be the same between her and Jacob. She wanted to shrug off the significance of that kiss. Wanted to pretend that there would be no consequences from that kiss. Wanted to forget that the blood in her veins had surged with that kiss.

The truth was undeniable. She was attracted to Jacob Smith. The man was a drifter.

Without faith.

A mystery.

And worming his way into her life.

Her heart lurched. That scared her silly. She would not care about this man. Especially since he behaved as if that kiss they'd shared had never happened. Yet that kiss shouted in the silence, tightened in her shoulders and shook in her hands.

She had to do something to cut the tension stretching between them like a taut rubber band about to snap. What could she talk about? "Commodore certainly put a damper on things last night."

"The man's scowl could topple a hot-air balloon."

"He's never been an easy man. But losing his only child… That wound won't heal."

"Maybe it would, if he quit picking at the scab."

"What do you mean?"

He glanced down at her. "Instead of harping at you about giving up this house, if he'd pitch in to help, he'd fill that chink in his heart."

Good deeds, exactly as Jacob did now repairing the crack in her ceiling, fixing the porch and rails, making the house livable, doing every conceivable chore to make her life easier and in the process becoming indispensable.

Well, she wouldn't allow herself to need him that way. Hardworking didn't equal trustworthy. Trustworthy meant everything to her. So why did his presence make her feel more alive, more energized and eager to greet each new day?

"Commodore blames the house for Martin's death," she said, determined to keep the focus on her father-in-law and off all these thoughts about Jacob.

"Until Commodore lets that go, he'll never find peace."

Would Commodore ever find peace as long as she lived

in this house? Her gaze traveled the crown molding, slid to the imposing chandelier, then dropped to the wooden floor she'd waxed until the boards gleamed. Most of the rooms in the house resembled this one—elegant, yet not fussy—and spacious, the height of the windows matching the lofty scale. The house wrapped her in a cozy cocoon of childhood memories.

She ran her hand along the windowframe in need of a fresh coat of paint. The house needed restoring, much as the unwed mothers who would fill its rooms—each with her own story, her own struggles, each with a heart—in need of mending. Here they'd find peace, acceptance and God's love. She'd see to that.

"I'm surprised that Martin's accident hasn't destroyed my love for this house, but, if anything, I cling to it more than before," she said softly.

"I've never had a place to call home, but I can see how this house reminds you of happy times with your family."

They both avoided the subject of that kiss and all it implied, pretending it meant nothing, when each small touch or glance sizzled. Still, more than attraction, more than that kiss connected them. She and Jacob knew the heartache of not having or losing family.

"You understand," she said, knowing he did, yet wishing he didn't. For that link was powerful.

As Jacob descended the ladder, her gaze locked with his. "I do." He smiled—a gentle, encouraging gift. "In some ways the house is your security and your father-in-law's adversary, or so he believes."

"With Commodore dead set against my living here, if I didn't love the house, I'd let it go rather than deal with his attitude. But the house means more to me than feeling at ease here. It provides plenty of room for Elise and her baby, and room for several unwed mothers who may need a harbor in the storm."

"Tell me why you want to open your home to these girls."

"They're wounded and desperate. I know how desperate." She swallowed against a sudden lump in her throat. "You see, my dearest friend, just sixteen years old, got with child. She and I were naive, barely knew the facts of life." She gave a wistful smile. "Nell was beautiful. Red hair, blue eyes, full of life…"

Life was fragile.

"She fell hard for a college boy home for the summer. When he returned to school, he wrote that he was engaged to someone else. Nell was devastated. She never told me about the baby. She never told anyone." Tears stung the back of her eyes. "Rather than face the shame of having a baby out of wedlock…"

The words stuck, but determined to make Jacob understand why she had to give these girls a home, she forced them out, each word scraping against her throat. "One night she slit her wrists and bled to death. Her baby died with her."

The sorrow on his face threatened to undo her. Unable to hold his gaze, she studied her hands. "The day before Nell took her life, she'd been examined by a doctor." She blinked rapidly, holding her tears at bay. "Otherwise, we'd have never known why she took her life.

"At her funeral, I made a promise. A promise that I'd never let another girl I knew go through that alone." She folded her arms across her chest. "I intend to keep that promise. These girls need someone to care about them. Someone to listen to them. Someone to help them without judging them."

Jacob cupped her face in his hands then drew her into

his arms. "I'm sorry about your friend. What a tragedy. I understand why you want to help."

That Jacob's arms felt like home made Callie step away.

"But, Callie, others may not see it the same way. Housing unwed mothers will bring trouble. You've got a lot to handle as it is, without dealing with opposition from the community."

"I can't let public opinion sway me. Not when I believe this mission is from God."

The skeptical look on his face only proved what she already knew. Jacob Smith didn't have faith. Didn't understand that God could speak through His Word, through listening to His quiet voice or by providing opportunities. Proving once again that Jacob Smith was exactly the wrong man for her.

"Why do you think you need to advise me?" She thrust the plaster mixture at him and stalked toward the door. "You can handle this job alone."

Jake didn't understand Callie at all. One minute, she'd been sharing memories, even a personal tragedy. The next, she'd stomped off like she couldn't stand the sight of him. Well, he'd have no problem handling repairs to Callie's ceiling alone. Though the job would take more time, as he ran up and down the ladder to mix and carry plaster.

Though he'd only been trying to help, his warnings upset her. Even if this was a mission from God, as she'd said, did that mean she couldn't look at the facts? He'd seen enough of life and enough of this town to know that Peaceful wouldn't allow her to give unwed mothers sanctuary without resistance. Trouble was brewing, starting with that biddy at church.

Yet he admired Callie's dedication. Yes, and that

very pretty mouth of hers. He sighed. How could a man think clearly when Callie Mitchell had stood mere inches away?

His heart tripped in his chest. If his mother had had someone like Callie in her life, someone to provide help instead of hindrances, perhaps she'd have kept him. Instead of leaving him in an orphanage, as if he wasn't worth the turmoil he'd caused. Why had she made that decision? He couldn't rest until he found the answer. Until he'd unlocked his past.

He just had to find the key.

Callie opened the newspaper to the Society page and a headline leaped off the page.

Callie Mitchell Opens Home to Fallen Girls

Mrs. Callie Mitchell hosted a dinner party in her home Tuesday evening, May 8. Guests in attendance were Sheriff and Mrs. Hal Frederick, Mrs. Mildred Uland, Miss Elise Langley, and newcomer Mr. Jacob Smith. Mrs. Mitchell's menu included beef roast, mashed potatoes with gravy, carrots and peas, dinner rolls and cherry pie.

Sources told this reporter that Mrs. Mitchell revealed that an unwed mother from out of town would soon take up residence in her home at 7133 Serenity Avenue. Mrs. Mitchell served a delicious meal, but her plans give this columnist indigestion.

News must be scant this week. Which of her guests had been the source? Certainly not Jacob. Elise was unlike-

ly. That left the Fredericks or Mildred. Whoever was
responsible, this item could be a blessing in disguise.

Callie had planned to wait until work on the house was
completed before raising funds for the unwed mothers'
home, but this publicity would give her an opening she
needed. Or breed more opposition. If so, what choice did
she have? The time had come to seek community support.
She'd go to the town fathers, to the newspaper with a plea
for backing.

But first she'd talk to Pastor Steele. If trouble brewed,
perhaps he'd help stem the tide of negative opinion.

*Lord, again I ask, if this endeavor is in Your will, please
provide as only You can.*

No time like the present. She grabbed her purse, slapped
her hat on her head, drove a hatpin through the crown, and
then tugged on her gloves.

As she left the house, Jacob strode up the walk, his
long strides swallowing the distance between them, a smile
lighting up his face. He took her breath away.

"Looks like you're heading out. Mind if I walk along?
I need to stop at the Mercantile and get supplies to fix that
chimney."

"I'll pay for them." Callie dug through her purse. "Any
idea how much?"

He laid a hand on hers. "I'll take care of it."

"I can afford to handle the expense of materials." She
frowned. "What I can't afford is to pay you a wage."

"Who'd want money and lose the great deal I have?
I like eating at your table…" His gaze locked with hers.
"…and having you near."

The intensity of his regard rippled through her. "I…I
like that, too."

And she did. Too much. She forced a light tone. "I may

not be back until time to fix supper. Don't worry. You'll get your next meal."

"I look forward to it."

Callie fought the desire to be that woman Jacob looked forward to. She wouldn't get wrapped up in a man who didn't love God.

They parted ways at the corner of Liberty and Serenity. He gave her one last lingering look, then turned west toward the Mitchell Mercantile. With her heart thudding in her chest, evidence that Jacob meant more to her than she wanted to admit, she turned east toward the church.

She found Pastor Steele in his office, preparing his sermon for Sunday. She took the chair across from him.

He gave her a warm smile, the kind of smile that welcomed confidences. "What do you have on your mind, Callie?"

"Perhaps you read in the Society page that another unwed mother will soon arrive at my home."

"I did." He chuckled. "Which I suspect has something to do with why you're here."

Callie leaned forward in her chair. "I'm here to ask you to support my plan to house unwed mothers, to provide for their needs and give them shelter from reproach."

"I applaud your plan. Too often these girls are thrown to the lions." He sighed. "And the babies' fathers go their merry way." He fiddled with the fountain pen on his desk. "Has it occurred to you that Peaceful might not welcome this home?"

The concern in his eyes dampened Callie's enthusiasm, but only for a moment. "I suspect a few will criticize, one in particular."

"We both know who that would be."

"But isn't that always the case with something new?"

"You make a good point. Far be it from me to try to talk

you out of what I believe is an important calling. But I need to warn you that it's possible more than a few will oppose this." He sighed. "Plenty of believers feel sinners deserve reproach. That they've broken God's commandments and should be ostracized. They forget the command, 'Judge not, that ye be not judged.'"

How could she ask? "Could you preach a sermon that would take a stand welcoming these girls to our community?"

"I'll preach on judging others, on forgiving others. Sermons based on God's Word. I can't endorse the unwed mothers' home from the pulpit, but I'll give my time and a donation and hope others will do the same." He peered at her over his glasses, then shoved them up his nose. "Human nature being what it is, I'll be praying this doesn't divide our congregation."

With the pastor's prayers and her own, surely God wouldn't allow that to happen. "I'll do the same. I'd hoped everyone could see the value of helping these girls."

"Everyone rarely agrees on anything, even the meaning of Scripture." He grabbed a sheet of paper. "There's much to consider here. If one of these girls leaves her baby after it's born, just slips away in the dead of night, you'll need the services of a lawyer."

Pastor Steele's words put a knot in Callie's stomach. She hadn't even considered such a possibility.

He wrote a name and address on the page. "I recommend a fine man in Indianapolis who can advise you. Write and explain what you're planning. He'll know the legalities involved."

"Oh, thank you." Callie took the sheet. "I'm going to have to keep you stocked in pie."

"If any of these young women are struggling with tough

issues like incest and rape, I'll be available to counsel them. With God's help, I'll try to help them find peace."

If only Nell had talked to her pastor.

Pastor Steele rubbed a hand over his eyes. "I suppose you could find yourself housing a prostitute."

Callie gasped.

"You'll need to make the rules crystal clear. Nothing illegal or immoral can go on while those young women are under your roof."

She'd need a list of house rules. Something she hadn't considered.

Pastor Steele took a look at Callie's face, then came around the desk and perched on the corner. "God has called you to this, but that doesn't mean you can ignore the important details of such an undertaking."

"You've given me a lot to think about. And act on." She released a breath. "I feel overwhelmed."

He smiled. "I feel the same way much of the time."

"All I know to do is take it one girl, one day at a time."

"When we're doing God's work, we can expect opposition. But these women will be blessed to have you on their side." He pulled a chair next to hers. "Shall we pray about this unwed mothers' home? Ask God to provide everything you need to make it a reality, including wisdom and support."

After the prayer, Callie left the church filled with peace. They'd asked God for His help. With His power, she'd strive to anticipate and deal with every obstacle, every problem. But, ultimately, the outcome rested with Him.

Pastor Steele would prepare hearts and counsel those who needed him. Mildred would donate funds to support it—Callie was sure of it. Perhaps even Commodore would contribute items to clothe fatherless babies.

Callie headed home, eager to share Pastor Steele's reaction with Elise. Perhaps even with Jacob. He'd lived in an orphanage. Surely he'd be pleased to hear that the pastor had given her counsel and supported her plan.

Jake finished his errand in town and arrived back at Callie's house, toting a bag of cement. A load of bricks would be delivered tomorrow. He saw no activity around the place, then remembered that Elise was visiting her mother. Callie hadn't returned from town. And shouldn't for a while, giving him the perfect opportunity to examine the newspapers.

He entered the house by the back door and strode to the main hall, then on toward the library. The door was closed. Not unusual with Callie's dislike of clutter. Inside he discovered that the piles had been separated by decades. Much easier to find what he wanted. Within minutes he found the year and month of his birth. To make sure he didn't miss a birth announcement, he'd check June as well.

He carried a stack to a chair and went over each one with painstaking care, searching for anything that would give him a clue to his identity.

And came up with nothing.

No one by the name of Smith appeared to have lived in the town. Had his mother given him an alias when she left him at the orphanage? If that were true, what was the likelihood that she'd stay in town to give birth? The only baby born on May 21, 1877 was a girl. If that was even the year he was born.

He rose and returned the stack to the desk. What to do next? With the newspapers a dead end, he'd talk to Mildred Uland, the woman most likely to know town gossip, especially from twenty-three years ago.

"What are you doing?"

Jake jerked toward the open door. Callie. He hadn't heard her enter the room. He stepped away from the desk. "I uh, thought I'd kill some time looking at these newspapers. Hope you don't mind."

Her accusing gaze locked with his. "Why didn't you ask permission?"

"I didn't think it mattered." He took in her tight mouth and the pucker between her slim brows. "Obviously, I was wrong."

She shoved back her shoulders. "Why go behind my back? I would have gladly shown you the papers."

"I'm sorry, I didn't realize you'd be upset."

"After that kiss… After what we've shared, I thought I could trust you. Obviously, I was wrong."

Jake wanted to deny her claim, to tell her she could trust him. To tell her the reason he needed to look at the newspapers. But if he did, she'd want to know more. He couldn't risk telling her everything.

By the look in her eyes, he'd not only made her mad, he'd hurt her. He hadn't meant to, but saying that wouldn't impress Callie. If anything, his denial would make her angrier.

A man's actions proved his trustworthiness.

From the frown puckering her brow and the icy chill in her eyes, she wanted him gone. He had money enough to stay somewhere else, but he wanted to be here, to make this house habitable for her and for Elise. With that crumbling, faulty chimney that risked their safety, he had to say something to ease her disquiet.

"I'm sorry. I should've asked first." He motioned to the newspapers. "I was looking for information on the Odd Fellows' building downtown. The edifice is unique, made me think of the work of an architect my boss talked about."

The guardedness in her eyes didn't ease.

He'd just lied to Callie. And she knew it.

"I want you to leave."

Her words cut into him like a knife. "I can't. Not yet. The chimney isn't safe. If it isn't fixed, you risk being overcome by carbon monoxide."

A flash of consternation swept across her face. "Nothing would make me happier than seeing you go. But I need to ensure the house's safety." She folded her arms across her chest. "We'll forget this happened." She turned to go, then pivoted back. "This time."

He heard the warning. She'd given him another chance.

If only he'd been able to tell Callie the real reason he'd needed to look at the newspapers. But if he did, she'd want to help. She'd want to get involved. She'd want to get close.

And that meant she'd learn the truth. The truth of who Jacob Smith really was. That he'd spent almost a year in prison. That *Smith* might not even be his real name. That a jury of his peers had judged him a loser.

But when Callie had looked at him, he'd seen a different reflection in her eyes. A faith in him that made him feel seven feet tall, instead of like a lowly worm. She'd made him believe in himself, something he'd lost.

If she discovered that he was a former convict, that look of respect he'd seen in her eyes would disappear forever. Better to endure her ire, and hope she'd forgive him, than lose her regard.

Callie watched Jacob leave the house and walk to the barn. His shoulders hunched like he carried the weight of the world on his back. She felt the same way. Until he repaired the chimney, she would try to put the incident with Jacob behind her.

What choice did she have? Unless the flue was repaired,

fumes could kill them all this winter. She couldn't take such a risk. A list of jobs he'd planned to do paraded through her mind. The windows on the north side of the house needed replacing. The house needed to be scraped and it needed a coat of paint. Nothing hazardous there, but the possibility that the house wouldn't be returned to its former glory sank inside her.

Jacob had entered her home without permission. He'd only needed to ask to see the newspapers. That he hadn't asked left no doubt in her mind. His excuse for examining the newspapers had nothing to do with architecture and everything to do with concealment.

Concealment had been Martin's forte. Her throat tightened as memories raced through her mind. Martin had hidden his selfish nature behind a jolly exterior. He'd hidden overspending, keeping bills from her until a storekeeper in town would ask her for payment. He'd hidden his frequent absences from work to go fishing and hunting by telling Commodore he was sick or handling a chore for her. A chore he never intended to do. Time after time, he'd lied to her. Each time had chipped away at her respect for her husband. Caught red-handed, he'd always been sorry.

Just like Jacob.

She'd thought Jacob Smith was the exact opposite of Martin—hardworking, dependable, a man who meant what he said. How wrong she'd been.

Loretta had said Jacob looked familiar. A chill snaked down Callie's spine. Could she have seen Jacob's face on a wanted poster?

No, Jacob might be devious, might not be the man she thought, but he wasn't a criminal.

Then what was he up to?

She'd thought they might have a future together. What a fool she'd been to even consider a relationship with a man without faith. With a man who kept things hidden. With another man who concealed his true nature.

She'd thought Jacob's past had left him wounded. That he didn't want to open that pain to others. Now she questioned the motive for his secrecy. Did he have a more sinister reason for not opening up and sharing his past?

The attraction between them was undeniable. Well, she wouldn't act on it. How could she have started to care for the wrong man?

Again?

Once he made the repairs on her house, he would leave, exactly as she wanted it. Her breath caught. Who was being dishonest now? For when he did, Jacob would take a piece of her heart with him.

That was all he'd get. She'd protect the rest with every particle of her will. And never let Jacob Smith get close again.

Chapter Twelve

Callie greeted Loretta, stepping aside to let her in.

Across the way, Jacob hauled bricks in a wheelbarrow toward the barn—no doubt, preparing to repair the faulty flue in her chimney. At the sight of him, her heart skipped a beat. She quickly looked away, tamping down the silly reaction to a man who was all wrong for her. A man who deceived. A man without faith.

Loretta handed Callie a basket of muffins, still warm from the oven, then wrapped Callie in a hug, eyeing her. "You're upset about something."

"Actually, I've had a good day." Until her run-in with Jacob, her statement was true. For some reason, Callie couldn't share Jacob's uninvited entrance into her house and obvious lie with her friend.

"Any special reason?"

"The water's hot. Join me for a cup of tea and one of these muffins." She inhaled. "They smell wonderful."

While Callie prepared a pot of tea, Loretta leaned against the counter, fiddling with the button on her dress. "How are you feeling?"

"Fine." Callie smiled. "Great, in fact. I'm not so tired these days."

With Callie carrying the pot and Loretta following with cups and napkins, Callie led the way to the table in her sun-drenched, sprawling kitchen.

As they took their seats, Loretta turned to her with a grin. "That handsome handyman of yours is getting more done in a few weeks than Hal accomplishes all year. Does he help with the chores?"

"He does." She wanted to deny that Jacob made her life easier, but she couldn't. Helpful or not, if Loretta knew the reservations Callie had about Jacob, she'd insist that Callie send him packing.

Callie would, as soon as he repaired the defective chimney. Others in town could do the repair, but the money to pay them would deplete funds needed for the unwed mothers' home.

Loretta lost her smile. "I saw the mention of your dinner party on the Society page and the columnist's reaction to your unwed mothers' home. That's why I'm here."

"I knew you'd want to help. Could you handle the funds while I took care of the details of housing the girls? We—"

Loretta raised a hand, cutting Callie off. "Before you get too far, let me explain. I didn't want to say anything in front of Elise, but I can't support your plan."

"You've been kind to Elise. I assumed…"

"Callie, its one thing to take in Elise, a neighbor girl we all love, but to bring total strangers with who knows what kind of pasts into your home is risky. Perhaps Hal's job makes me wary, but I'm afraid of what this unwed mothers' home will bring to our town."

"I thought you'd be my biggest supporter. Might help with fundraising." She sighed. "Everyone in town listens to you."

"I'm sorry. But, to speak frankly, I think your idea is crazy."

Loretta's words landed in her stomach like a stone. "Why?"

"A home for unwed mothers will cause trouble. Trouble this town doesn't need. Right now we have a close-knit community. People will take sides. One thing will lead to another until Peaceful is anything but."

"Once people get used to the idea, they'll see the importance of providing a refuge for these girls."

Loretta's eyes narrowed. "Those girls could be lawbreakers, have arrests or jail sentences in their pasts. We can't risk opening our children or this community to riffraff."

"Riffraff?" Callie's cup hit the saucer with a clink, splashing tea onto the table.

"Right now Hal doesn't do much to ensure the peace. Other than an occasional fracas in the saloon, the cells in the jail sit empty. That's the way we want to keep it."

"I want the same thing." She laid a hand on Loretta's sleeve. "You're overreacting. I'm taking in young women, not hardened criminals."

"Your heart is in the right place, but I can't go along with this idiocy."

"Have you prayed about it?"

"No, I guess I haven't." She moved her arm away. "But don't think making me feel guilty will change my stance. I have personal reasons for objecting to this unwed mothers' home."

"Like what?"

"Our boys are seventeen and eighteen, at that age when… Well, when young ladies are fascinating creatures. They're inexperienced and fool enough to fall for some girl's helpless charms. One or both could offer marriage to solve a need for a daddy for her baby and a husband to take care of her bills."

"Then tell your sons not to get involved with them."

Loretta harrumphed. "You have a lot to learn about parenting. Our boys are at an age when telling them what to do will only make them sneak around to do just the opposite."

"These girls will have been burned. I doubt they'll be hunting for a man, but—"

"You're naive. Who knows why these girls end up pregnant? Their babies could be the result of rape, even incest. Or maybe they'd slept with several men and have no idea who fathered their babies."

"You're expecting the worst, but—"

"Okay, let's give them the benefit of the doubt." Loretta rose and paced the floor, then stopped in front of Callie. "They've made a mistake like Elise. They're good girls who want to start over. And give their babies a happy life. But you can't know which kind of girl will be coming to your home. If you expect them to be honest about their pasts, you're mistaken."

Callie had to convince Loretta of the worth of her endeavor. "Sit down, please. Let's talk calmly about this."

Loretta did as Callie asked, but with a frown on her face.

"The Bible tells us to love our neighbor. Sometimes giving that neighbor what he needs is a risk, as it was for the Good Samaritan. While he ministered to the injured man, he could've been beaten and robbed. But he didn't consider the cost. Instead, he gave his time and his money to see that the man received good care and recovered fully."

Loretta threw up her hands. "The Good Samaritan

stumbled across the victim. He didn't go looking for some-one in trouble."

"Loretta, surely you remember what happened to Nell." Unable to continue, she bit her lip.

"I do. And I'm sorry, Callie, but surely you care about my sons more than girls you've never met. Give up this plan for George and Henry's sakes."

"Your boys know right from wrong. And who's to say— maybe these girls will be God's answer for their wives."

Loretta gasped.

Callie took Loretta's hand. "You don't really believe these girls deserve forgiveness, do you?"

"You're wrong. I'm not judging them. I'm afraid of where this will lead."

"All I know is that you're putting up roadblocks to these girls' chance to start over. To be loved while they carry and deliver their babies. Whether you see them as a mistake or not, these babies are created by God."

"Are you being honest with yourself? Is concern for these girls the real reason you want to do this? Or are they replacing the family you've lost?"

Callie winced. Loretta's words stung like a slap in the face. Yet she'd heard the truth in them. Her motive for the unwed mothers' home might not be as Godly as she'd thought, but that didn't make her decision wrong.

"It's true that I love having Elise with me. The house was like a tomb before she moved in. But the promise I made Nell at her funeral is my reason for this step. I'd even talked to Martin about it. Not that his reaction was any better than yours."

"You can't know that these girls won't come to a horrible end, like Nell. If so, you'll be left to pick up the pieces."

"I can't run my life expecting the worst." She shivered, suddenly unsure if she could handle the job.

"I'm sorry, but my sons and the other young people in town are more important to me than these girls. Their loose behavior could spread like a rotten apple through a bushel. Our children might think intimacy before marriage is acceptable." Loretta rose. "Too much is at stake. I will fight you on this."

"What will you teach your children by your stand? That you don't trust them to do what's right? That you won't heed God's leading if doing so involves risk?"

Loretta's jaw jutted. "I'll do anything to protect my boys. You'll understand that better when your baby arrives."

Tears sprang to Callie's eyes. "You believe I'd make decisions that would harm children? I'm trying to help children."

"I'm sure your intentions are good, Callie. We both know where they lead."

With that her friend left by the back door. Without sharing their usual hug. The unwed mothers' home had put a rift between them. A rift that might never heal.

Oh, Lord, am I doing the right thing? Am I following Your will? Is my unwed mothers' home contrary to Scripture?

In the parlor, she pulled her Bible from the table and onto her lap. Grateful for privacy, she looked up Scriptures about orphans, about Jesus's treatment of prostitutes and sinners of every variety. Nothing she found convinced her that caring for these girls displeased God.

Quite the opposite.

In the back of her mind, a nagging worry took hold. Would this unwed mothers' home split the community? Peaceful had been good to her, had rallied around her. The possibility of her friends and neighbors turning against her twisted in her stomach.

What if Loretta was right that her motivation for

establishing this home was to fill the hole in her heart rather than to fulfill a need for these girls?

Right motivation or not, she felt called by God to house unwed mothers. How could she refuse? She would obey. No matter what the cost.

Lord, help me be strong. Strong enough to handle the job.

Except for God, she might be handling it alone.

Callie sat across the table from Elise. Rain poured down the kitchen windows, all but hiding the outbuildings from view. Jacob had mentioned that the roof of the lean-to leaked during the last rain. He'd been too busy repairing her chimney and cracked ceilings to see to his own comfort. Here she sat in a snug, leak-free house, thanks to him. Even if she was still upset by the excuse he'd made for sneaking into her house, she couldn't allow Jacob to stay out there getting drenched.

"You should invite him in."

Callie turned toward Elise, her stomach fluttering at the prospect of having Jacob in the house again. In this kitchen. The place where he'd massaged her feet. But she wouldn't admit that to Elise. "You read my thoughts. Will you make some popcorn while I go out to the lean-to and invite him?"

"I'll get out the dominoes, too."

Callie wrapped her fringed shawl around her shoulders, grabbed the umbrella and slipped out the door, raising the umbrella over her head. Picking her way between puddles, she arrived at the lean-to door and knocked. "Jacob, it's Callie."

The door opened to the ping of water hitting metal buckets. One pail sat in the middle of the floor. The other stood between her and Jacob like a sentry. Her heart squeezed at the dismal cramped space where he spent his nights.

Jacob planted a hand against the frame and leaned toward her, his muscles bulging through the sleeve of his shirt. "Hi," he said flashing a lazy grin. The hollow in his cheek put a hitch in her breathing and rooted her to the spot. "Why are you braving this downpour?"

"You can't stay out here with the roof leaking. Come up to the house. Elise is making popcorn."

"Are you sure you trust me inside?"

She heaved a sigh. "I trust you inside the house, or I wouldn't have invited you. But that doesn't mean I believe your excuse for looking at the newspapers."

"I'm sorry, Callie. I shouldn't have lied."

She waited. No explanation came. What was he hiding? "You're not going to tell me why, are you?"

"Can you just trust that I have my reasons? Good reasons that I'm not able to share with you. Not yet."

Her eyes traveled his face, searching for furtiveness but seeing only candor. Yet, his admission didn't provide the answers she needed. She couldn't force him to confide in her, but she wouldn't open her heart to a secretive man.

"I guess I'll have to. Let's go before we both get soaked."

He shrugged into his jacket, then took the umbrella and wrapped an arm around her, shielding her with his body. As they navigated the puddles to the house, the heat from his skin drew her to him like a moth to a flame. She knew where that led.

Inside, Elise greeted them along with the aroma of popcorn. Elise dished up the snack into a large bowl, Jacob poured apple juice while Callie gathered napkins.

Elise set the bowl on the table. "Did you feel like a drowned duck in that leaky lean-to?"

"A smidgeon," Jacob admitted with a grin. "But my feathers are well-oiled."

Elise giggled. "At least you're not waddling like me." She proceeded to do a good imitation of a duck, as she moseyed to her seat.

Laughing at her antics they all sat and turned the dominoes black side up.

With Jacob at her side, taking up more space than a mere man should, the intimacy of their last private moment in the kitchen rose between them like a living, breathing thing. Callie vowed she'd never make the mistake of being alone with him again.

Her hand brushed Jacob's as they both reached for popcorn and every rational thought fled. Why did the slightest touch of this secretive man affect her this way?

"Remember you score if the dots total anything divisible by five." Elise laid down double-fives, grinning from ear to ear. "That makes ten." She wrote the number under her name. "I have a feeling I'm going to win."

"We'll see about that," Jacob said, plunking down a piece with five on one end, ten on the other. "That makes twenty."

Elise harrumphed and wrote the number under Jacob's name. "Are you sure you haven't played dominoes before?"

"Not this way." He grinned. "But it doesn't seem hard."

Callie had no play. Moaning, she drew a domino. This one played. She added her piece to the string of dominoes but didn't make any points.

Eyes dancing with mischief, Jacob rearranged his dominoes and cocked his head to her, looking handsomer than a man should. "Looks like things aren't going well for you."

"As if you care," she said, rolling her eyes.

As Elise studied her options, Jacob's gaze locked with hers. "Oh, but I do. More than you know," he said.

At his words, Callie's heart skipped a beat. His jade eyes continued to burn into hers with an intensity that left her insides quivering like a field of grain on a blustery day. To avoid his eyes and cool the heat in her veins, she reached for her glass of apple juice and practically drained its contents in one long swallow.

"You must be thirsty," Jacob said. "Let me get you more."

"It's the popcorn," she choked out.

About to make her play, Elise furrowed her brow. "Did I add too much salt?"

"No, a hull got stuck in my throat. I'm fine now."

Jacob leaned toward her. "I'd hate to lose a player to a hull injury, especially a player who looks to be losing."

While Jacob continued to grin as if he knew exactly what was bothering her, he proceeded to add a domino. "Give me twenty more points," he said, sending a satisfied smirk in Callie's direction.

"You sound mighty sure of yourself, Mr. Smith."

Cocking his head, he eyed the line of dominoes in front of her. "The evidence is hard to deny, Mrs. Mitchell."

She laid down a double-ten. "That'll be twenty-five." Folding her arms, she smiled at Jacob.

"Appears you're getting the hang of it."

"I'm not one to give up."

Jacob took her hand and gave it a squeeze. "One of the many things I admire about you," he said, then released it.

Leaving Callie feeling bereft, which made no sense at all. She would concentrate on the game. Not that the outcome would've mattered one whit normally. But tonight, she couldn't let him best her.

"Papa likes to play dominoes." Elise put out her piece then lifted her eyes to Callie's. "I miss him."

"Have you thought about going home for a visit, Elise? Maybe he's had a change of heart."

"He still insists I give up the baby, either to a married couple not from here or…an orphanage."

"If your father ever spent time in an orphanage, he'd change his mind about having his grandchild there."

Elise sighed. "He's so upset he doesn't act like my baby's even human, much less his grandchild."

Callie took Elise's hand. "I'm praying that your father will change his mind once the baby arrives. Who couldn't help but love a newborn?"

"Oh, thank you. I hope you're right." Elise turned to Jacob. "What was it like in the orphanage, Jake?"

"Life was regimented. We were lined up and marched to meals that we ate in silence." He gave a wry smile. "Nothing resembling your meals, Callie. We didn't starve, but we came close. There never seemed to be enough food."

Jacob had gone hungry? And hadn't known the joy of conversation at mealtimes?

Elise's eyes filled with sympathy. "I had everything I needed and more."

Callie patted her hand. "We were fortunate."

"Depravation comes in many forms. We worked. We slept. No hugs at bedtime. No praise. Not that all the kids deserved it. Bullies terrorized younger kids. Disobedience was a problem. Every day some kid, sometimes several, got a switching or hit with a razor strap for serious or even slight infractions."

Callie gasped. "I've never been whipped."

Jacob grinned. "I earned a few. The belt didn't hurt as much as the lack of reconciliation afterward, no making up and being forgiven. Some kids cried most nights." He met her gaze. "You learned to be tough."

From what Callie had seen, a lesson Jacob hadn't forgotten. Everything he'd said about the orphanage twisted inside her. "Talk to Elise's father. Tell him what you've told us." She laid a hand on his. "Please."

"Maybe I will," Jacob said, playing his last domino. "Next time I need a haircut. Though, like most folks, I suspect he won't appreciate the interference."

"Can't you talk to him sooner? Elise's baby will be here before the month is out."

Jacob avoided her gaze. "I'll see what I can do."

"Thank you for trying," Elise said, then added up the scores. "Looks like Jacob won."

"Nothing to this game." Jacob grinned.

Callie cocked her head at him. "Are you sure you're a novice?"

"It was the luck of the draw," he said, trying to look humble but failing, his eyes twinkling with humor. "Or I'm a fast learner."

Callie laughed, enjoying this fun side of Jacob. But even more importantly, pleased he'd agreed to talk to Mr. Langley. "Let me know when you're going to speak to Elise's father. Elise and I will pray." An idea seized her mind and wouldn't let go. "Even better, let's pray now."

At the suggestion, Elise smiled, but Jacob looked as if he'd swallowed a persimmon. Still, she reached out her hands. Elise took her left. Jacob hesitated then took her hand in his. The solid strength of his callused hand, evidence of his occupation, filled her with reassurance. She gave him a smile, then bowed her head.

"Father God, Jacob has agreed to talk to Elise's father about his experience of living in an orphanage. We pray that Mr. Langley will listen and their talk will go well.

And Lord, please meet the needs of orphans and all Your children, no matter who or where they are. Amen."

Jacob dropped her hand, as if the experience scorched his conscience. She doubted that he valued prayer. But perhaps, along with Elise's father, God would teach Jacob Smith a thing or two. She sent up a silent prayer that the experience of talking to Elise's father would somehow bring Jacob closer to God.

They'd just finished their second game when Elise yawned. "I'm tired. You'll have to play without me. I'm going to bed."

Jacob rose. "I'd better leave."

Elise walked to the window and peered out. "It's still pouring."

"A little water won't hurt me."

"Don't be silly." Callie packed away the dominoes. "Wait until the rain stops."

Elise said goodnight, then left the kitchen. The memory of the last time she and Jacob were alone in the kitchen brought Callie to her feet. She refilled the bowl of popcorn, moved about the kitchen, wiping grease off the stove, cleaning out the pan, straightening the hand towel, keeping her distance.

"Don't worry, Callie." Jacob shot her a teasing grin. "You and those pretty feet of yours are safe with me."

Her cheeks heated. "I'm not afraid of being alone with you."

"That's not what I'm seeing. I promise to keep my distance. Come sit before you wear yourself out and the wooden planks on the floor."

"You're imagining that." She set the bowl of popcorn down on the table, then took a seat across from him, careful to tuck her feet beneath her skirt.

Though every nerve in her body zinged at being alone

with Jacob, a man who made her feel things she'd never felt before and didn't want to feel now, she didn't want the evening to end.

Jacob took her hand, rubbing his thumb across the palm. "I've had a wonderful time, playing a game with you and Elise, sharing a bowl of popcorn. It was like being a kid again."

She pulled her hand away. "What, ah, kind of games did you play as a boy?"

"When our chores were done and weather permitted, we played outside—kick the can, dodgeball, racing games and, of course, baseball. In winter, we had snowball fights and built forts." He chuckled. "Most of us had runny noses all winter."

"I was afraid from what you said that you never had fun."

"Kids find ways to have fun. Sometimes at others' expense, like the time we hid a frog in the silverware drawer." He laughed. "We scared the cook so badly she refused to fix our supper."

"You were an imp."

He grinned. "That's a kind description. What was it like at your aunt's?"

"Aunt Hilda liked to play board games and dominoes on winter evenings. In the summer I spent every moment I could outside playing jump rope, hopscotch, roaming around town." She giggled. "Getting into trouble."

"You?"

"No more than most kids."

"You were never punished?"

Callie laughed. "Occasionally, Aunt Hilda gave me a scolding. Once I had to sit in my bedroom without supper."

"What did you do?"

"I lied to her. I learned my lesson and haven't told a lie since."

He raised a brow. "Never?"

Their eyes locked and everything within her stilled, as a surge of connection to this man swept through her. Evidence that she was lying right now, to herself. No matter how much she wanted to deny it, no matter how wrong he was for her, Jacob Smith had gotten under her skin.

She wouldn't let him get close. Not until she knew what brought him to Peaceful and why he wanted to look at those newspapers. He'd admitted that he'd lied about his reason, but hadn't confided in her, either. Never again would she fall for a man without seeing what lurked beneath the surface.

"What about you, Jacob? Perhaps you're not telling a lie, but…" She took a deep breath, afraid of his answer. "Are you living one?"

A flicker of something lit in his eyes. He dropped his gaze. What had she glimpsed in their depths before he turned away? Something wary, something secretive, something leery.

Her breath caught. How could she have fallen for another deceiving man?

Chapter Thirteen

Jake had hightailed it out of Callie's kitchen last night before the rain had stopped, dashing to the lean-to, each footfall drenching his pant legs and his spirits. Callie had pushed to ferret out his secret, destroying the camaraderie they'd shared. Before she learned the truth, he'd finish his search for his mother and get out of town.

With a grunt, he shoved the wooden handles of the hedge shears together, cutting off the branches of the overgrown evergreens blocking Mrs. Uland's windows. A chore he'd offered to do, hoping to question her about the gossip she'd heard about the Squier family. But the search for his mother didn't preoccupy his thoughts. All he could think about was Callie.

Better to sever the relationship, as he did these branches, than to let her become involved with him, a man who'd rubbed elbows with depravity and ugliness in jail and smelled the stench of it in his nostrils still. A man who had no idea how a proper husband behaved. Or, for that matter, what it took to be a good father. Callie deserved better than him.

Not that he could take the risk of getting close, even if he hadn't spent time in jail. He'd been burned by an

indifferent foster family, a woman he'd thought loved him
and an unscrupulous best friend.

As much as he felt Callie incapable of such treachery,
he couldn't seem to let go of his mistrust. To avoid Callie
and her questions, he'd gulped down breakfast, mentioning
his plans to trim Mrs. Uland's shrubs on his way out the
door. Callie hadn't tried to stop him. She knew as well as
he did that Jake wasn't the man for her.

Mrs. Uland would no doubt insist on paying him, but
he'd refuse. He had money, which he didn't need to use as
long as he stayed in Callie's lean-to and ate at her table.
But his time here was running out. Soon the unwed mother
from Bloomington would arrive. Before she did, he'd be
gone.

The thought of leaving drenched his good spirits like an
April downpour. He tried to tell himself that his reaction
had more to do with not finishing the renovations on the
old Victorian than an interest in Callie.

But, no matter what Callie claimed, he'd never been a
good liar. Since the age of seven, he hadn't even been able
to lie to himself.

He swiped sweat from his brow in the crook of his
elbow. A man had no problem staying warm working at
this speed. He dumped the last armload of branches onto
the tarpaulin, grabbed two ends and hauled it to the back
of Mrs. Uland's lot. On a windless day, he'd burn them. Not
today. He glanced toward the fast-moving clouds. Today
was better suited to flying kites.

The idea of holding on to the string with Callie beside
him, watching a kite soar into the sky, the tail whipping
in the wind, held him in its grasp. He could visualize her
delight, the huge smile she'd wear as she looked upward,
holding on to her hat. He'd wrap an arm around her—

In reality, the blustery day would be better spent mucking

the barn. Odors didn't linger on a day like this one. He'd handle that chore when he finished here. And forget what he couldn't have.

Jake stowed the hacksaw, clippers and tarpaulin in the small shed near the rear of her property, then walked around to the front door.

Mrs. Uland answered his knock, wrapped in a bulky shawl. "Gracious, you're a whirlwind on two legs! I'm practically dizzy from watching you. Come in, dear boy. I have coffee made."

He flicked evergreen needles from his sleeve. "I'm a mess. Just wanted to let you know I'd finished trimming your bushes. I'll burn the branches when this wind dies down."

"I've been walking between the windows, enjoying the view. My neighbors probably thank you as much as I do. All those overgrown shrubs looked like a hermit lived here with something to hide." She laughed, obviously not the least concerned about what her neighbors thought. "If you're sure you won't come inside, let me get you a cup of coffee to ward off the chill."

"Coffee sounds good."

"Sugar? Cream?"

"I like it the way it comes."

"I prefer to dress it up with both." She laughed. "My hubby said I didn't like coffee, only what went into it. He might've lived long enough to greet old age, if he'd indulged." She shot him a look. "You might want to give that a try."

He bit back a smile. "Yes, ma'am."

Accompanied by her dog Sandy, Mrs. Uland returned carrying a tray holding two mugs and a plate of gingersnap cookies sprinkled with sugar. "The older I get the more I can't tolerate the cold."

"Your windows may need caulking."

"That or my bones." Her grin crinkled the corners of her eyes. "Maybe that would stop their creaking."

Jake grinned, taking a seat in one of the wicker rockers on the porch across from Mrs. Uland's. Sandy laid his nose on Jake's leg. He gave it a pat. The porch was comfortable in the morning sun and they were somewhat protected by the wind.

He could set Mrs. Uland's house to rights in no time, but he'd move on before someone discovered his past. Though maybe this quirky dowager, who didn't appear to care what anyone thought and wasn't easily rattled, wouldn't be thrown by the news that he'd spent a year in jail. Perhaps, just perhaps, Callie wouldn't be undone by the information, either. Not that he'd take a chance by telling her.

Mrs. Uland wrapped both hands around her mug and took a sip. "This is nice. Help yourself to the cookies." She motioned to the plate on the table between them. "Don't waste them on Sandy. He's not fond of them, silly dog. My ma baked gingersnaps every week. They gave me a sore tongue, I ate so many." She chuckled. "That's what I got for being greedy. But they're still my favorites." She inhaled, closing her eyes. "The aroma makes me think of my childhood."

He took two. "I didn't realize I was hungry till I got a whiff of these." He took a bite. "They're delicious. Cookies are my favorites. At Christmas, a nearby church would bring gingerbread boy cookies to the orphanage. One for each of us."

"Ma made those, too."

"I'd prolong eating mine for as long as I could." He grinned. "I'd start with the legs, then the arms and finally the body. Left the head for last."

"Now why was that? I always ate the heads off first."

Jake shrugged. "I guess I...liked their smiles."

"You must've been a sweet little boy to care about that. You make me feel like a monster," she said with a laugh. "So we both have good memories of cookies."

A list of memories from his childhood tromped through Jake's mind: his mildewed pillow, beans of every kind, scratchy towels, limp shirts, a pile of work, the sting of a razor strap. The giant old bush behind the shed, the place disobedient boys were sent to get their punishment. He'd never smell a lilac without thinking of that bush. Odd that, now, he didn't mind the scent.

Mrs. Uland dunked another cookie into her coffee. "When you go shopping for a wife, make sure she can make gingerbread cookies. Your house will always smell like home."

To Jake, cookies—any kind of cookies—each individually made, often with kids in mind, were a small serving of affection. He used to help the cook in the kitchen, cleaning up, peeling potatoes, shelling beans. On rare occasion when cookies made the menu, she'd sneak Jake a couple of extras. He'd carry those cookies in his pockets as he'd roamed the woods or fished the pond. Just knowing he could munch on them whenever the notion struck put a smile on his face.

"Are you looking?"

"Pardon?"

"For a wife?"

"No, ma'am."

"I'm thinking Callie might change your mind about that."

Jake choked on his coffee. Curled at his feet, Sandy raised his head then lowered it again.

"Not just yet, you understand, what with her only months since Martin's death. But a woman needs a man. I'm a rudderless ship since my husband passed." She sighed.

"Keeping up this house is more than I can handle. Those bushes should've been trimmed years ago, but I didn't know who to ask. Not Martin." Mildred shook her head, tsk-tsking. "He was a congenial fellow, but not partial to work."

"I got that impression."

"Take my advice. Don't say as much to Callie. She doesn't cotton to criticism of that husband of hers. I admire her loyalty. We've both lost husbands. Mine was a saint." She smiled. "I never deserved that man. The only time he made me mad was when he up and died on me, leaving me to manage without him for twenty years." She rolled her eyes Heavenward. "Or for however long it'll be before the Good Lord takes me home."

Jake didn't know how to respond to this talk of Heaven. Shifting in his chair, he let his gaze roam the house's exterior. "I'm impressed with the construction of these Victorian houses. They're solid. If properly cared for, they're almost indestructible."

"Changing the subject doesn't fool me, Jacob Smith. Call me a busybody, but you and your Maker need to have a talk."

If only he could believe. "Reckon you're right about that."

"Don't be waiting too long. As for that house of Callie's, it was hard to watch it fall into disrepair. Couldn't understand why the senator built a lovely home then left it to rot."

Here was the opportunity Jake sought. "Wonder what makes someone move under the cover of dark and never return?"

She tapped a finger against her lower lip. "None of the rumors made any sense. Some said the house was haunted." She chuckled. "Such foolishness, but people talk. Make up something if they don't know the facts." She sobered. "Another story, which makes more sense was that votes were the reason he left."

"Votes? How so?"

"He never did one thing unless he thought it'd get him a vote. Near an election, he'd attend church, faithful as you please. Sat in the front row. Once elected, he didn't darken the door, that is, till the next ballot. He'd attend Peaceful's festival in September if there was an election in November. Shake his way from gathering to gathering. But otherwise never joined in, never took part."

"Seems like people would've caught on and not reelected him."

"Reckon they thought he'd done a good enough job, but they weren't fooled, if that's what you're thinking. Folks aren't fooled long by a user." She narrowed her gaze. "Make sure you don't do the same thing, Jake. I don't know what brings you to Peaceful. I suspect you've got your reasons. An agenda, some call it, for coming and not joining in. We got enough folks living on the sidelines. Don't be one of them."

Jake felt heat climb his neck. In a couple sentences, Mildred Uland lumped him together with Senator Squier, discrediting them both. "I'd say I've joined in by repairing Callie's house."

She raised a palm. "That work you do isn't what I mean and you know it."

Jake hated to admit that Mildred was right, even to himself, but he'd managed to stay on the sidelines most of his life.

"Now Lillian and their daughter, Irene, were nothing like the senator. They took an active part in the community."

"They only had one child?"

Mildred nodded. "Irene was a pretty little thing, petite,

not much over five feet tall. Never understood why they'd uproot her with only another year till graduation from high school."

"Maybe the commute to Indianapolis got old." He took a swig of coffee.

"He didn't run for another term." She frowned. "Bothers me that I have no idea if Lillian and Irene are alive or dead. Guess that makes me nosy."

"I don't think so. When someone disappears without a word to anyone, folks want answers." He met her gaze. "Perhaps something bad happened here that ruined the house for them."

"Can't imagine what." She nibbled on a cookie, thinking. "Reckon I'll have to accept I'll never know. A mystery— that's what it is." She shook a finger his way. "Kind of like you." She turned questioning eyes on him. "You're mighty interested in the Squier family. Why is that?"

He forced a grin. "Making conversation is all. The family means nothing to me," he said, though he heard the wobble of his reply. He rose. "I'd better get to mucking out Callie's barn. Thanks for the coffee and cookies."

"Jake." Mrs. Uland held out the plate of cookies. "Take these with you." She walked to the step, Sandy at her heels, and handed them to him. "You're giving Callie's house new life. From the bounce in her step, you're giving it to her, too. Make sure you don't hurt that girl. She's had enough heartache."

"Yes, ma'am." He doffed his hat. "Thanks for the cookies."

If what Mildred said was true and Callie cared about him, even a little, he'd better hurry his search and get out of town. He would only bring Callie trouble.

As he strode toward her house, he relived the conversation. He'd said the Squier family meant nothing to him. But if Senator Squier moved his family because Irene got in a family way, that could mean she was his mother. Though he didn't have evidence to support that conclusion, he couldn't dislodge the idea from his mind. If she had given birth to him, she no longer lived in Peaceful. Where was Irene Squier now?

Mildred was obviously puzzled about that, too. Thankfully, she'd given Jake a name to go on. He'd see if he could discover why the senator gave up politics. And what had happened to the family. He might have to make a trip to Indianapolis. Whatever it took, he intended to pursue the only lead he had.

One thing he knew. If a senator's daughter had given birth to him, her family had possessed the material resources to raise him in their home, and a motive to avoid scandal.

Hiding a baby in an orphanage would've been a convenient solution to the problem of an illegitimate grandchild. At his sides his hands fisted. Convenient and corrupt.

If Irene gave her baby up to save her father's career, then the ploy had backfired. Senator Squier hadn't run for a second term. Why?

Perhaps Jake was making too much of the family's disappearance. Yet, the fact that they'd left in the middle of the night, and appeared to have dropped out of sight, certainly raised his suspicions. What did all this speculation mean? He might be no closer to the identity of the woman who gave him life than when he first arrived in town. But he wouldn't know the truth until he investigated this new lead.

Mucking out the barn could wait. He'd head to the depot and buy a ticket for the first train to Indianapolis.

Yanking a leggy weed and tossing it to the ground, Callie wished she could do the same to Jacob. He'd finished trimming Mildred's bushes hours ago, then said he had an errand to run and left. If that errand involved purchasing supplies, he should've been back by now.

Where had he gone?

She sighed. This was yet another example of Jacob's secrecy. When they'd parted last night, she'd asked Jacob if he was living a lie. He'd laughed off the question as if she'd been joking, but from the disquiet in his eyes, he knew better.

Well, she refused to let that man ruin the joy of today. Soon another unwed mother would arrive. She'd help the newcomer get settled in and see what she could do to make Refuge of Redeeming Love feel like home.

While she waited, Callie took the opportunity to clear dried leaves and weeds from the front flowerbed. Thankfully, the wind had died down. The bonnet she wore protected her face from the late-afternoon sun, warm through the sleeves of her dress.

Across the way, Stripes rose on his haunches and batted at a moth. A dog barked. Most likely, Sandy had treed a squirrel. A robin flew off with strands of dead grass to incorporate in its nest. All around her, Callie saw and heard the signs of life, of renewal—all part of God's plan. She loved spring.

Though she still had three months before her baby arrived, this bending and stretching was getting difficult. She chuckled, hoping she could get to her feet once she finished. Elise was off visiting her mother while her father cut hair at his shop.

Callie hoped the newcomer—Grace—would fit in. She'd grown accustomed to Elise in the house and Jacob nearby. As time went on, more women would come. Each one would affect the tone.

A sound alerted her to someone's approach.

A woman, carrying a satchel, her dark hair pulled into a severe bun, wearing a plain skirt and shirtwaist and, from her expression a chip on her shoulder. Her no-nonsense look fit Callie's image of a spinster schoolmarm more than an unwed mother.

The woman glanced at the newly painted sign Callie had hung that morning alongside the front door. Grace wasn't as young as Callie first thought, probably older than Callie herself.

"This is the home for unwed mothers."

"It is." Callie smiled a welcome. "You must be Grace."

She gave a cursory nod.

"If you'll give me a hand up, I'd appreciate it."

Grace took Callie's hand and with one fluid motion pulled Callie to her feet.

"Whew, you don't mess around." Callie tugged at her skirts.

"Some would say that's exactly what I did." Grace's tone held the biting edge of a well-honed knife.

The smile on Callie's face faltered. "I'm Callie Mitchell." She offered her hand, which was ignored. "Welcome to Refuge of Redeeming Love."

"How much does it cost to stay?"

"I'd ask for help with groceries if you can afford to pay. If not, you're still welcome. We share the chores."

Grace nodded, but didn't look pleased. Callie had an urge to chastise her for that haughty attitude but her conscience walloped her in the stomach. If God blessed His children according to their gratitude, there'd be far fewer rays of sunshine, drops of rain and bites to eat.

"I didn't catch your last name."

"I didn't give it."

Callie waited.

"Grace. I'm not saying more."

"Are you on the run?"

"Not from the law, if that's what you mean."

"From your family?"

"What's it to you?"

"I own this house. I don't want trouble, not here or in town. If we fail to keep the reputation of Redeeming Love spotless, I could be forced to close."

"No one's looking for me."

Every trace of disdain in her eyes evaporated, replaced with a raw pain that shut off Callie's questions. This girl needed someone to care.

"I'll show you to your room."

They walked to the house, Grace trailing a few steps behind. Along the way, Callie pointed out the location of the privy and other outbuildings. Inside, they climbed the stairs without Grace making one comment about her surroundings. A disappointment to Callie, who enjoyed seeing the house appreciated.

Sensing that the girl needed privacy, she led Grace to the back bedroom, the furthest from hers and Elise's. The space to rest, to cry, to work out whatever had happened to put that baby in her belly and bring her here.

"I hope you'll find your room comfortable."

Grace glanced at the double bed topped with a blue and white quilt, the dresser, washstand and armoire. "It's better than I expected."

Not exactly praise, but it would do. "Unpack, take a nap if you'd like. Or you might take a walk around the grounds and the house."

"I could use a nap."

"How did you get here?"

"Hitched a ride on a wagon. Walked the rest of the way."

"You must not live far."

"I won't be answering questions about where I'm from or who the father of this baby is. If that ain't acceptable, then say the word. I'll leave before I muss the sheets."

At the hostility in her voice, Callie frowned. "Who should I contact if you get sick?"

"No one cares if I live or die."

Callie folded her arms across her chest. "There are things I'll need to know."

"Like what?"

"Like how far along are you in your pregnancy?"

"Six months."

"Have you seen a doctor?"

"No."

"I'll get you in to see Doctor Wellman."

"I don't need no doctor."

"If you're worried that you can't pay, he's agreed to tend to residents of Redeeming Love whether they can afford a doctor or not."

She shrugged, as if medical care didn't matter, one way or another.

"I'd appreciate help preparing dinner. Come to the kitchen around five o'clock. It's at the back of the house behind the dining room. There's food to make, the table to set, cleanup after."

Grace's eyes turned cold. "I've worked as a domestic. I know what needs doing."

A piece of information Callie would remember. "Well, I'll leave you to unpack." She stepped toward the door. "Unless you need something before I go."

"What I need you can't give."

"Are you sure about that?"

"I'm sure."

"Well, if not me, then God can provide for your needs."

"If you're into preaching, I'm leaving."

"I don't preach, Grace. But talking about my faith is who I am. I did before you came and I will after you leave. If that's not all right with you, maybe you should walk out that door."

The young woman glanced at her feet. "I need a place to stay," she said in a subdued voice, without a trace of belligerence.

No matter what the woman claimed, Callie could provide a need—the roof over Grace's head. "I'm glad to have you."

Grace turned her back, walked to the window, all but dismissing Callie.

"Well, I'll be in the parlor. I've done all the gardening I care to for one day."

No response, as if Callie hadn't spoken. She left the room with the warnings Loretta had raised dancing through her mind. Most likely, Grace wasn't a lawbreaker. But her cold demeanor left no doubt. She wasn't interested in building relationships.

What had happened to her?

Well, whatever Grace had experienced, God had brought her here. Time would help. Affection would help. Prayer would help.

Or so Callie hoped. Yet doubts nagged at her. How would Grace's presence affect the household?

With three pregnant women under one roof, and who knew how many more to come, Callie wondered if she was equal to the task of keeping everyone's spirits up and trouble down. She'd gotten used to harmony in the house. Harmony she had no idea how to maintain.

She'd never felt more inadequate.

And more like giving Jacob Smith a piece of her mind.

Just when she needed him most, the man was nowhere to be found.

A knot twisted in her stomach. When had she started relying on a drifter?

As Callie made coffee, she glanced out the window. Rays of morning sun bounced off the barn's tin roof. A glance at the kitchen calendar reminded her of the Peaceful Ladies Club's Spring Tea later this morning. She'd agreed to bring a buttermilk coffee cake. Mercy, with the confusion of Grace's arrival yesterday, she'd forgotten the event, much less her contribution.

Donning an apron, Callie's hands stilled on the sash. This tea would be a perfect opportunity to lift Grace's spirits. Normally, she'd have obtained permission to bring guests, but all women eighteen years and older were welcome. There would be plenty of refreshments. Two more wouldn't matter.

Humming to herself, Callie set about the task. She'd use her talent for preparing food to help Grace feel welcome in the community. Along with Elise, they'd have a lovely time. And for a while forget their troubles. And have fun— something their situations may have denied them.

Callie measured flour, baking soda, baking powder and salt into the sifter then squeezed the handle back and forth, back and forth, mixing and refining the ingredients that dusted to the bottom of the crock.

God sifted his people, too, pushing them together to improve the whole. He'd used Grace's sullen attitude to show Callie that she could handle Grace's hostility. Without turning to someone exactly wrong for her. Jacob.

The man hadn't appeared for supper last night. Nor breakfast this morning. What did she care? Hadn't she learned not to rely on a man?

When Elise and Grace came into the kitchen, Callie talked long and hard to persuade Grace to attend the tea. She'd finally agreed, more to appease Elise, who wanted to go badly.

Finally, they'd dressed and walked the few blocks to the Ladies Club. Callie carried the coffee cake. Elise wore a smile of anticipation. Grace wore that chip on her shoulder.

Inside the front door, a knot of women chatted, oohing and aahing over each other's goodies.

Mrs. Sunderland noticed them first and stepped forward. "This is a private club."

Callie leveled a steely glance. "We've never turned anyone away, Mrs. Sunderland."

Coming around beside her, Loretta shot Callie a look of understanding. "I'm sorry, Callie, but we're not prepared for guests today."

Not taken in by that nonsense, Callie wanted to say as much, but doing so would only embarrass Grace and Elise more. Though with that scowl on Grace's face, Callie was surprised anyone dared confront them. Poor Elise looked ready to faint.

Mrs. Sunderland shook her head. "I can't believe how far you'll go to pursue your agenda."

Callie's mind went blank. "My agenda?"

"Everyone knows you need money to repair and keep up your house. Soliciting funds for unwed mothers is a clever way to look out for *your* interests, not the community's." She swept a hand. "Or these girls. Elise should be home with her parents." She folded her arms across her chest. "Honor your father and mother is a commandment, yet you've aided her rebellion."

Callie wouldn't break Elise's mother's confidence. But even if she knew that Sarah supported her daughter's actions, Mrs. Sunderland wouldn't be moved. She didn't have a heart.

Tugging Elise along, they headed out the door. Grace shot her a glare. "You're using us for your own benefit." She scoffed. "I knew your motives were too good to be true."

"Grace," Elise said, taking her arm. "Mrs. Sunderland will say anything to destroy Redeeming Love."

As they retraced their steps toward home, Callie could barely put one foot in front of the other. What a fool she'd been to expose Grace and Elise to censure. She'd wanted to give hurting women some fun. Her intentions had been good. But everything she'd planned had gone awry. She'd failed. Yet again. Only this time, Elise and Grace had been affected by the consequences of her bad decisions.

After this, Grace would probably never trust her.

Where would all this lead?

Chapter Fourteen

Jake hadn't seen Callie since his return from Indianapolis. He hoped his absence hadn't built another wall between them, but he still wasn't ready to talk about his mother.

The hours he'd spent at the State Capitol hadn't produced any solid evidence about his birth mother. He'd talked to several senators. Only one had served in the Senate with Wesley Squier. He'd remembered conversations they'd had about his wife and daughter. Told Jake that Squier had lost his appetite for politics, moved back East to his wife's hometown, though he couldn't recall where. He assumed Irene had gone with her parents.

Jake checked records at the courthouse and back issues of newspapers in the city's library, but found no mention of Wesley Squier, except for his announcement not to run for a fourth term. The article didn't mention his wife or daughter.

Wherever the family had gone, they apparently hadn't lived in the area for years. Irene couldn't have mailed those postcards, which meant he'd been on a wild goose chase.

With his lack of success weighing him down, he slogged toward the barn to get the tools he'd need to repair the water-damaged parlor ceiling.

Across the way, Callie plopped the milking stool and pail down alongside the cow. Soaking up her presence, he brushed off the setback, wanting only to make Callie's load easier. "Hi," he said. "Let me do the milking for you."

At his greeting, Callie jerked up her head.

Her beauty socked him in the gut. He'd missed her, as if he'd been gone for days instead of less than twenty-four hours. His gaze swept over her, then settled on her eyes. Eyes as turbulent as stormy seas and weary, as if she could barely keep her seat.

His pulse ratcheted. "Are you feeling all right?"

"I'm fine."

She didn't look fine. Or sound fine for that matter. Was she upset about his absence? "Is something bothering you?"

She glanced away, as if she didn't want to confide in him. Disappointment at the remoteness between them sank to his belly. "Are you angry that I didn't tell you where I've been?"

"Why would you think I care?" she said in a tone as frigid as a mountain stream. "You have a right to come and go as you please."

"That look in your eyes suggests otherwise."

"If you must know, I didn't sleep well last night. I couldn't get Grace off my mind."

"Who's Grace?"

"If you'd been around, you'd know Grace is an unwed mother and a resident. And she and Elise were refused admittance to the Ladies Club this morning."

"Why?"

"Why do you suppose?"

"Mrs. Sunderland at work?"

She nodded. "I had every right to bring visitors, but no one spoke up, even Loretta."

"You care too much. You're going to get sick if you don't keep your distance emotionally."

She harrumphed. "That's occurred to me. And not merely regarding Grace."

It didn't take a genius to understand her meaning. Unable to meet that probing gaze, he looked away.

She sighed. "I believe God brings people into my life for a reason. I just need to understand what purpose He has for me." She rose and strode to Jake. "As for you, at first I thought God brought you here to repair my house. But now I believe His reason is far bigger, far more important."

Jake turned on a booted heel. "Well, if you're sure you don't need help, I'll be in the parlor plastering the chink in the ceiling. Purpose enough for me."

"Whatever reason you're in Peaceful, Jacob, *your* purpose may not be God's objective."

The comment stopped him, made him turn back. How could he respond to that?

With every particle of his being, he wanted her touch. Wanted her with a desperation that left him shaken. But what Callie needed, he couldn't give, didn't even possess. "I don't believe God works in a doubter's life."

She gave a gentle smile. "God works in anyone's life He chooses, even those who haven't accepted Him." Then she returned to Bossy, putting her back to him.

Callie's behavior left him baffled. One minute she appeared upset with him, the next she talked about his purpose as if she cared about his life. What man understood a woman's thoughts? All he'd wanted to do was give her a helping hand. Not dig into purpose and faith.

He gathered the ladder and tools, trying to put Callie out of his mind the only way he knew how—with hard work and steely determination to find his birth mother.

If she left Peaceful to give birth, she could've returned with no one the wiser. He'd talk to Mildred Uland again. See if a woman in town had disappeared for months then come back.

In the parlor, a woman he'd never seen before had holed up on the couch. She looked up from leafing through a magazine and shot him a scowl. Dark hair, dark eyes, dark disposition. This had to be Grace, the newcomer.

"Hello," he said, forcing a smile he didn't feel.

She gave him a cursory nod, not exactly friendly, but then he hadn't been, either.

"Excuse the interruption. I'm here to repair the ceiling."

"Fine with me."

"I'm Jake Smith. I'm remodeling the house for Callie."

She shrugged. Not giving her name.

While ignoring Callie's latest arrival and her attitude, he cleared out the furniture and rug, set the ladder beneath the water damage and went about the task of laying a thin coat of plaster.

He had no interest in getting to know Grace, but he would like to know why she had gotten involved with a shiftless man who lacked the decency to propose marriage. Who lacked one grain of commitment or responsibility, gave not one thought to the consequences of his actions.

The realization that he'd just described his father landed in Jake's belly with a thud. Why had he blamed only his birth mother all this time? Those postcards were the reason. How could a mother send an annual birthday greeting, yet make no effort to see her child?

His hand tightened on the handle of the trowel, digging into the wet plaster, marring the repair. With care, he added plaster then smoothed the edges until he could no longer see the gouge. He climbed down the ladder, leaving the repair to dry.

As he turned to go, something about Grace reading a magazine while everyone else worked struck him as wrong. "Callie's out milking. Elise is gathering eggs. You could be helping with chores instead of sitting here like a princess on her throne."

"I'm no princess. No mind reader, either. If she wants help, she should ask."

"Callie probably assumes that you're not up to working and is excusing you for not carrying your weight. Someone like Callie can't imagine that some people are takers, not givers."

Grace's eyes turned icy. "You're no doubt taking a wage. You hardly have room to talk."

"My wages are the same as yours. A roof over my head and three meals a day." He folded his arms across his chest. "I don't sit idle."

She shot him a glare. "Mind your own business. And I'll mind mine."

"Callie's having a baby, too. She shouldn't be waiting on you hand and foot."

At the reference to her pregnancy, the woman all but snarled. "Get lost."

Before she ruined her health, Jake would suggest that Callie set up a schedule to divide the work. Not that she'd appreciate his interference. But in a couple of weeks, Elise would give birth. A baby would make even more work for Callie.

If only he could stay until Callie's baby was born, and Callie was back on her feet. But the unwed mother from Bloomington could arrive at any time and identify him. Then all havoc would break loose.

* * *

Pretending to sip a lukewarm cup of tea, Callie sat on the fringed sofa in her mother-in-law's heavily draped parlor, surrounded by an abundance of knickknacks of every size and shape—a signed baseball, bronzed baby shoes, a tarnished silver rattle—all reminders of Martin. Martin's pictures filled the mantle and piano, lined the walls. With the stuffy room closing in on her, Callie couldn't wait to leave.

Dorothy sat at her side, her gaze traveling the room, the lone worshipper in a shrine to her son.

With a shaky hand, Callie set the teacup on the saucer with a clatter. She'd spent the last half hour choking down cup after cup, looking for an opening in the conversation to discuss the financial needs of the unwed mothers' home.

Once she broached the subject, Callie felt certain she could count on Dorothy's support. Unlike Jacob, who'd dared to disapprove of Grace's behavior. As if he had the right to object to anything. Why couldn't he see that Grace's fragile emotional state proved the newcomer needed their understanding and patience?

The sensation of a tiny moving arm or leg rippled across Callie's stomach. Awed at the miracle of the baby growing inside her, Callie laid a hand over the spot.

"Is the baby moving?" Dorothy leaned closer. "Can I feel it?"

Callie moved Dorothy's hand to her abdomen and held it there. At another kick, Dorothy closed her eyes, almost as if praying. "It's your grandma, sweet baby."

She lifted her gaze to Callie. "Bless you, dear. This child you're carrying will give us back a piece of our son. It breaks my heart that he'll never see his child." Tears sprang to her eyes. "Oh, we miss him. His absence aches in our bones, blankets our every moment with sadness."

Uncertain what she could say that would comfort Dorothy, Callie simply patted her hand. The promise of Heaven and assurance of seeing loved ones again eased but didn't eliminate the heartache for those who grieved.

Dorothy heaved a sigh laden with pain and weariness. "I know Martin wasn't a perfect husband. That's hard to admit about my only child." She gave a shaky smile. "He was gregarious, spontaneous, fun-loving and…irresponsible and self-centered." Dorothy's gaze clouded. "Commodore and I are at fault for that. We spoiled our son."

"I'm sure I'll do the same with my baby," Callie said, trying to soothe Dorothy's regrets, yet knowing Martin's mother spoke the truth.

Fighting for control, Dorothy looked around the gloomy space, more mausoleum than living room. Callie wanted to rip off the heavy curtains covering the windows, open the casements. Fresh air would do Dorothy good, more than anything Callie could say or do.

She wrapped her mother-in-law in her arms. "Martin had a kind heart. He never said a harsh word to anyone."

"You were patient with him. You gave our son happiness," Dorothy said, a tremor in her voice.

"His strengths were the reason I loved him."

"I understand." Dorothy fiddled with the narrow gold band on her finger. "More than you know."

How many women could acknowledge such a thing about their only child, especially after his death? Callie's breath caught. Perhaps a woman who lived with the pain of her own troubled marriage?

Fighting to regain her footing after Dorothy's emotional admission, Callie wondered if she should broach the subject of money. But with two unwed mothers in the house and their babies on the way, Callie needed funding now.

As she got to the reason for her visit, Dorothy

straightened. "I agree with your unwed mothers' home. In principle. But I can't support it. I'm worried that you're being foolhardy and not putting your baby first." Dorothy plucked at something on her sleeve, lint or a thread perhaps, only visible to her. "I hate to tell you this, dear, but I thought you ought to know…before the letter arrives."

A python of foreboding wrapped around Callie's throat and squeezed, shutting off her air. "Letter?"

"The members of the Peaceful Ladies Club met yesterday and voted to revoke your membership."

"What?"

"Oh, Callie, I'm sorry." Her eyes flashed. "The women believe your unwed mothers' home is in conflict with Ladies Club bylaws and God's commandments."

Callie wanted to protest but the words lodged in her throat.

"They assert that providing refuge for these fallen girls is, in essence, coddling sinners and sending a message to the youth of this town that contradicts Scripture."

Callie's pulse pounded in her temples. These women thought she'd broken God's commandments. "I can't believe they'd do this. Aunt Hilda was one of the founders of the Ladies Club."

"I reminded them of that, but the leadership felt the home would bring nothing good to Peaceful. You'll get a detailed summary of their objections and action."

These women were her friends. They'd been there for her when Aunt Hilda died. When Martin died. They'd hugged her. Prayed for her. And she'd done the same for them. She'd served on Ladies Club committees, hosted meetings and social events, taken food into their homes in times of crisis. Last year, she'd cared for the president's children when Karen came down with influenza.

Now they were tossing her out.

"You know, Callie, you leaped into this without a plan in place. You don't have the money to finance the home, yet you have two unwed mothers living there. You're ruffling feathers of the people you need to help you. If you'd paved the way, perhaps they would've seen the unwed mothers' home from your perspective." She sighed. "I'm sorry, but I can't support what you're doing, especially when the consequences could hurt my grandchild."

"I'd never do anything that would harm my baby."

Dorothy's praise of Callie's treatment of Martin was mere words. She wanted to defend herself, to demand that the women of the Ladies Club show a Scriptural basis for kicking her out. The injustice of it all churned within her.

Vengeance is mine sayeth the Lord.

No, she didn't want vengeance. She wanted vindication.

Be patient.

She took a deep breath and counted to ten. These women would discover that the town wouldn't be turned upside down by these girls, as it feared.

Or would it? God had a way of doing that very thing. A flipped view of their world might be what the folks in this town needed.

"I have more bad news." Dorothy didn't meet Callie's eyes.

Every muscle in Callie's body tensed, sensing that losing her membership in the Ladies Club was only the beginning of the trouble ahead.

"I want you to understand that I don't believe a word of this gossip. I know you. Know your faith. But all this trouble with these girls is turning this town into something ugly."

"What are you saying?"

"Gossip has it that you and Jacob Smith are…" Dorothy sighed "…intimate."

"That's a lie!"

"Or course it is. Commodore doesn't believe a word of the gossip about you and Mr. Smith, either. Though, he is suspicious of the man."

Who wasn't?

Callie had met with disapproval. She'd endure removal. But slander? Where would this ugliness end?

How much would the unwed mothers' home cost her?

That evening at supper, Jake pulled out a chair for Elise, then another for Callie, who thanked him but didn't meet his eyes. Why? Grace had deigned to come to the table, undoubtedly reluctantly if her demeanor meant anything, scooting into her chair before Jake could assist her.

After blessing the food, Callie passed the serving bowls. Elise chatted away about her knitting, her baby, while Grace picked at her food, ignoring attempts to include her in the conversation. Elise shot furtive glances at the newcomer, obviously uncomfortable with Grace's stony silence.

Jake glanced at Callie. "The food is delicious."

Callie nodded her thanks, her gaze distant. Something had happened to upset her. Had her visit with Dorothy that afternoon gone badly? Or was she still angry with him for suggesting she divide the work? Hoping to dispel the gloomy atmosphere, Jake said, "How are you feeling, Elise?"

She sighed, resting her forearms on her belly. "Ready to have this baby."

"Won't be long now." Callie gave Elise a sweet smile, a smile Jake would've given anything to have directed at him.

"Have you made…uh, plans for your child?" he asked.

"If you're asking if I'm keeping my baby, the answer is yes. I thought you knew that's the reason I'm here."

"I wasn't sure if you'd changed your mind. Raising a child alone is a huge responsibility."

"My baby won't end up in an orphanage. After what you told me, I'd never allow that to happen."

Grace's head shot up. Her eyes darted to Jake then to Elise. "Easy for you to say." She snorted. "You two have all the answers. Passing judgment, condemning women. You don't know anything." She plopped the glass she held on the kitchen table, sloshing water and glaring at him. "You bellyache about that orphanage, Jake. Why? You had food in your stomach and a roof over your head."

Had Grace lived on the streets? What had happened to put that sneer on her face?

Callie reached a hand to Grace. "You make a good point. Many children aren't given up by choice. Parents die." Jake heard the tremble in Callie's voice. Knew she still suffered from the loss of her family. "Or they can't provide." She sighed. "It's far easier to name the problem than to solve it."

Had an inability to provide motivated his parents to give Jake up? Maybe they didn't have two pennies to rub together. An orphanage would be better than living on the streets.

"I know of at least one couple in this town who'd love to raise a child," Callie said. "No baby born at Redeeming Love need end up without a family. God will provide."

"Another pat answer! I've lost my appetite." Grace shoved back her chair, tipping it over. As it crashed to the floor, Jake jumped to his feet. Grace stomped from the room.

"What's wrong with her?" Elise burst into tears.

As Callie pulled Elise into her arms, she met Jake's gaze, her eyes wide with alarm. "Grace is having a rough time adjusting. We'll need to be patient with her."

Jake righted the chair then stood by helplessly with no idea what to do or what to say that would restore harmony.

"I'm not hungry," Elise said, though she hadn't finished her meal. "I'm going to see my mother while Papa's at the shop."

The front door banged closed, the sound echoing in the silence. Grace might be troubled, but she'd brought strife into the house. Not good for anyone. Especially for Callie, who gave and gave, trying to make life better for those in her care. No doubt she'd see Grace's reaction as some failure on her part, rather than laying the blame at Grace's feet, where it belonged.

With the force of a tidal wave, awareness slammed into Jake. Grace reminded him of someone. Someone he knew all too well. Someone who'd railed at life. Someone embittered and spewing blame.

Himself.

Swallowing hard at the similarities between him and this troubled young woman, his gaze surveyed the kitchen. The stormy scene they'd witnessed was at odds with the beam of sunlight streaming in through the window, lighting the vase of peonies on the table, their scent mixing with the aroma of beans and ham.

This cozy nest Callie had created, along with that warm way of hers, had softened his edges. Perhaps in time, she'd do the same for Grace. But at what cost? Plenty, if the look of dismay on Callie's face meant anything.

Jake wanted to make amends for Grace's behavior. To protect Callie from this strife. Protect her from any ugliness.

He reached a hand. "Grace is upsetting you. Having her here isn't good for you or your baby."

"I didn't ask for your opinion." Eyes snapping, Callie slapped her napkin on the table. "You're leaving. So keep your advice to yourself."

Chapter Fifteen

As he hauled manure to Callie's garden, Jake bent into a gust of wind. Except for an occasional fast-moving cloud obstructing the warmth of the sun, the breezy day was pleasant, invigorating. Spring carried the promise of new beginnings. New beginnings he wanted but couldn't see, not with the shadow of prison eclipsing his every tomorrow.

He glanced toward the stoop where Callie washed clothes. Even from here, he could feel the tension between them, as thick and high as fortifications at the penitentiary. Her anger last night made it perfectly clear. Callie didn't want advice from him. She didn't want anything from him.

She heaved a heaping laundry basket to her middle, wrestling with it. He dropped the handles of the wheelbarrow and loped toward her. At his approach, she tilted her chin in that stubborn way of hers, as if she'd refuse his help.

Maybe if he started small, helping with the laundry, he could restore the harmony between them. "Let me carry that basket."

"If you insist." Callie looked away, as if she couldn't stand the sight of him.

"I do." He took the basket from her arms.

Callie pivoted and headed for the clothesline stretching between two poles, leaving him to follow along behind.

With hammer and nails, he'd taken care of the hazards threatening the women in the house. He could fix any object with the right tools, but he didn't know what it would take to fix things with Callie.

Jake watched the sway of her hips, wanting nothing more than to pull her into his arms. But after the way they'd parted last night, she wouldn't welcome his embrace. Callie understood the futility of building a relationship with a man like him.

At the clothesline, he lowered the basket to the ground. She reached for a lump of white just as he did. Their hands collided, zipping a flash of attraction from the tips of his fingers to the base of his spine.

"I'll do that," he said. Before she could protest, he pulled a sheet from the pile and unfurled it. The wind caught the cotton, whipping it in the air between them.

Callie grabbed clothespins from her apron pocket and pegged the first corner to the line, then the middle. When she jabbed the last pin in place, the sheet hung between them, a wall of sorts. They were in close proximity, but miles apart.

Sometimes Callie's determination to handle things alone had Jake clamping his jaw in exasperation. Perhaps, married to Martin, she'd had to do everything on her own and knew no other way. Was he any different? Empathy for this woman, a survivor like him, made him long to pull Callie into his arms.

Jake stomped past the sheet, determined to do that very thing, determined to tell her how much he cared. One glance at her belly stopped him. Her child would need a father. Jake had no idea how to handle that role. Getting out of her life was the kindest thing he could do. The fact that he cared about her kept his arms at his sides. His mouth closed.

He yanked a towel from the stack and draped it over the line. She pegged. He draped. Neither spoke, yet the air fairly crackled with friction as every touch and glance burned into Jake's awareness like a hot branding iron.

When he could stand the tension no longer, he threw up his hands. "Callie, why don't you just tell me what's on your mind?"

She whirled toward him. "What's the point? You'll do what you please, no matter what I say."

A cloud covered the sun, throwing them in shadow. He took a step closer. "You're putting barriers between us and not just with this laundry. You know I'd stay if I could."

"I know no such thing. You have no job to go to. No family waiting for your return. For once, drop the pretense and be honest. With me. With yourself."

Her words slashed at him. He hadn't been honest with her. He hid his past and his purpose the same way that cloud overhead hid the sun. Perhaps he could tell her why he'd come to town. Why he kept his past a secret. And she'd react differently than others had.

She turned back, as if she meant to talk to him, then her gaze fastened on something in the yard.

A few feet away, he spotted a baby robin hunched in the grass, its little beak opening and closing with soft chirps. The mother hovered nearby, fluttering her wings, panicked or maybe merely showing her offspring what to do. From the looks of it, the baby didn't get the message.

"Jake. Look." Callie pointed across the lawn.

Out of the corner of his eyes, he saw Stripes slink forward, eyes locked on its prey. The mother robin flapped her wings, hopped closer, alarmed by the stalking feline, but the baby bird remained huddled on the ground.

Callie crouched down, trying to shoo the cat away. Stripes kept coming.

Slowly, Jake moved toward the birds, then squatted in the grass. The baby bird looked weak, defenseless, its feathers stirring in the breeze. The mother robin flitted about, her dark, beady eyes on Jake. Wary. Scared.

"Do you think he's hurt?" Callie lowered herself in the space beside Jake.

"I don't think so." He kept his voice soft and low, but still the mother robin's gaze held trepidation. The baby let out a squawk. "Falling is part of learning to fly."

"What if he's not ready yet? Maybe he needs to go back to the nest."

"Maybe."

Jake studied the baby bird. Under its thin skin and feathers, he could see the delicate bones that would one day carry this small bird through the sky. At times like this, Jake marveled at the order and beauty of nature. Could a Master Planner have designed this world?

Callie laid a hand on his arm. Her gentle touch slid through him. "You need to put him back. I'd do it, but..." She waved at her belly. "Will you, Jake?"

That Callie needed him for more than repairs to her house filled some ache inside him. Still, moving the bird might not be the right solution. "We need to give him a chance to fly. We'll chase off the cat—"

"Stripes will come back." Worry flooded her eyes. "I can't bear to think of him down here, helpless, with the cat out there, watching. Waiting."

"If I touch it, the mother may not accept the fledgling."

"The mother can't get it back in the nest. Someone has

to." She turned pleading eyes on him. "Isn't it better to try than to let the cat get it?"

He glanced at the baby she carried inside her. He couldn't do anything for that baby, but he could do something for this baby bird.

He edged forward, one small step at a time. The mother bird flapped her wings, squawked a protest, but Jake kept closing in. The mother froze. Watched. Her heart beat so fast that Jake could see it through her breast. Stripes stepped closer and closer. With one last glance at her baby, the robin took flight and perched on a branch above his head.

Yanking his gloves from his back pocket, Jake shoved his hands inside, reached down, scooped up the trembling baby bird, and cradled it in his hand. It weighed almost nothing.

The warm smile Callie sent Jake slid through him, easing the impasse between them. "Any idea where the nest is?"

She pointed behind him. "Up in that tree."

As soon as the words left her mouth, the robin flew to a branch far above him. Jake grabbed a low limb and clamored up the trunk, heaving himself along with one hand and holding the bird in the other until he reached the spot where the robin waited. There he found her nest balanced between two branches, a miracle of twigs, dried grasses and loose threads. Occupied with two chirping siblings, beaks open wide, ready for a meal.

As he gently deposited the outcast alongside his family, Jake grasped in that moment that one of nature's creatures had placed its trust in him.

Him. Of all people.

He retraced his path, much easier with both hands free, then jumped to the ground. A foot away, Stripes sat on her haunches, eyeing Jake with reproach. "You're a mom. Shame on you."

Relief plain on her face, Callie chuckled. "Stripes is not happy."

Jake removed his gloves and stuffed them back into his hip pocket. "The wanderer is back in the nest."

"Thank you," Callie said then threw her arms around Jake, burrowing into him with a sob.

What was wrong? The bird was safe. Who would've thought a baby bird that had fallen out of its nest would bring this self-sufficient woman to tears? Yet that Callie needed him, even for a moment, slid through Jake. Filled with a sense of the rightness of having Callie in his arms, he rubbed her back, murmuring an endearment near her ear.

She jerked away, wiped her tears with both hands and shot up her chin. Back to her strong independent self. Unwilling to rely on him for anything. Anything except repairs.

"The baby bird would most likely have survived," he said. "Mother birds push fledglings out of the nest because they know the time has come to try their wings. It's what's best for them."

Callie's eyes locked with his, in their depths Jake saw tenderness. For him? "Do you think it's possible, Jake, that sometimes… Sometimes human mothers do the same thing?"

"I don't understand what you mean."

"I'm saying a mother may do what she sees as best for her baby, but the child may not see her actions that way."

Callie's words held a significance she wanted him to grasp. Why wouldn't a child understand his mother's actions? Unless…

As understanding dawned, he wrestled with the insight.

"You think my mother believed that giving me up was the best choice for me?"

"It might have been. You don't know what she faced. What your life would have been like if she hadn't given you up."

The ground shifted under his feet, as if the earth had moved on its axis. Jake saw the truth with sudden clarity. "All these years, I've resented her decision. Until I know her circumstances, I can't say her decision was right or wrong."

Callie touched his face with a gentle palm, offering approval or maybe solace.

"That insight came through a baby bird. And you, Callie, the most merciful person I've ever met. You've taught me by your example how to live." He laid his hand over hers. "I need to give my mother the same clemency."

A smile bloomed on Callie's face. The beauty of it socked Jake in the gut. He wanted nothing to stand between him and this special woman. A woman he trusted enough to divulge his stint in prison, his search for his mother.

Grace called to Callie from the house.

Callie gave her a wave, then pivoted to Jake. "You're a good man, Jacob Smith. God is working on you." She gave him a smile, then walked to the stoop, tucked an arm around Grace's waist and walked her inside the house.

As Jake tramped toward the barn, filled with gratitude that the incident with the birds had led not only to an understanding about his mother, but to an easing of the rift between him and Callie.

One thing stood between them, a Grand Canyon of an impasse. He didn't believe in God. If only he had Callie's faith.

Perhaps the amazing order of nature wasn't an accident. Perhaps everything in this world had been designed by a

Higher Power. If so, that lesson would outweigh all the others.

Jake had doubts. Still, he would examine them. Open that Bible of his. And see where it led.

Callie stared out the back kitchen window facing the tree Jacob had climbed that morning to return a lost baby robin to the nest. Sometimes she felt just as lost, unsure which way to turn. Had she been foolish to test her wings with this unwed mothers' home when her own baby's arrival was imminent?

The incident with the baby bird had made Callie realize that she wasn't taking care of her own baby as well as she'd thought. She'd put other things first, before her own child. That sense of failure had driven her sobbing into Jacob's arms. Her mind was a jumble of confusion. Her emotions were in shambles.

In such a state, how had she thought she could help Elise and Grace? Or any other unwed mother who appeared at her door?

Laying her hands on either side of her abdomen, Callie bowed her head. *Lord, give me wisdom. Help me put my baby's welfare first. Enable me to make plans that ensure his well-being, not put him at risk.*

Her baby had lost his father. Her breath caught. Had God brought Jacob into her life for that very reason? Not that she'd fall in love with an unbeliever, but she felt Jacob's softening toward God. Saw it in his attentive posture during Pastor Steele's sermons. Saw it in his growing forgiveness toward his birth mother. Saw it in his kindness toward Elise and, of late, Grace.

Callie glanced at the plate of food warming on the stove. Grace had skipped the noon meal, not something an expectant mother should do. If nothing else, perhaps God gave Callie this mission to ensure that Grace got proper nourishment.

Holding the plate, Callie walked upstairs and rapped on Grace's door. "It's Callie. May I come in?"

The door opened a crack. "What do you want?"

"I brought your food up. You need to eat."

The door widened. "I'm not hungry."

"Please, eat anyway, for my sake. If you don't, I won't get a wink of sleep tonight."

The door swung open. Callie breathed a sigh of relief. Grace looked pale, defenseless as if she didn't have the strength to keep on her feet. "No one has ever cared about me enough to lose sleep."

Callie set the plate of food on Grace's nightstand then put an arm around her. "I'm sorry you've never had some-one in your life who cared."

Stepping away from Callie's arms, Grace turned to the bed, smoothed a wrinkle from the quilt with her palms. "Not many folks worry about a servant."

Underneath those quiet words, Callie heard Grace's res-ignation to her status in life, as if her job determined her worth. She had to make Grace understand that God loved her. And that made her a person of significance. But food for the body came first. "Eat while it's still warm."

Amazingly, Grace sat on the edge of the bed and took a bite of the chicken and noodles. "You're a good cook."

"I don't feel like much of a cook when you can't keep your feet under my table."

Suspicion rode in her eyes. "So why are you doing this? What's in this unwed mothers' home for you?"

Perhaps Grace had seen through her and suspected that her motives weren't entirely selfless. "I thought I wanted this home because of what happened to a friend of mine.

But it's possible I want it so I can surround myself with people and forget the losses I've had, the loneliness."

Grace's gaze darted to her plate. As if Callie's admission was a hot potato she couldn't juggle.

This young woman needed to share her wounds with someone. If she chose to confide in her, Callie prayed her response wouldn't make matters worse.

While she ate, Grace looked at Callie's wedding ring. "What happened to your husband?"

"He passed away last November."

Toying with the band, Callie admitted that her marriage had been a disappointment. She'd been both wife and mother to Martin. Some days she'd felt more like a warden, trying to keep tabs on his whereabouts, his choices. He hadn't understood that she hated that role. Oddly, he'd never blamed her for taking it. She wondered why she still wore his ring. Maybe she saw it as a badge of legitimacy for her baby.

Grace took a sip of milk, then set down her glass. "That's tough. I thought maybe you and Jake... I noticed a spark between you."

Callie gulped. Was the attraction between them that obvious? What did it matter? Nothing good would come from furtive glances, pounding hearts or stolen kisses. She wouldn't care about Jacob. She wouldn't care about another man who deceived. But even as that thought came to her, Callie knew it was already too late. She did care about Jacob Smith. But she'd never let him know.

"Jacob will be moving on." She forced a smile. "But thanks to him, this house is livable. I have much to be thankful for."

Grace took the last mouthful on her fork, wiped her lips then dropped the napkin on the plate. "I'm not interested in a list of your blessings."

Grace used that sharp tongue of hers to keep people at a distance. If Callie hadn't cared about Grace, hadn't taken the time to look into her weary eyes laden with pain, she'd never have seen past that wall she'd erected. Grace was wounded. What could Callie do to help?

The young woman rose and set the dishes outside the door, as if unable to tolerate one tiny thing out of place, then walked back to Callie, her expression closed. "Thanks for the meal."

Callie smiled. "You're very welcome."

"I'm sure you have things to do." She glanced at the door, an invitation to leave.

But Callie wasn't budging. Not yet. "What happened to your parents, Grace?"

As if her legs gave way, Grace sank to the mattress. "They died."

Callie sat beside her. "What did you do then?"

"I lived on the streets, like thousands of immigrant kids." Her brown eyes, dark as storm clouds, met Callie's. "No matter what Jake says, an orphanage is better than sleeping in alleys, huddling together for warmth, eating garbage."

A huge lump formed in Callie's throat. Trying to clear it and the image Grace's words evoked in her mind, she swallowed convulsively. "That explains why you're upset with Jacob."

She sighed. "I'm not. Not anymore. I haven't walked in his shoes."

This young woman had endured a horrid life. Worse, Callie suspected that what Grace had told her revealed only the tip of the iceberg, that more was frozen below the surface.

"If we all did that, this world would be a better place." Callie faced Grace and took her cold hand. "I want you to know that you're a child of God. That makes you worthy. Servant and master, rich and poor, all are the same in the eyes of God."

Tears sprang to Grace's eyes. She squared her shoulders, obviously fighting powerful feelings inside her. Callie waited.

Grace swiped at her eyes. "So what happened to that friend you mentioned?"

Changing the subject, another tactic Grace used to put the focus on anyone, anything, but her. Well, Grace deserved to know. She explained Nell's pregnancy and suicide.

"Some boyfriend." Grace shook her head. "Women rave about the guys they love. But men get what they want then move on."

"You're not an admirer of men."

Grace motioned to her protruding belly. "Should I be? Prince Charming exists only in fairy tales." She yawned. "I'm tired."

"Sleep well, Grace."

As Callie left the room, she thought about the make-believe castle of her childhood and the prince she'd envisioned riding up on a powerful steed to rescue her.

An image of Jacob popped into her mind. He was a far cry from her vision of Prince Charming. True, he was handsome, strong and capable. He'd made the house safe, helped with chores, did whatever he could to make her life easier. All things she appreciated. But when it came to giving his heart—

This prince hid his past. Had no interest in sharing a castle.

She'd go through life caring for her baby, handling this home and steering clear of men. Grace was right. Prince Charming existed only in childhood dreams.

Her baby thumped against her belly. She laid her hand on the spot. This precious baby growing within her deserved a father. A father to toss a ball. A father to demonstrate how to pound a nail. A father to give piggyback rides on his back. No matter how much Callie wanted to believe that she could be both father and mother to her child, the absence of a father would leave a void in her child's life.

She'd come to Grace's room to see that she ate and help however she could. And she'd left burdened with her troubles, problems she didn't know how to solve.

She'd never felt lonelier.

Chapter Sixteen

That morning, Callie had taken Grace to see Doc Wellman. After the visit, Doc had taken her aside. "Give Grace understanding, love, your time," he'd said. "Something is wrong. Very wrong, but she won't talk to me. I feel she's slipping away, as if she doesn't want to live."

Back at the house, Callie poured Grace a glass of milk and set out the wheel of cheddar she'd bought at the grocer and slices of homemade bread. "I always treat myself after a doctor's visit. The baby and I like cheese." Callie grinned, cutting off a slice.

Ignoring the food, Grace sipped the milk.

"You barely eat enough to keep a bird alive." Callie cut another slice and offered it to Grace.

Grace turned her head away, as if the sight made her sick to her stomach.

"Don't you like cheese? It's good for you."

Grace looked at her. In the depths of her eyes, Callie saw something that made her shiver. Something so horrible she said a quick prayer.

"I hate cheese."

"Oh." Surely that didn't explain the horror she'd seen in Grace's eyes. "Does the smell bother you?"

Grace swallowed convulsively. "It…makes me…remember."

Barely able to swallow the bite she'd taken, Callie rose and put the cheese in the icebox.

Grace lurched from the chair and staggered to the window, turning her back to Callie. Callie moved closer, put a hand on her shoulder. The seconds became a minute. A minute became two.

Just when she'd decided that Grace wouldn't explain, the young woman turned to her, perspiration beaded on her forehead, her face pale as paper.

"I've never told anyone." She lowered her eyes to the floor.

With a strong sense of foreboding tightening every muscle, a desire to run slid through Callie. But she held her ground. Whatever Grace had to say, Doc Wellman believed it needed to be said.

Callie's breathing grew shallow. *Lord, help me. Help Grace. Help us both.*

"My employer's husband…asked me to store some clothes in the attic. While I was putting the last of the things away, he…" She took a breath, as if the effort of saying that much had winded her. "He came in and locked the door behind him."

The air left Callie's lungs.

"He said—" She pivoted to the window. Callie heard a sob. "He said his wife was visiting her mother for a couple of days." She lowered her forehead, rested it on the glass. "He'd given the staff the time off." She gave a strangled laugh. "I wondered if it was with pay."

She began to sway back and forth, back and forth in front of the window. The chill in Grace's voice and that rocking churned in Callie's stomach.

She put an arm around Grace, grasping her cold hand

and turned her away from that window. "You're here with me. You're safe."

Grace fastened her gaze on the far wall. "I fought… but…couldn't stop him." She tore her hand from Callie's and clasped it over her mouth. A sob. "He dragged me to the floor." Another sob tore from her throat. "And…raped me."

Callie laid her cheek against Grace's face. Their tears mingled with the pain of her gut-wrenching admission.

"He came back time and time again. For three days, he…returned to the attic. At the end of each day, he'd bring water and—"

A moan escaped Callie's lips. "Cheese."

Legs giving out from under her, Grace slid down the wall to the floor, leaning back, eyes closed, as if trying to shut out the images. Images burned into her soul with the branding iron of brutality.

Callie sat beside her, held her trembling hand. "I'm sorry, so sorry." Yet nothing she could say or do would erase the horror of those days in the attic.

Birds chirping, Mildred's Sandy barking next door, the whistle of a distant train—ordinary sounds drifted in through the open window. As if this day were like any other. But Callie, a woman who'd never been mistreated, and Grace, a woman who'd been subjected to every cruelty, wounded to her core, clung to each other, and knew innocence was gone forever.

"On Monday, the day the staff and his wife were due back, he came in before dawn. He said he'd kill me if I told his wife or the police." She gave a harsh laugh. "Then he raped me one last time, unlocked the door and told me to clean myself up. Said not to worry, he wouldn't touch me again." Her chin quivered. "I was…used goods."

Inside Callie, anger raged. She wanted to hurt that man.

To make him pay for what he did. *Oh, Lord. Oh, Lord, help us.*

"His wife and the staff returned within hours. He never bothered me after that. I needed that job. Entering that house each morning took everything I had. Fear kept me silent until the morning I knew I was pregnant. I saw him leave for work and followed him outside. When I told him, he said, 'Who's the father? Or do you even know?'" Grace beat a fist on the floor. "I hate him! I'll hate him till the day I die."

Callie tugged Grace into the circle of her arms. "He should be shot." And she meant it. That frightened her even more.

"I can't bear to see the face of this baby I'm carrying." Tears slid down her cheeks. "Yet as often as I thought about it, I couldn't end its life."

Callie shuddered. That baby, that poor baby, would always be a reminder of the violence of its conception.

Grace's trembling fingers found her lips. "What if… What if it resembles him? What if looking into that face the rest of my life is a reminder of everything he did to me? And I grow to hate the child, as much as the father?" She turned her face away. "Don't you see? Putting my baby in an orphanage would be a kindness."

Callie thought of Jacob. There were so many reasons a mother might abandon her child.

"I'd hoped I'd feel better once I told someone. But…" She sobbed. "I feel worse."

"I wish I could take away your pain."

"You won't despise me if I can't keep my baby?"

"Oh, Grace, I have no idea how I'd react if I had to endure that horror. I'm proud of you. Whether you keep your baby or not, you're giving him life, a chance. If you decide to let him go, I know a couple here in town who would love your baby and would give him a good home."

"What if… What if my baby is evil? Like him?"

Callie shook her head. "God is merciful. Your baby will be gentle, sweet."

A sob escaped Grace. "I can't keep it. I'm too filled with hate to be a mother."

Again thoughts paraded through Callie's head that she dare not examine, couldn't admit out loud. She wanted to track that evildoer down. She wanted him to pay for what he'd done. She understood in that moment the hate Grace carried.

Yet that hate festered, destroying Grace's future. Hate meant that brute would be victorious. "Don't let him win, Grace. Don't let hate destroy you."

"It already has."

"No! You're not destroyed. You're strong. That's why you didn't harm your baby. That's why you're here. That's why you will survive. You're battered and bloody, wounded, body and soul." She tucked a strand of hair behind Grace's ear. "We're going to clean, anoint and bind your wounds. With God's help and His power, you'll heal."

"I've been so ashamed."

"Of what? Not being able to stop a monster far stronger than you? God knows what happened. He knows your innocence. The suffering you endured. He hasn't left you. He loves you."

"I feel dirty." She sobbed. "I washed and washed, but I can't get rid of his hands on me. His mouth."

Callie laid both hands on Grace's shoulders. "You're not dirty! The love of God covers you. That man who raped you is dirty. He'll have to answer for his crime. One day he will. If not here on earth, then in eternity."

Grace twisted a hand in the folds of her dress. "Don't tell anyone. Promise me."

"I promise."

But someone should tell. What if he did that to another woman? Callie shivered. Perhaps he was doing it now?

"Thank you for trusting me enough to tell me what happened. But you need to tell someone else. Doctor Wellman. Or Pastor Steele. Someone who knows how to help."

Grace swallowed convulsively and let out a soft groan.

Laying her hands on either side of Grace's jaw, Callie peered into brown tormented eyes. "You've done nothing wrong. You've done nothing to be ashamed of."

A sob. Two.

In silent entreaty, Callie opened her arms. "Let it go, Grace. Let it go."

Burrowing into her arms, Grace wept. Callie wept with her.

God was faithful. Callie prayed that He would restore Grace, give her a new beginning as only He could do.

Callie hoped God would forgive her desire for vengeance. Perhaps Nell's suicide contributed to that. Nell had kept her pregnancy secret.

Grace had kept the crime against her secret, too. Letting it eat at her, nibbling away at hope, joy and love.

Secrets destroyed.

Her breath caught. Jacob Smith kept a secret. She saw it when his eyes grew wary. Felt it when he held others at arm's length. Heard it when his tone turned guarded.

Whatever Jacob hid, when that secret came out, there'd be consequences. Callie suspected that she'd also pay a price. Better to confront him now, with her defenses firmly in place, then wait for that secret to catch her unawares.

* * *

Bent over the hoe, sweat dripping off his nose, Jake hacked at the weeds in Callie's garden, exposing their roots to the sun. Freed from the soil that fed them, the weeds would wither and die. If only he could as easily cull the debris choking his heart. With every passing day, the tension between him and Callie intensified. How long could they go on like this?

"Looks like you could use a cold drink."

Jake pivoted. Callie leaned on the fence watching him, tendrils of her chestnut hair teasing her neck. A crisp white apron covered her skirt, the ribbons fluttering in the breeze.

She took his breath away.

With his forearm, he swiped the sweat off his face and smiled. "Nothing would taste better."

"I'll bring a glass of iced tea to the gazebo. We'll have a chat."

The afternoon sky encasing her silhouette brought out the startling aquamarine of her eyes, yet… The softness he usually saw in those eyes had grown watchful, conveyed a warning. A chill snaked through him.

"Sounds good. I'll meet you there."

As he watched her go, Jake wondered what Callie had on her mind. That somber demeanor of hers suggested that she intended to uproot him as he had these weeds. Only instead of a hoe, she'd remove him with a swift, sharp spoken word.

Across the way, Grace left the henhouse carrying the egg basket. She waved at him and he returned the gesture. He couldn't help smiling at the new spring in her step. Callie hadn't told him what had transpired between them, except to say that Grace had shared her story. Everyone had a story. Perhaps sharing that story with a trusted friend was the first step to healing.

When he finished the last row, he strolled to the gazebo. Inside, Callie sat on the swing, a cold drink on the table at her side.

"Thanks," he said then swigged half the glass. "Hits the spot." He pulled up a chair and sat across from her. "You always know what I need."

Her eyes narrowed. "Are you willing to do the same thing, Jacob? For me?"

"What do you mean?

"I need something from you."

"I'd do anything for you, Callie."

"Anything?"

An alarm went off in his head. "If I can." His mind scrambled for footing. Where would this lead?

"You can— I'm sure of it. But the question is, will you?" She folded her arms across her middle, as if shielding her baby. "From that very first day you arrived looking for work, I sensed that you carried a secret. Hid something you didn't want anyone to know." She clenched and unclenched her hands in her lap. "I've tried to tell myself that you're just a private man, but…" Her eyes clouded. "Lately I've realized that keeping secrets isn't beneficial. Not for the one holding the secret. And not for the one taken by surprise." She met his gaze. "You see, secrets have a way of coming out."

From the very beginning, Callie had suspected that he hid something, yet hadn't pushed him for answers until now. The hard shell around his heart softened. That proved she cared about him, about their relationship. He could trust her with his past.

"Some things are hard to talk about, but you're right. I have kept something hidden." He took her hand. "I want to tell you."

As if his tension became hers, the spark in her eyes

dimmed. "From your expression, what you're about to say is bad news."

His gaze dropped to her small hand, the feel of her calluses rough against his own. "I'm hoping you won't see it as bad news. But, even if you do, you deserve to know." He took a deep breath and met her eyes. "I thought once I'd found love. Love of a woman I met in Bloomington."

Callie lowered her eyes to their clasped hands. "What happened to her?" she asked, so softly that Jake could barely hear.

"Susan's actions proved that she didn't…love me. Never had." How could he find the words? Would she believe him? "I was accused of stealing from a jewelry store. Lloyd, a man I considered a friend robbed the store." His throat convulsed. "He left my wallet behind to…" his voice grew raspy, harsh "…make it appear I'd committed the crime."

She squeezed his hand. "Why would a friend do such a thing?"

"He wasn't a friend at all. He wanted someone else to take the blame. He picked me so he could have Susan."

"I don't understand."

"The woman I thought loved me didn't believe in my innocence." He gave a chilling laugh. "She turned to Lloyd for comfort, exactly as he'd planned, while I cooled my heels in jail."

Tears sprang to Callie's eyes. "Jail?"

He swallowed past the lump in his throat. "Because I didn't have an alibi and with that wallet as evidence, the jury found me guilty." He sucked in a gulp of air, trying to get enough oxygen to finish. "I spent almost a year behind bars for a crime I didn't commit."

"Oh, no!" Her hand covered her mouth her eyes wide

with horror. "That must've been terrifying." She tightened her hold on his hand.

"I'd be there still, except Lloyd got careless. He gave a necklace to Susan. She recognized it from the description on the list of stolen items I'd supposedly taken and went to the police. They searched Lloyd's room and found more stolen property. I was released. Lloyd stood trial and now he's in jail."

Tears slid down her face.

"Life behind bars was…" He shook his head, refusing to return to that place, even in his mind. "It wasn't an easy time." He swiped the tears off her cheeks with his thumb. "I've allowed those months in jail, those years in an orphanage to make me bitter, to keep me in a prison of sorts."

"Those experiences would wound anyone."

Suddenly, unable to meet those sad, compassionate eyes, he jumped to his feet and turned away. Did she see him as pathetic? He wanted her respect. But could she respect a jailbird? Even one falsely accused? Or would the indignities he'd suffered in jail disgust her? Build a wedge between them?

She rose and put her arms around him. "I'm sorry, Jacob. So very sorry."

"Don't pity me."

"Pity you? Never! If I could, I'd erase that nightmare." She gazed up at him, her eyes glowing with what looked like admiration. "You survived a terrible ordeal. I'm proud of you. Of the man you are."

The snap of a broken twig.

Jake spun on his booted heel, searching beyond the screened enclosure. He didn't see anyone, but someone had been there.

"What's wrong?" Callie whispered.

"Someone may have overheard me. I'm sorry. That'll only complicate your life."

She shrugged. "I can't see how that'll make the attitude of this town any worse."

He wished he shared her opinion. "I've never known anyone like you. You're brave and kind and good and strong. Yet your life hasn't been easy. Your example has made a huge impression on me." He cupped her jaw in his palm. "I've learned to trust again, Callie, because of you."

"Don't put me on a pedestal. If you knew all the anger I've struggled with, the doubts about God's leading, you'd know how much I fail."

"Your actions say otherwise." He grinned. "You're even humble. See? You're perfect."

"Hang around long enough and you'll see the real me."

"I'd like that," he said, his heart in his throat.

"You would?"

"Yes, I would."

"I wish you could've trusted me with this sooner."

"I'm sorry. Nothing in my life made me believe I could trust anyone."

"I'm the one who's sorry. Sorry Susan and Lloyd betrayed you." She laid her head on his chest. Surely she could hear the wild beat of his heart. "But if all that hadn't happened, I would never have met you."

He'd never thought of it that way.

"Thank you for sharing your past, Jacob. Now no secrets lie between us."

As his throat constricted, Jake pulled her to him, wrapping her in his arms. He had one more secret. But if Callie knew why he chose Peaceful, she wouldn't rest from the search until she'd turned over every stone and examined it under a magnifying glass. With the controversy over the unwed mothers' home, Callie was coping with enough. Now with the strong likelihood that someone had overheard his confession, she'd face even more trouble.

She'd come to him determined to uncover his secret. He could only hope the price she paid for that discovery wasn't too steep.

At the entrance to Mitchell Mercantile, Callie tightened the hold on the bag she carried and released Jacob's arm. If only she hadn't pushed him into talking about his stint in prison. Whoever had overheard hadn't taken long to get the word out. The news had spread faster than wildfires on an arid prairie.

At the grocery yesterday, several people had come up to Callie, warning her to send that jailbird packing before he robbed her blind. She'd made it clear that she stood by him. Eventually, the gossip would die down. And Peaceful would once again live up to its name. Or so she hoped.

"I'll just be a minute," Jacob said, then headed toward the hardware section of the store. As he strode past aisles milling with customers, they put their heads together, no doubt whispering about his time in prison.

It didn't seem to matter to anyone that Jacob had been falsely accused and released with an apology. How could people add more pain to the injustice he'd endured by gossiping?

Sighing, Callie moved to the counter teeming with jars of every size and shape crammed to the top with gumdrops, peanut brittle, taffy, hard candy and pretzels. Fresh-baked goods were tucked under glass. Barrels of pickles and crackers lined the floor. One barrel with a spigot held vinegar.

On the other side of the counter, her father-in-law sat at

his desk, examining a ledger. As if he felt her presence, he looked up. "Hello, Callie." Smiling as if he were glad to see her, he shoved back his chair and stepped toward her.

Seeing his good mood, hope leaped inside her. Perhaps he'd accept her proposition. "You look busy."

"Taking care of these books is a full-time job." He thrust the pencil he held behind his ear. "What brings you out today?"

She pulled the blanket Elise had made from the bag. "I'd like to barter Elise's hand-knit items like this lovely blanket and jars of my jams and maybe some pies, in exchange for store credit." She forced a smile. "Or, better yet, for cash."

"You're looking to raise money for the unwed mothers' home, aren't you?"

"That's true, but…" Her hands trembled on the blanket. "Frankly, I'm not sure I can put food on the table for me and my child, much less others, unless I get a steady income."

"I see." His brow furrowed as if her words pained him. "I don't agree with your plan, but I'd never let you or my grandchild go hungry." He sighed. "I haven't been as generous as I should've been, hoping you'd give up this foolishness." His jaw jutted then eased. "Reckon you're even more stubborn than I am." He chuckled. "I'll buy as many of your jams, pies and knitted items as you two can make. Pay a good price for them, too. They'll fly off the shelves."

"Thank you." She slid the bag toward her father-in-law. "In that case, I'll leave these with you."

Commodore opened the cash register and took out a wad of bills. "I'll let you know when we run out." He handed her the money. "You've always been able to stretch a dollar." His eyes filled with misery. "The ones my son didn't spend. This is a small way of saying thanks."

"You're a blessing, Commodore."

At that moment, Jacob laid his purchases on the counter and wrestled his wallet from his hip pocket. From Commodore's cold, penetrating stare, trouble brewed between the two men. Jacob suspected that Commodore had spread the news of his imprisonment and looked ready for a showdown.

Her father-in-law rang up the wood fill and plaster, bagged them and took the money, all without saying a word to Jacob.

As Jacob reached for the sack, Commodore covered it with his hand. "I can see you're trying to get close to Callie. No jailbird is raising my grandchild. Look at you, drifting from town to town. You really think you can stop here and become a father?"

"Commodore!"

"Let me handle this, Callie." Jacob turned to her father-in-law. "I'm innocent. My record's been erased. I'm no more a criminal than you are."

Leaning close, Commodore put his face mere inches from Jacob. "So you say, but this town is up in arms about that stint in jail. I won't have Callie's good name dragged through the mud. I want you gone."

"My name isn't being tarnished by befriending Jacob. He's done nothing wrong."

Jacob fisted a hand. "I've got an urge to plow a fist into your yakking jaw. But my principles won't allow me to harm Callie's baby's grandfather."

Commodore took a step back, no doubt suspicious of the strength of Jacob's principles. "Your reputation in this town is ruined. Gossip about you two is rampant. If you care about Callie, you'll leave."

"He can prove he's innocent," Callie said.

"Innocent or not, the damage is done." Commodore

pointed a finger at Jacob. "Who'd hire you in this town? Who'd trust you in their home? Who'd want to share a pew with you in church? You've seen enough of Peaceful to know I'm speaking the truth. If you truly care about Callie," Commodore went on, "you'll get out of town. Her baby's future is what's important."

The uncertainty filling Jacob's eyes tore at Callie. "You might want to consider your stance, Commodore, if you care about seeing your grandchild."

"See what you're doing, Smith? Because of some misguided loyalty to you, she's threatening to cut me off from my son's child. Are you proud of yourself?"

"Don't blame Jacob for that. You're the one causing the problem."

"Only a few minutes ago, I was a blessing. Maybe you should remember, young lady, which side your bread is buttered on."

The threat squeezed against Callie's lungs. Before she said more than was prudent, she thrust the money in her pocket, took Jacob's arm and rushed from the store.

Outside, Jacob laid a hand on hers. "What Commodore said is true, whether it's fair or not. I won't be the reason this town hurts you and your baby."

"You could leave? That easily?"

In the end, didn't everyone leave?

Or deceive her at every turn?

Commodore had accepted her proposal, paid her well even praised her cooking and management skills, and then threatened to retract their deal unless she toed the line.

"I'm sorry, Callie, but sometimes a man has to make hard decisions to protect those he cares about."

No doubt Commodore believed he was doing the same thing. "If you could toss me aside at the first hint of trouble, that's evidence of how little you care." She yanked free of his hand then clipped along the walk, refusing to look back, every step thudding against her bruised heart.

Well, she needn't have worried. No steps sounded behind her. What did it matter? Without faith in God, Jacob was the wrong man for her. They had no chance of a future together.

This impasse was for the best. With Jacob out of the picture, Commodore would keep his end of the bargain, ensuring that the unwed mothers' home would survive. She needed nothing more than her baby and to help these women.

So why did a future without Jacob leave her feeling so lost and alone?

Chapter Seventeen

Nothing. Not a single clue.

Jake stretched his arms over his head. He'd been sitting here with Callie for hours, flipping through past issues of *The Peaceful Chronicles,* looking for some nugget of information that would reveal his mother's identity or help Callie write the town's history.

To restore the peace between them, Jake had come clean about his reason for landing in Peaceful. As he knew Callie would, she'd joined his search, eager to find any detail that might lead to his mother's identity. If Callie learned during that search that his mother had no interest in a relationship with him, Jake knew she'd never think less of him.

Grace had gone next door to clean Mildred Uland's house after Mrs. Uland's cleaning lady had quit. Elise had helped for a while, then said she wasn't feeling well and went upstairs to lie down, leaving just the two of them holed up in the library.

Across the way, Callie hunched over a newspaper, caught up in some article. He drank in the curve of her cheek, her upturned nose and tendrils of hair curling around her neck. Memorizing each small detail, storing them in his mind for the day she sent him packing. Though they'd forged a modicum of peace, thanks to some fast talking on his part, he didn't doubt that day would come.

Still, he'd been wrong to fall for Commodore's ploy to get him out of town. Not that Peaceful would ever accept him. On that much he and Commodore agreed. But he'd see the quest of finding his mother to the end and help Callie make her dream a reality. During one of his chats with Mildred, he'd given Callie's neighbor money for the home's support, asking her not to reveal the source. Mildred had added her own funds, then opened a bank account for Refuge of Redeeming Love.

That much Jake could do for Callie.

He returned to skimming titles, searching for names of the men and women who'd played a role in settling the town and helping it grow and flourish. He looked for significant dates, events and even human-interest stories that would bring Peaceful's history alive on the page. They'd clipped anything that looked promising and tucked each one into labeled boxes. From those clippings, Callie hoped to condense it into an interesting narrative. But to Jake, most of this information was as dull as unvarnished wood.

Callie took a sip of tea, then pointed to an article. "This lists the winners at the Marion County Fair. My grandmother's quilt won a blue ribbon." She swept a hand over the clippings. "Find anything of interest to you?"

Yes, nothing held his interest like Callie, but he wouldn't say that. "Not yet. But I'm grateful for the chance to look."

She picked up another issue of the newspaper. "I'm keeping an eye out for clues to your mother's identity. Have you been reading the Society page?"

"No, I'm sick of reading descriptions of ladies' hats and who attended the latest tea. I'm saving those tidbits for you." He pointed to the box labeled *Gossip*.

"Oh, I found something." Callie picked up the paper to read the words to him. "Listen to this: 'Occupants of a house on Serenity Avenue may wish to dub the street Stressed Avenue, since a young man from the wrong side of the tracks has been seen calling on their daughter.'" Callie laid down the paper. "Could that be a clue?"

"To what?"

Callie rolled her eyes. "If the columnist is referring to *this* house, then the daughter would be Senator Squier's."

"And?"

"That could mean some young man was courting Irene Squier."

"There're lots of houses on Serenity. But I suppose it's possible."

"And he could've… Well, might've gotten her pregnant."

Jake reached a hand. "What else does it say?"

"Nothing." She thumbed through the stack of issues. "Let's see if more is said about this in later columns." She turned to the next paper's Society page and read the gossip column. "Nothing in here, but I'll look through the next several issues."

Jake picked up the column and reread it. "Even if the gossip referred to the occupants of this house—and we have no evidence that it does—Irene moved away from here. Remember?"

"True. What's the date of that paper?"

"September 1876." Jake's breath caught as he did the math. "I was born in May of the next year."

Callie gasped. "Could Irene be your—?"

"Mother." Just hearing the word off his lips, a desire to know Irene Squier sprang to life inside him.

The date of the family's departure and this column were significant. He thought back on his conversation with the state senator in Indianapolis. The man had said Wesley and Lillian Squier had moved back East. He'd assumed Irene had gone with them. If she had, she couldn't have mailed those postcards.

But what if she hadn't left?

What if she resided in Peaceful? His heart pounded. What if he'd passed her on the street?

Callie gathered a stack of newspapers. "I've looked at the gossip columns for the remainder of the month. No mention of this relationship. But until we read them all, we can't be sure we're on the right track."

Jake grabbed the box labeled *Gossip* and leafed through the clippings they'd snipped earlier. A few minutes later, he found another mention of a romance on Serenity. "Here's another one! With a later date." He half rose from his chair. "'Young love on Serenity Avenue will find a way—better under the watchful eye of a chaperone than under cover of dark.'" Jake cleared his throat. "Sounds like they were sneaking off together."

"I wish we had more to go on."

He flipped through the rest of the gossip articles. "No sorrier than I am. I've looked at the columns in May, near my birthdate. There's no mention of a baby born to someone on Serenity."

"Wouldn't it be something if the young woman who lived in this house was your mother?" She glanced around the room. "It's as if this house were meant to shelter unwed mothers."

"Perhaps we're making too much of this. Serenity's a long street. Several families could've had a daughter."

"Of courting age? It's the first lead we've had."

He reread the article. "Where was the wrong side of the tracks?"

Callie pointed south toward the downtown area. "The

Monon railroad tracks cut Peaceful down the middle. Mildred might know more about the area south of those tracks."

"I'll see what she knows. She hadn't remembered Irene courting anyone, but this article might trigger her memory."

Again Jake thought about his visit to Indianapolis. He hadn't shared that trip with Callie, thinking that what he'd learned amounted to nothing. But now he was tempted to return. See if Senator Davis might have an address for the Squier family, something more to go on.

Callie jumped up and shot around the desk. "What an adventure this is turning out to be! Let's go see Mildred."

He gazed into her lovely, animated face. Callie appreciated the importance of family. Combing the newspapers had become important to them both. When had anyone cared that much about him?

"We'll go." He tugged her into his arms. "But before we do, I know another quest that interests me."

He lowered his head. The softness of her lips under his elicited a groan. She melted against him, encircling his neck with her arms. The gentleness of the kiss intensified with an urgency that set his heart knocking in his chest.

The door banged open. Jake and Callie jerked apart.

Elise stood on the threshold, her face twisted in pain, her hands supporting her bulging belly. "I think it's time," she ground out.

Springing into action, Callie rushed to Elise's side. "I'll help you upstairs." She motioned to Jake. "Get Doc Wellman. On the way, stop at the Langleys'. Tell Sarah that Elise has gone into labor."

"Consider it done."

Callie shot him a smile, then wrapped an arm around Elise and walked her out of the room.

On the way to the front door, Jake's stomach plummeted like a runaway wagon on a downhill slope. Not just about the arrival of Elise's baby, though his disquiet that her time had come surprised him. But after almost giving up on finding his mother, Callie had stumbled upon gossip columns that might be a clue to his roots. Who would've thought gossip would ever have merit?

Soon life would change forever. Certainly for Elise. And perhaps, if the clue meant anything, life would change forever for him. Where would those changes lead?

Jake paced the kitchen floor, tending the teakettles on the cookstove, as Callie had asked. With no idea what else he could do, he felt lost, like a man in the backwoods without a compass. He wanted to shut out the moans from upstairs, yet couldn't leave—as if his presence made an iota of difference. Poor Elise was suffering. The doctor had been here for ages. Her mother had arrived. Why wasn't that baby coming as well?

Maybe the baby was like his grandfather—too stubborn to come. How Mark Langley could refuse to be there for his daughter baffled Jake.

"Jacob."

He whipped around. Callie stood in the doorway. "What's wrong?"

"Nothing. Nothing at all." Callie's calm demeanor eased his stomach, righted his off-kilter world. "Doc Wellman says it won't be too much longer. I came down for hot water."

Wanting to protect her from that kind of pain, he touched her cheek, soft beneath his fingers, "Are you afraid? Knowing you'll go through that in a few months?"

"Bringing a baby into this world can be hard, but I'm not afraid." She laid her hand over Jake's. "Some things are worth any amount of pain."

"I've heard of women having ten-pound babies." He glanced at her petite frame. "It could be difficult to—"

She laid her fingers across his lips. "When did you become such a worrywart?"

He wasn't. Normally. When had Callie become his world?

He tugged her to him. She laid her head against his shoulder and snuggled close. Jake rested his chin on her forehead and soaked up the peace he felt at having her near. With Callie in his arms, life's concerns faded. All felt right with the world. This is where she belonged.

"Callie." She glanced up at him with those startling sea-blue eyes of hers. "I care about you—"

Abruptly, she broke away, clearly avoiding his declaration. "I'd better get that water," she said, not meeting his gaze.

Everything that had softened inside him, hardened. Callie didn't want him. He couldn't blame her. "I'll get it."

Jake followed her upstairs, carrying a hissing teakettle and a steaming pot by the handle. Outside Elise's bedroom door, he handed them over to Callie. "Let me know if there's anything else I can do."

"Pray all goes well and this baby arrives soon. Elise is tired." She sighed, no doubt remembering he wasn't a praying man. That sigh nearly did him in.

Jake knew one thing he could do. He raced down the stairs and strode out the front door, all feelings of abandonment inside him shoving to the surface. He'd do what he could to ensure Langley didn't abandon Elise.

At his knock, Mark Langley opened the door, looking as lost as Jake felt. "Is Elise all right?"

"The baby hasn't arrived yet. Callie says it's normal for babies to take their time coming."

Her father nodded, but didn't look comforted. Obviously, he cared for his daughter. But what about that child she would bring into the world?

"I'm here to tell you what it's like to spend your childhood in an orphanage." Then, not waiting for Mr. Langley's permission, he proceeded to do so. When he finished, he looked deep into Langley's eyes. "Be a father to your daughter. Be a grandfather to her child. The only thing you have to lose is your pride. If you don't, you'll lose everything that matters."

Without a word, Langley headed for the door. Jake had to hurry to catch up.

In Callie's parlor, Elise's father perched on the edge of a dainty chair. "Thanks for telling me about your childhood. It's got me thinking about a lot of things—"

A shriek from above brought him to his feet. "What's taking so long?" Pacing the rug like a caged coyote, he rubbed a hand over his eyes. "If anything happens to that girl, I'll never forgive myself."

"She'll be all right." Jake gulped. She had to be.

Langley stopped and looked at Jake. "Things aren't good between us. Haven't been in a long time. I wanted a boy," he said, choking out the words. "Never could relate to Elise and all that girly stuff. I loved her…but didn't show it much." He shuddered. "I wonder if I drove her into that scalawag's arms."

Langley feared his daughter had fallen for a smooth-talker to fill the void of a distant father. Jake had expected families to be warm, loving, supportive, never failing one another. He'd seen that few people had picture-perfect families. Yet they managed to go on and forge their way, hopefully as Elise and her father would do.

Langley went on pacing. "I couldn't deal with Elise having a baby." He sighed. "My baby having a baby. Just couldn't take that in. I wanted the problem to go away. That's how I saw the baby—as a problem."

"It's not too late to set things right between you and Elise. She's a generous, forgiving person."

"I said a lot of things I shouldn't have."

"What about the baby?"

The eyes he turned on Jake filled with misery. "That's my grandchild Elise is bringing into this world. A baby, not some shame I can shun." His voice broke. "Elise and I got to the point that I couldn't figure out how to mend things."

Jake would give anything if he had a relationship with his parents. Even with all that had happened. Even with the hurts he'd buried inside. If he ever found them, and they showed him one bit of interest, he'd forgive their abandonment. Family mattered. Families stuck by one another. Families worked it out.

"Just be there," Jake said. "Be there when Elise needs you most."

Another shriek, then another and another until the air all but vibrated with Elise's cries. Both men froze. Then they heard the high-pitched wail of a baby that sounded so hopping mad, Jake couldn't help but chuckle.

Mark Langley's face lit up. "It's here."

Jake shook his hand. "Maybe that boy you always wanted."

Elise's father shook his head. "I hope it's a girl. If it is, I'll show her girls are special. That is, after I show her mother."

Callie appeared in the parlor and stopped at the sight of

Mr. Langley, her wide-eyed surprise changing to a huge smile. She motioned for the two of them to follow her upstairs.

The door to Elise's bedroom opened. Doc left the room, carrying his medical bag. "Elise and the baby are fine. You're a grandfather of a healthy baby girl."

"Thanks, Doc. Thanks for taking care of my girls," Langley said, in a shaky voice.

Callie ushered them inside. Elise sat propped up in bed, her face weary but wearing a stunning smile, her baby tucked in a yellow blanket and wrapped in her arms.

Mrs. Langley sat beside the bed. "Mark," was all she said, but Jake heard more in that word than an entire sermon on forgiveness.

Mr. Langley walked to his daughter. "I'm sorry, Elise, for everything I've said. Can you forgive me?"

"You're here, Papa. You came." Elise's voice strangled with tears. "You came when I needed you most." She pulled back the blanket to expose all of her baby's face, reposed in sleep during this momentous family reunion. "Meet your granddaughter, Kathryn Marie Langley."

Mr. Langley caressed the baby's face with one finger. "She's beautiful, Elise. Like her mother."

"Oh, Papa."

Elise laid the precious bundle beside her on the bed and lifted her hands to her father.

Mark Langley wept in her arms.

Callie led Jacob through the hedge to Mildred's, the only person they trusted who might remember the young man from the wrong side of the tracks who could've courted Irene Squier.

Mildred ushered them into her parlor. "Have a seat."

Every surface, shelf and chair was stacked with books

and keepsakes. Not unusual these days while Mildred spent endless hours going through mementoes. All treasures Callie knew, but from the shocked expression on Jacob's face, he saw nothing but junk. Callie picked up a stack of books on one end of the sofa and set them on the floor.

With an apologetic smile, Mildred cleared books from the other end. "You'll have to excuse the mess. I'm going through things, trying to cull them out, but…" She picked up a McGuffey's reader and opened the cover. "This belonged to my husband. Has his name right here." She looked away. "It's hard to let go."

Callie understood the difficulty of letting go. Not with things, but with loved ones. Jacob had difficulty letting go of a past that affected him still.

"I'll get refreshments," Mildred said, then left the room.

Jake leaned toward Callie. "A house this size no doubt has a library. Isn't it large enough to hold her collection of books?"

"Like she said, she's been going through things. I think all these keepsakes make her feel closer to her husband." She sighed. "Now you can see why her cleaning lady quit. Grace will do the job as long as she can. Her way of helping with expenses."

Mildred returned, carrying a tray with three glasses of lemonade and a plate of those gingersnap cookies she loved. Callie shoved aside a box of postcards on the table to make room for the tray.

Mildred cleared the chair of today's newspaper and plopped down. "You're here for more than my cookies," she said. "Anyone with ears knows about your time in jail, Jake." She offered him the plate. "I'd like to hear your version."

After he explained, Mildred leaned toward him. "Life's

not fair, plain and simple. But you hold your head up. In time, people will lose interest."

"Perhaps, but my past is tainting Callie's reputation and giving this town another reason to turn against her."

Mildred cocked her head at him. "Why not tell me why you're in Peaceful, Jake?" She raised a hand. "Better yet, let me guess. Considering how many times you've asked questions about the women in this town, about the Squier family, especially their daughter, Irene, I suspect you came here looking for your mother."

He met her gaze. "Yes."

"Why did you believe your mother was in Peaceful?"

Jacob told her about the postcards.

"Have you found her?"

"That's why we're here, Mildred. We found a few references in newspaper gossip columns that could be a clue. The columns suggest a young man from the wrong side of the tracks courted a young lady on Serenity. We're hoping that was Irene. Do you know who that young man might have been?"

Mildred munched a cookie, then leaned back, closing her eyes, hopefully deep in thought, not nodding off as she was prone to do. Her eyes popped open. "The wrong side of the tracks is easy enough. The folks with money lived on this side. Folks south of those tracks lived in small bungalows, a few in shanties." She furrowed her brow, staring at her shoes, as if the name of the young man was written on the toes. "What year was that?"

"Most likely the fall and winter of '76."

"That explains it. The reason I don't recall Irene having a suitor is my husband took sick about that time. He died a few months later, that next spring. I spent every moment at his bedside. I wouldn't have noticed if Irene had spooned with a young man on her front porch—or on mine for that matter. I'm sorry. I wish I could've been more help."

Disappointment sank to Callie's belly. "You were a wonderful wife, Mildred. Everyone said so."

"I hope you figure it out. Maybe talk to the folks south of town." She nailed Jacob with her gaze. "I've got a question for you. Are you planning to run? Or stick with Callie here?"

The shocked look on Jacob's face said it all.

Mildred harrumphed. "Don't let a little gossip direct your steps. Let me tell you, Jake, God expects better of you."

"God doesn't know me."

"Ha! You've got lots to learn, my young friend. Stay put. Open your heart to God. You're in for the ride of a lifetime."

Callie had come hoping to learn more about Irene Squier. Instead, Mildred had tried badgering Jacob into faith and into caring for Callie. Callie knew what Mildred had forgotten. Before a man could ride, he had to be willing to get in the saddle.

Jake sat in Callie's parlor holding Elise's baby against his chest. Inside the blanket, the poor little thing drew her knees up, screeching like an alley cat in a midnight skirmish. And Jake didn't know the first thing about comforting her. He'd never even held a baby before.

Not that he planned to hold this one for long. He'd come in from feeding the stock and surely didn't smell good enough to hold a newborn baby. But, with Callie off to a prayer meeting and Grace holed up in her room, Elise had come to him, close to tears from walking the floor with Katie.

He couldn't turn her down. Not after she gazed up at

him with exhausted eyes and asked for his help, as if he knew the first thing about babies. He'd taken the tyke into his arms as gingerly as an explosive device with a short fuse and sent Elise off to bed.

Elise surprised Jake by staying at Callie's after she and her father had made peace, hoping Katie Marie would soften Grace's heart toward her baby. But Grace avoided the newborn. Even took food to her room if the baby showed up at meals.

How could she not open her heart to this baby? Katie Marie was perfect. Helpless. Tiny. And madder than a hen with a broken beak.

Patting her back, Jake walked the floor, swaying with her. Not enough to hurt her. He hoped. He kept patting. Kept walking. Every muscle tense.

What if he hurt her?

What if something was wrong?

Should he get Doc?

Where was Callie? How long could one person pray?

"Looks like you could use some help."

Callie stood in the parlor smiling at him. The relief of having her there washed through him clear to his toes.

An explosion erupted from Katie's mouth. A belch of gigantic proportions, one a teenage boy would be proud of, was followed by a stream of curdled milk that dampened his shirt, and an odor that left him gagging. Surely that couldn't have come from this dainty creature.

But the baby kept on crying, as if her little heart would break and Jake felt like joining her.

With an amused smile, Callie took Katie Marie from his arms, easing the baby into the crook of her arm and cooed softly to her, then tucked the baby up against her middle, swaying to the rhythm of some unsung lullaby.

Immediately Katie quieted. Her eyelids drifted closed. She slept.

Callie sat on the sofa. Jake sank beside her as wrung out as an old dishrag. "I'm thankful you got home when you did." He grabbed the cloth Elise had left with him and dabbed the milk from Katie's rosebud lips, then mopped his clothes. "You're a natural mother."

"You were managing just fine."

Jake knew better. Commodore had said Jake wasn't cut out for fatherhood. He hadn't doubted Commodore's assessment. His failure to soothe Katie had added further evidence.

Callie lifted her gaze to him. "Isn't she beautiful?"

"She is."

Jake touched the soft folds of the baby's neck, ran a finger over the silky strands of her hair and along a tiny fuzzy ear. Katie emitted a soft sigh and snuggled deeper into the yellow blanket, a picture of contentment, tugging at his heart with a strength that left him dazed.

This precious infant would grow up without a father. Something hot flared inside him. Better to have no father than a bad one. At least she'd have one good parent.

"I can't wait to hold my baby," Callie murmured, ending on a soft sigh.

"Your baby is blessed to have you as a mother."

She smiled at him, beamed really. "Thank you, Jacob. I want what's best for my child."

"What's best for your child isn't me."

"Oh, you worry too much. Few feel up to the task of parenthood." She chuckled. "What's best for this little one is her bed. I'll put her down."

As Jake watched them go, tears stung the back of his eyes. Callie hadn't understood what he'd tried to tell her. Even as the admission stabbed like a knife to his heart, the truth was undeniable. Callie's baby needed a good father. How could Jake be such a thing when he'd had no role model? He'd heard enough from Pastor Steele's sermons to know a husband should lead his family. Yet Jake lacked the faith that would help guide a child and head a home.

The harsh truth of his incompetence sank inside him. He had to walk away. Leave this house. Leave the ministry to unwed mothers. Leave Callie. Leave everything and everyone who had become important to him. He'd vowed to toughen himself against caring, against opening his heart—

He'd failed. Callie Mitchell had his heart. He'd found what he'd been looking for all his life. Nothing in his past had prepared him for his feelings for this woman. Her presence made the bleakest day beautiful, the toughest task easy, and the most monotonous day exciting. She was merciful. Kind. Generous. Everything good.

He loved Callie. Completely, totally.

Only a few days old and Katie Marie had already taught Jake Smith a thing or two. He hadn't had a family. Never knew the privilege of sharing a home or of having the support of loved ones, but this baby had given him a peek at the responsibilities of fatherhood.

He wasn't fit to raise a child. To love this woman. Especially in a town that would never accept him.

He'd never tell Callie he loved her. If he did, it would be asking her to choose him over what was best for her child.

Even a faithless jailbird wouldn't stoop that low.

Chapter Eighteen

Wind howled in the trees, whipping the limbs into a frenzied dance. Rain pelted the windows, striking the glass with the clatter of hail. Callie prayed a tornado wasn't brewing and heading their way. Jacob had raced to Mildred's to cover a leak in her roof with a tarpaulin. Yet, even with nature blowing up a tempest, her house was sturdy and would weather the storm.

Katie Marie's cry drifted down the staircase. Within minutes, she quieted. Her needs met by Elise. Remembering the way Jacob had handled the newborn last night, holding her like a piece of crystal, as if she'd break, Callie smiled. His tender, awed expression proved he was smitten with the baby. He would be a good husband, a wonderful father.

For someone. Not for her.

What's best for your baby isn't me.

Jacob's statement didn't sink in—at first—but it hadn't taken Callie long to realize he meant every word.

She'd prayed and prayed for Jacob to come to God. Though she'd seen a change in his attitude in church and he'd acknowledged reading the Bible, he hadn't taken that step. And from his own mouth he'd dispelled the prospect of that changing.

He shared her concern for unwed mothers, understood her troubled background. She'd had hope that he might be part of God's plan for her life. But she and her baby needed a God-fearing man to lead their home. God would not send her a man without faith.

A knock at her door jarred her out of her thoughts. Who would be out on such a night? Whoever braved this weather was getting drenched. She hurried to answer it.

On the other side of the door stood a stranger wearing a long navy macintosh over his suit, lowering a silk umbrella. She shivered in the damp, chilly wind.

The man tipped his bowler, revealing his pate, bald and pale as a peeled onion. She noted the case in his hand. Surely even the most ambitious salesman wouldn't be out in this weather. "I'm sorry, but whatever you're selling—"

"Ma'am, I'm Robert Lovell, attorney with the Indianapolis law firm of Lovell, McGahan and Lovell." He replaced his hat. "I'm looking for Martin and Callie Mitchell."

At the mention of her deceased husband, Callie's grip on the door tightened. "I'm Callie Mitchell. Martin's widow."

"I'm sorry for your loss, Mrs. Mitchell."

"What's this about, Mr. Lovell?"

"May I come in? I'd rather explain my business in the comfort of your parlor than out here in this storm."

"Please excuse my bad manners. Come in." As Callie led the way, her stomach roiled like a vessel on a storm-tossed sea. What business would a big-city lawyer have with her?

She felt an urge to ask him to wait for Jacob, but that was silly. Whatever this was about, it had nothing to do with Jacob. The time had come to stop relying on that man.

They took seats at the parlor table. After an apology for dripping water on her carpet, the attorney reached inside his case and pulled out a ream of papers. He glanced through them, then met her eyes. "Just to verify, I'm at 7133 Serenity Avenue in Peaceful, Indiana."

"That's correct."

"This house was previously owned by Senator and Mrs. Wesley Squier."

"My father-in-law, Commodore Mitchell, purchased the Squier house at auction two years ago this month."

"The senator and his wife died in a trolley accident that same year. Their daughter, Irene, preceded them in death."

Something tightened in Callie's chest, pressing against her lungs until she could barely breathe. If Irene was Jacob's mother, she was dead. How could Callie break the news to him? "I had no idea. What a tragedy."

He cleared his throat. "Indeed. Senator Squier and his wife had moved back East. At the time of their death, as their attorney, I had a copy of their Last Will and Testament. Or so I believed." He mopped his brow. "As it turns out, not all their legal papers were in my possession. Recently, a safe was uncovered containing a later will, written in Wesley's own hand with the seal of a notary, negating the earlier one. A judge in Maryland has ruled that the later will is binding."

Through the window, lightning flashed, casting eerie shadows in the room. "What does this have to do with me?"

"Mrs. Mitchell, the house Commodore Mitchell bought shouldn't have been up for auction. The Squiers left this house to someone else."

Callie's pulse throbbed in her temples with the rhythm

of rumbling thunder overhead. "I don't understand. Commodore paid for the house."

"I can appreciate your confusion. But, as I said, the house should not have been sold. It was left to Irene's son, Jacob Squier Smith."

All these years Jacob thought he had no family, but he did. He had a family that had looked out for him, left him in their will… That meant—

The room tilted then righted. Callie knew, in that moment, nothing would ever be the same again. She was losing her home, her baby's home and the refuge for unwed mothers. *Lord, help me handle this trial.*

"Could this be a mistake?"

"No mistake. I'm sorry."

Her body went cold. She shivered.

"A letter attached to the updated will explained that after Irene died in childbirth, Senator Squier placed the infant in an orphanage, giving Jacob an alias, the surname *Smith* to protect his daughter's good name. These documents were found weeks ago, but we haven't been able to locate Jacob Smith. The orphanage had no address for him. As you can imagine, we wanted to make sure Jacob Smith survived before we broached this rather sticky situation with you."

Should she get Jacob from Mildred's? He needed to hear the news, had a right to know. But to hear something this devastating from a stranger seemed cruel. "Mr. Smith is here in town, but not available at the moment."

The attorney smiled. "That's good to hear. I'm staying at the Liberty Inn tonight. Please give him my business card and ask him to meet me there tomorrow."

She nodded, taking the card.

"I suspected that he was in the area. A few days ago, Mr. Smith spoke to a friend of mine in Indianapolis."

Callie's head snapped up. "What?"

"Mr. Smith came to inquire about the Squier family. The state senator he talked to, David Davis, is a friend of mine. David knew I represented the Squier family and was looking for their heir. I'd never given David the name of the man I sought, but he thought Jacob Smith's inquiry might be important." He smiled. "It was."

"Jacob came to Indianapolis, asking about my house?"

"I'm not privy to every topic of their conversation." He handed a copy of the will to Callie. "You can rest assured that these documents are legal and binding."

The name Jacob Squier Smith leaped off the page. Callie's hands trembled so badly that she laid the document on her lap.

"Do you have the deed in your possession, Mrs. Mitchell?"

"Yes."

"Would you get it, please? I will make the necessary change of ownership in the recorder's office in the Marion County courthouse."

Callie's head pounded, fire filled her veins. Jacob Smith had lied to her again. Even his name had been a lie.

No wonder he'd been willing to make repairs without a wage. No wonder he'd worked from dawn to dusk to restore her house. No wonder he'd been reluctant to tell her about his past. Jacob Smith had manipulated her.

For two years, she'd lived in the shelter of these rooms, more shabby than stately, but home. Wasn't possession nine points of the law? "I will fight this, Mr. Lovell. I have no intention of turning over the deed to this house." She shook the papers. "This document could be a fake. I don't know you or your law firm." She rose. "Good day, sir."

Mr. Lovell's jaw jutted, but he got to his feet. "I assure you, these documents are legally binding. There is no mistake," he said, his tone steely.

"I assure you I won't be fooled again. I will look into this with an attorney of my own."

Not that she had an attorney or the money to hire one. She'd find a way. Perhaps Mildred would lend her the money. With the bond between Mildred and Jacob, the prospect of telling her neighbor about his deceit sank inside her like a stone.

She showed Mr. Lovell to the door, bracing against the wind then closed it after him.

Now she understood why Jacob told her he wasn't best for her baby. His reason wasn't some concern for her baby's welfare or a lack of faith. No. He knew he'd set up this betrayal.

What a fool she'd been.

Jacob Smith—no, Jacob Squier, a man she'd trusted, a man with a horrific past dominated by loneliness and injustice. She'd made his burdens her own. For this? Once again she'd missed what lurked beneath the surface of a man.

Yet that didn't eradicate Jacob's image from her mind, didn't block those intense green eyes, the dimple in his cheek, that chiseled jaw—

Something Commodore once said stuck in her mind and came back to her now: *A drifter has something to hide. As soon as someone gets close to his secret, that's when he leaves.*

Jacob Smith hid secrets. But Commodore had been wrong about one thing. Jacob wouldn't be leaving. Not when he expected to move into the main house.

Jake had managed to get the tarpaulin in place before the brunt of the storm hit. The wind practically blew him from Mildred's to Callie's. Thankfully, the rain had let up enough to make the distance without getting drenched.

Callie opened the door to his knock. He brushed the rain off his hat, smiling. "I've battened down the hatches at Mildred's." He took another look at her. "Everything all right here?"

She moved aside to let him in. "How nice of you to take an interest in your house."

"What do you mean?"

She glared at him. "How could you do this to me?"

Her icy tone stopped him cold. "I don't know what you're talking about."

"I've had a visitor."

"In this weather? Who?"

"A Mr. Robert Lovell, an attorney who claims this house doesn't belong to me." She took a step toward him. "That it was wrongly sold."

"What?"

"A more recent copy of the Squier Last Will and Testament was found. How convenient to find that will after you've increased the house's value." She gave a choked laugh, verging on hysteria. "But then you know all about that."

Lightning struck nearby. Thunder shook the house. Callie never flinched. She didn't appear to notice the storm, but Jake could see by the glint in her eyes, the rigid set of her jaw, she had one raging inside of her.

He reached for her, but she batted his hand away. "I don't understand what you're saying. Callie, talk to me."

"You lied. How could you? I trusted you. I cared about you. Even thought, I lov— What a fool I've been!"

Another bolt of lightning, a clap of thunder. He pleaded with her, his composure crumbling. "Lied? I told you about my time in jail, the reason I came to Peaceful. I've told you everything."

"You're quite the actor." She poked a finger into his sternum with surprising force, as if wanting to give him pain.

What was going on?

"Don't pretend! I had all the deception I could stomach with Martin. Always pretending, always telling me what I wanted to hear and hiding what I didn't." She poked again, harder. "I trusted you! You and Martin are cut from the same cloth." She thrust the papers at him. "This proves you're lying!"

With an unsteady hand, Jake took the paperwork, never taking his eyes off Callie.

Her chest heaved. "Read it!"

Jake glanced at the page. Phrases jumped out at him. *The house at 7133 Serenity left to Jacob Smith.* Why?

"This doesn't make sense." The sneer suffusing Callie's face forced the air out of his lungs.

He read on—*Jacob Squier, also known as Jacob Smith, son of Irene Squier, born to her on May 21, 1877.*

His pulse ratcheted. The date of his birth. "Irene Squier's my mother." His gaze leaped to Callie and he looked into eyes as turbulent as storm-tossed seas. Unable to bear the coldness there, he dropped his gaze to the papers in his hand. *Irene Squier died in childbirth.*

Dead? She was dead? Died giving birth to him?

Again and again he read the same words. With each reading the horror of them shuddered through him. As he read them one last time, the pieces came together in his mind. Comprehension slammed into him, doubling him over. He sucked in air. All the time he'd resented his mother for not coming to him, she'd been dead.

Tears filled his eyes. He'd never get to know her. Never get to see her face. Never get to tell her he was sorry for years of blaming her for deserting him.

"I thought *you* were an answer to my prayers. How wrong I've been."

Jake straightened, tried to focus on Callie's words. But she didn't make sense—nothing made sense. He tried to tug her to him. Maybe in his arms, she'd listen. "I didn't know about this."

She laughed. The eerie sound slithered along Jake's spine.

"Do you expect me to believe that your coming here to Peaceful, to this house looking for work was a coincidence?"

"The waitress at the café suggested you—"

"Lies. All of it. Lies!" Her voice broke. "You were living in my lean-to, waiting like a vulture for the pickings."

"I'm not lying!"

"Do you deny that you went to Indianapolis?"

He frowned. How did she know about that? "No, but—"

"You set all this in motion!" Battling tears, she flung a card at him. "You're supposed to meet the attorney at the Liberty Inn tomorrow."

The anguish on her face tore at him, clawed at his heart, ripped it to shreds. Instead of thinking of Callie and what this meant to her, he'd been focused on his mother, on his loss. Callie was losing her home. To him. He wouldn't let that happen. He picked up the card: Robert Lovell, Attorney at Law. Tomorrow he'd contact the lawyer and get this straightened out.

Callie pointed a hand toward the door. "Get out of my house. I won't be moving, not until I'm forced. Stay in the lean-to tonight." She snorted. "I couldn't send even a dog out in this storm."

With that she turned on her heel and stomped off.

Callie was tossing him out. The closest thing he'd had to

a family had been destroyed while he'd stood there holding that card in his hand, powerless to stop it.

The family he wanted and thought he'd found was exactly like that foster family so many years ago.

A figment of his imagination.

Jake slapped his Bible shut and stretched out on the cot, his back propped against the pillow. The storm had passed, but that hadn't eased the storm raging between him and Callie.

At first, her accusations had baffled him, then filled him with shock. Shock turned to anger.

That Callie believed him capable of treachery when all he'd ever wanted was to help, not harm, churned inside him. But he'd moved past his own pain and had seen hers. Everything between him and Callie lay in ruins.

Yet, even knowing that, he still listened for her footsteps outside, hoping she'd come to him. That she would admit she knew he'd never wrest the house she loved from her. She hadn't come.

No matter. He'd go to her. Surely, she must be calmer now. Together they'd work this out. If the will was legitimate and the Victorian did belong to him, he'd sign the house over to Callie. He'd ensure that she and her baby had a roof over their heads, as well as all the unwed mothers and their babies, both now and in the years ahead.

He leaped to his feet, striding to the door and opened it. Dusk had fallen but he could see Callie, standing at the back door, talking to a woman heavy with child. Then she ushered her inside. Callie had gone on with her life while he could barely function. She'd settle the newcomer in, as only she could do, and give the woman a sense of belonging.

As she once had him.

He closed the door and dropped to the mattress, tucking

his hands under his head. Something about that woman nagged at him, hung on with the tenacity of a gorging tick. He'd seen her before. Where?

He jerked to his feet. With the turmoil of the afternoon, he'd put the incident out of his mind. Until now.

That morning he'd gone into Mitchell Mercantile to buy work clothes. He'd seen that same tattered cloak, that same disheveled woman, a furtive expression on her face, shoving something in her pocket as she slipped out of the store. No one appeared to notice anything amiss.

Most likely she was a downtrodden woman, down on her luck. He'd give it a few minutes then knock on Callie's door. Make sure the newcomer wasn't a problem. Then he'd tell her his plan to set things right.

First thing tomorrow, he'd talk to that attorney. They'd work this out. Everything would be fine. Picturing Callie's reaction, he grinned. If he handled it right, she might even let him give her a hug.

By now, Callie would've settled the woman in. He shoved on his boots, crossed the lean-to floor in a few strides and opened the door.

He found himself staring into the remote eyes of Sheriff Frederick, his hand raised as if to knock. Or break down a door.

"Money's missing from Commodore's cash register. He's thirty dollars short. He saw you in the store. Know anything about that?"

Jake shook his head. "I didn't take any money. Not from the Mercantile. Not from anyone."

"Mind if I check your room?" Not waiting for an answer, Frederick rummaged through Jake's bedding, his clothes folded on the chair, rifled through his Bible, as if a man would hide evidence of his sin in that book. Then jerked open the drawer and pawed through his personal items, his boss's reference, the fragile postcards, ragged from scrutiny and age.

The only connection he had left of his mother. A powerful urge to knock the sheriff into the next county seized him. But that satisfaction wouldn't accomplish anything except to give Frederick another reason to haul his hide to jail.

He slammed the drawer shut. "Where's the money?"

"I told you—I didn't take that money."

"Maybe cooling your heels in jail will improve your memory."

Jail. Reflected in the sheriff's eyes, Jake saw his guilt. Reflected in the tone of Frederick's voice, Jake heard his guilt. Once again, he was facing jail for something he didn't do.

Frederick wrapped a beefy hand around Jake's arm.

"Let go of me," Jake said, his tone rigid, "I'll come of my own accord."

Anyone seeing the two of them on the walk to the jail would've thought they were taking an evening stroll. But for Jake, each step relived another walk. A walk he'd taken from the courtroom to a cell, his fate sealed by a jury. He'd been no guiltier then than now, but innocence didn't keep a man free.

The prospect of being caged like an animal shoved against every nerve, every tendon, every muscle. A compulsion seized him—to run, to fight—to stop the inevitable clank of that barred door. But he kept moving, kept putting one foot in front of the other, holding tight to his control. The only thing he had.

Inside the jail, Frederick threw open the door of a cell. Jake flinched. Then with sheer strength of will, he took the last steps inside.

The door closed with a bang that ricocheted through

the block of cells and echoed with a familiar finality that made his stomach heave.

Mere months before, he'd been in another prison where an innocent bump could send a man into a rage. And someone could end up dead. He'd learned to watch his back, always prepared for trouble. Trouble was a daily visitor in jail. Conditions made that inevitable. The bullpen, that dim, airless exercise room with inmates herded together like doomed cattle in the stockyards. The stench of unwashed bodies and urine invaded his nostrils. The slime of spit, slippery beneath his feet had him gulping for air. He couldn't survive that again.

Shoving the memory aside, he dropped onto the cot in the dim cell, elbows on knees, hands dangling, focusing on the fibers on his frayed cuffs. Those frayed cuffs had been the reason he'd gone into the Mercantile. Odd that something so trifling as wanting a new shirt determined a man's fate. He plucked at the fibers, unraveling from the times he'd scraped against shingles, plaster, lumber— typical in his line of work.

Yet, far more than his cuffs was unraveling. His life was unraveling, too.

That woman he'd seen in the Mercantile could've taken the money before she slipped away. Yet he had no way to prove it. Considering Callie's anger at the will, she wouldn't come to his defense.

Jake's throat knotted. He'd lost everything that mattered. His mother. His woman. His freedom.

Once again, he was confined to a cell, no one to hear, no one to care. Swallowing against the bile pushing up his throat, Jake understood with clarity. He didn't know how to handle his life. He didn't know how to handle even one night in this cell.

Tears stung his eyes. All he'd ever wanted was a family. Was that too much to ask for?

That yearning had brought him to Peaceful in search of his mother. In a way, he'd found her. His mother had lived in Callie's house during its grander days. Both he and his mother had walked those floors, spent time under that roof, been sheltered by those walls. Not much of a connection but something. Something he'd cherish. All he had.

A sob tore from his lips. All those years he'd resented his mother for not coming she'd been *dead*. Irene Squier, still in her teens died giving him life.

Someone should care that she no longer lived. Someone should mourn her. He did. He cared, yet too late to tell her.

Too late to thank her.

Too late.

He had nowhere to turn. No one in this town would help him. He hauled himself to his feet and walked to the window, staring at the star-studded night through the bars. Across the way, he spotted the silhouette of Callie's church steeple, pointing toward the sky. The Heavens, people said, God's home.

Did God exist? Were all those words in the Bible true?

He dropped to his knees in the striped moonbeam on the floor, gazing up at that scrap of sky, the only visible link to God, if He even existed.

Jake had read the Bible stories. There'd be no burning bush for him. No parted waters. No water into wine.

All he knew for sure was that he couldn't go on alone. He couldn't make it through another day under his own power. He'd prided himself on his skill with hammer and nails, on hard work, on his physical stamina. But he had nothing left. He was a hollow shell of a man.

A sob shoved up his throat. *If You're real, God, if You're up there and You...care about...me, help me. Please. Help me accept the loss of a mother I never knew. Help me find my way. Please, be that arrow Callie talked about. Show me the way.*

The arrows he'd been following had taken him to a dead end.

I've tried to live by my own strength, but I don't have any strength left. I don't have enough strength to spend the night in this cell. I don't have enough strength to fight Commodore's charge. I don't have enough strength to convince Callie to love me.

I love you.

Jake swiveled on his knees, searching the small space, the corridor. No one was there, but he'd heard a voice. A voice that was crystal clear, real. The tone gentle, with the warmth a loving parent would use with a frightened child.

Some child. *Him.* A twenty-three-year-old jailbird unable to handle his life.

He staggered to the window, peering into the night, searching for some change, some concrete evidence that the voice in his head, dare he think, was the voice of... God.

No falling stars, no flashes of lightning, no howling wind. A regular night. But in that moment, a night like no other. A blessed sense of peace filled him.

God was real. God cared. God loved him.

Jake felt that love. Felt that forgiveness. Nothing about his new conviction made sense. Yet with bone-deep certainty Jake knew God was there in that cell with him.

Him.

A man who'd walked this life alone. Or so he'd thought. Now he knew that choice had been his, not God's. God had been there all along, waiting for him. At Jake's first step of trust, at his first plea for help, God had answered.

He'd read about Jesus in the Garden of Gethsemane. How he'd cried out to God the night before he hung on that cross. If Jesus could handle *that,* Jake could easily handle this night.

Tomorrow he'd share his faith with the only woman whose opinion mattered. He had the promise of a fresh beginning. It seemed so simple. Yet, so complex. To a man like him, who'd never been loved, the love of God was a mystery.

He had a father now. A Heavenly Father.

Thank You for loving me. Thank You for saving me. Thank You for never leaving me when I rejected You countless times. Help me be and do what You want.

Certain of what he must do, Jake closed his eyes and gave his burdens to the One who controlled the universe, even this small chunk of it. Let go of the anguish of those lonely years in the orphanage, the heartache of waiting for a mother who never came, of being framed by a friend for a crime he didn't commit, the months of degradation and fear in that other cell, of losing Callie's regard. All that weight lifted from his shoulders.

He still remembered every moment of his past. How could he forget? But his past no longer dominated who he was. His todays. Or his tomorrows. He felt reborn.

Hope spilled into every crevice. With God's help, he and Callie could be a family. He could be a good husband, a good father. He stretched out on the cot and slept.

Chapter Nineteen

The morning brought bright sunshine and chirping birds, but nothing was light about the load of uncertainties Callie carried. Yesterday's storm had moved on, as storms always do. But the storm within, the pain of losing her home, of losing Jacob raged. How could she have allowed herself to depend on him?

As she'd made her way to the barn, she hadn't seen Jacob. Not that she expected to after the way they'd parted last night. He'd no doubt already gone to meet that lawyer about his inheritance and would succeed in ripping the house out from under her and her baby. In effect, destroying her dream and leaving some desperate women homeless.

Leaning into Bossy's side, Callie bit back a sob. Now, she'd be forced to move in with Commodore, but at least she had a place to go. But what would happen to Grace and Joanna?

She had to tell them, though they might react as Mildred had when Callie had seen her neighbor earlier—with total faith in Jacob's integrity—insisting that he hadn't known about his mother's death or the Squier will. Once Mildred took Jacob under her wing, she had a blind spot when it came to him.

Callie rose, picked up the milk bucket and left the barn with Stripes at her heels.

"Callie!"

Hand on her hat, Loretta hurried toward her, skirts flying. What was going on?

When she reached her, Loretta took the pail and they continued walking toward the house. "Hal arrested Jake last night for stealing from Commodore's store."

"What?" Callie gripped Loretta's arm, slopping milk out of the pail.

"After closing yesterday, Commodore discovered thirty dollars was missing from his register. Jake had been in the store that morning."

Callie whirled on Loretta. "That's the only reason Commodore had for accusing him?"

"Hal said Jake looked more dead than alive when he walked into that cell. I think he felt sorry for him, but once a jailbird—"

"How can you condemn a man with no real evidence?"

Loretta's gaze sought the ground. "I'm sorry." She raised her eyes to Callie's. "But Commodore swears he knew everyone who stepped inside the store the entire day, had known them for years. Who else could've done it?"

Callie reached for the bucket, Loretta's question slowing her hand. Jacob had betrayed her but this act of thievery didn't ring true. "I have no idea."

"I can see you're upset. I thought you'd want to know."

"I'm glad you told me. I'm just sorry you always jump to conclusions about people."

Loretta worried her lower lip with her teeth. "I don't know why I do that. Maybe because I don't want anyone I care about to get hurt." Tears brimmed in her eyes. "I know things haven't been good between us, but I care about you, Callie."

With that declaration Loretta hurried off before Callie could respond. As she walked on to the house, Callie acknowledged that she cared about Loretta, too, though her friend didn't always make caring easy. She'd have to make amends for that hurt in Loretta's eyes. Her entire life seemed to be falling apart.

Inside the kitchen, one by one the others came in, dished up oatmeal, poured tea and coffee, and took seats at the table. Callie went through the motions, greeted Joanna, Grace and Elise, kissed Katie Marie's soft cheek, but the food in her stomach churned. She didn't have the heart to tell them about the Squier will and all that would mean.

Had she been wrong? Maybe Jacob hadn't known about the will. But he hadn't said one word or taken one step that indicated he'd refuse his inheritance. Her breath caught. Had she given Jacob a chance to explain before they parted last night? He couldn't very well come to her when he was locked in a cell.

Still, she couldn't expect a man who'd never had a home to relinquish ownership of a house he admired.

Brought out of her reverie when Grace and Joanna rose and cleared the table, Callie realized they'd finished their breakfast. "Jacob's been arrested for stealing cash from the Mercantile," she blurted out. She wouldn't mention the will until she knew for certain that she'd lose the house.

"What?" Elise, eyes spitting fire, laid the baby on her shoulder and patted her back. "I don't believe it!"

Joanna studied her fingernails, indifferent to the predicament of someone she'd never met.

Grace's eyes filled with disquiet. "Do you think he's guilty?"

That first day when Callie had asked Jacob if he'd steal from her, his jutting jaw attested that he'd found her question offensive. No wonder with the horror of being unjustly jailed for theft. She sighed. He'd never appeared to care much about money. He might not be candid, might've kept his purposes to himself, but he had principles.

"He'd never steal," she said and knew she spoke the truth. The man was innocent.

Elise's eyes snapped. "If you don't think he's guilty, how can you let him rot in jail?"

Dear sweet Elise, dramatic and loyal. "I won't let an innocent man be railroaded to prison," Callie said firmly. Even if Jacob had stolen her house. And her heart. She rose. "I'm going to the jail. Make sure Hal gets off his duff and looks for the real culprit. After that, I'll try to convince Commodore to drop this ridiculous charge."

Katie Marie gave a resounding belch, as if offering her displeasure at Jacob's treatment. "That's my girl," Elise said, grinning at her baby as she tucked Katie into Martin's wicker baby carriage. "I'm coming with you."

"Me, too," Grace shoved back her chair and lumbered to her feet.

Joanna lifted downcast eyes. "I'll go, too."

The women in this house knew the pain of being judged and convicted by a merciless town, yet had the courage to unite in Jacob's defense. Callie had never been prouder of anyone.

"On the way, we'll stop for Mildred. Hal had better be prepared. The women of Peaceful are on the march."

Leaving the dishes and the oatmeal sticking to the pan— not Callie's way—she strode out the back door, the others bringing up the rear.

Up ahead, Commodore and Albert Thompson, the sheriff's deputy, headed into the lean-to. With her entourage behind her, Callie hurried toward them.

"We're here to search the lean-to, Callie," Albert said. "Another set of eyes is—"

"A waste of time. Once you come up empty-handed, perhaps, Commodore, you'll drop this absurd charge against Jacob."

"I never thought my son's widow would fall for a jailbird."

Heat climbed Callie's neck. How dare Commodore use that hateful label for Jacob? "I haven't fallen for anyone." Callie planted her palms on her hips. "Admit it. You're accusing Jacob of theft because he fixed up this house and thwarted your plan to force me to move in with you."

Commodore harrumphed. "Think what you will. I knew every single person who came into my store yesterday."

Joanna tugged her sleeve. "Shouldn't we get to the jail?"

Callie nodded, then turned back to Commodore. "You often work on accounts at your desk. You can't see everyone who enters your store."

"I haven't run a successful business for years without keeping an eye on the clientele."

Which said plenty about her father-in-law. "Don't you trust anyone?"

Commodore stared into space. "Not much in my life has given me reason to. Maybe I don't even trust myself."

The air of despondency in his eyes pinged against Callie's heart. She took a step toward him but he turned away, avoiding her touch. "The deputy and I will be examining Smith's quarters with a fine-tooth comb."

For a moment there, Callie had felt sorry for Commodore. But she wouldn't waste time arguing with a man whose compassion died with his son.

Sheriff Frederick didn't use a cattle prod or whip. His method of getting Jake to confess was far less painful, yet monotonous enough to threaten his sanity. But in an attempt to conduct himself in a way that honored God, Jake bit his tongue. A tongue that was getting sore.

"Were you in the Mitchell Mercantile yesterday?" Frederick began again.

"Yes."

"What time was that?"

"Around eleven o'clock."

"What were you doing there?"

"I told you, Sheriff. I went in to buy a work shirt."

"Did you get that shirt?"

Jake exhaled. "You know I didn't."

"Does it strike you as odd, Smith, that a man would go into a store for a purchase, find what he needed, yet leave without it? I've got to wonder if that man went in for something all right, but it wasn't a work shirt. And he didn't leave empty-handed."

"For the fifteenth time—I didn't take the money."

The door banged open. Callie led the way, a warrior leading the charge, her expression resolute, eyes blazing.

Jake had never seen her look more beautiful and been gladder to see anyone.

The sheriff rose to his feet. "Callie, you can't come in here during an interrogation."

"You can't arrest a man based on his past."

Callie had come to his defense, even if it hurt his pride that she hadn't declared him innocent. Her action gave Jake a smidgeon of optimism.

Frederick rubbed his neck. "Jake's under suspicion, that's all. No point getting riled up."

"Why did you send Albert and Commodore out to search my lean-to?"

"Looking for evidence."

Cradling Katie Marie in her arms, Elise came up behind Callie. Grace on one side of her, the new resident on the other. The newcomer glanced at him, her eyes laden with guilt, but quickly looked away. He hadn't seen the woman take anything, but he had a feeling in his gut she'd taken that money. As soon as he could, he'd pull her aside and make her see the path she headed down was wrong.

Mildred came next, slower but no less spirited, if those narrowed eyes fixed on the sheriff meant anything. "Why's Jake in custody, Hal?"

"It's not exactly custody, Mildred. We're just talking."

"No need to spend the night behind bars to talk." She folded her arms. "What evidence do you have?"

"Two witnesses saw Smith leave the store in a hurry."

Callie huffed. "A guilty man wouldn't draw attention to himself. Did you ask Jacob why he left?"

"Claims he noticed something that made him suspicious, but can't or won't say what it was."

Mildred harrumphed. "Then we owe Jake our thanks."

The sheriff snorted. "Mildred, a toddler could come up with a better excuse."

"Hal Frederick, I diapered you more than once. Don't go getting uppity with me."

Elise giggled. "You're outnumbered, Sheriff."

Frederick's gaze swept the ladies, every one of them glaring at him. "You all need to settle down."

These women had come to Jake's defense. He hoped he wouldn't make a fool of himself and cry. But he didn't like them worrying. "Don't fret. God will take care of it."

Callie leaned toward him. "Did I hear you right?"

He shot her a smile. A smile she returned.

The sheriff motioned Jake to his feet. "Come with me. You're staying in that cell for as long as it takes to get to the truth."

"I'm the one you want," a soft voice said behind him.

Jake spun around to the speaker, the newcomer he'd seen in the store.

Callie put an arm around the girl. "Joanna, what are you saying?"

"I took the money."

The room turned silent.

Joanna reached inside the cloak she wore, odd for a warm spring day, and pulled out a wad of bills, shoving them into the sheriff's hands. "It's all there, except for the price of a bowl of soup and a glass of milk. I'm sorry." She laid an arm over the swell of her baby. "I was starving. The cash register drawer was open and I took it."

Jake took Joanna's hand. "I understand desperation, being alone in the world with no one to turn to." He glanced at the sheriff. "Ever known hunger, Sheriff? Ever seen it drive people to desperation?"

"Reckon I have."

"The waitress at the café told me about the home for unwed mothers, where it was. Callie took me in without one question. She fed me, gave me a bed to sleep in. If I'd known people like Callie Mitchell existed, I never would've done something so desperate. So wrong." Tears spilled down Joanna's face. "I was afraid to admit I took it. Afraid I'd have my baby in jail and they'd take it away." She sobbed. "But I couldn't let someone else take the blame."

Grace moved to her side. Soon all the women surrounded her.

Jake met the sheriff's eyes. "I'll pay the rest."

The sheriff nodded at Jake, his face clearing. "Case closed. You're both free to go. Smith, with my apology."

A surge of joy shot through Jake. *Thank You, God.*

Callie smiled. "God did take care of it."

Jake wanted to tell Callie he loved her. But he couldn't until he'd told her about his newfound faith. He'd taken a long time to see that when a man didn't walk with God, he wasn't much of a man. At least not the kind of man God intended.

And he understood why. Faith gave believers more than a clean slate. It also gave them strength, wisdom, purpose.

His new purpose would be a legacy to his mother. Even if the only part Callie allowed him to play in helping unwed mothers was signing over his mother's house.

Pastor Steele appeared at the door.

Callie gasped. "Oh, goodness, with everything that's happened, I forgot all about our meeting this morning."

"You folks feel free to come, too," Pastor Steele said. "We'll be talking about ways to help Refuge of Redeeming Love."

As Jake strode beside Callie on the way to the church, others questioned where they were headed, then joined the group until a crowd had formed. His imprisonment and the confession of the hungry newcomer swept through the throng. Some exchanged puzzled glances, more expressed doubts, a few grumbled about the riffraff invading the town. Obviously, everyone had an opinion and wanted their say. This was turning into a three-ring circus with Pastor Steele as the ringmaster.

Before they reached the church, Jake wanted Callie to know what had transpired in that cell last night. "I need to talk to you." He pulled her to the side, under the canopy of maples.

Off to their right, a family of ducks climbed out of the brook running alongside the town. Bringing up the rear, the last duckling struggled to keep up. So like Jake, the last one to find his way. "Callie, you may have already guessed from what I said at the jail, but I wanted to tell you straight out. I've found God."

A smile bloomed on her face. "Oh, Jacob. I thought you looked different. Happier than I'd ever seen you."

Dare he hope she cared? That the mixup over the house hadn't ruined his chance with her? Or was she just overjoyed that he'd found God, as she would for any nonbeliever?

"I've been reading the Bible, the prophecy, the promises fulfilled in the baby and sealed on the cross. But it all had seemed…illogical. Last night, in that cell, I had nowhere to turn. Callie…God showed up." He swallowed, fought for control. "I wasn't alone in that cell. I heard His voice. Not an audible voice but unmistakable, as clear as if He stood beside me."

Tears spilled down Callie's cheeks. She took his hands in hers, hanging on as if her life depended on it. Or knew his did.

"I put control of my life in God's hands." He grinned, wanted to shout from the rooftops. "And look, I'm free. Free from jail. Free from my past. Free from my sins."

God had answered Callie's prayers. She threw her arm around Jacob's waist and gave him a hug. "I'm so happy I could burst!"

"No more than I. I don't understand why the existence of God could seem irrational one minute and reasonable the next, but that's what happened."

"You opened your hardened heart, Jacob. That made all the difference."

"I credit you for the example of your life. For caring about where I spent eternity. I can never thank you enough."

Smiling, he took her hand and together they walked the short distance to the church and joined the others gathered out front. Pastor Steele stood on the steps, about to go in.

Across the way the family of ducks she and Jacob had

seen earlier marched across the road, the hen in the lead, the babies in a straight line behind her, the drake bringing up the rear. But one duckling meandered alone, searching for something in the grass.

"Let's wait," Pastor Steele said, then stepped into the street and slowed traffic. "Make sure the ducks make it to the other side."

A buggy and wagon slowed for the parade of ducks, as the mother duckling led her babies across. The last duckling remained on the other side. The mother halted in the middle of the road and waited as the drake turned back and rounded up the duckling, shepherding it back in line. Once he waddled to the end, the mother moved ahead.

Pastor Steele's gaze swept the crowd. "I don't know about the rest of you, but those ducks are a lesson to me. They know by instinct what we need to learn—each one in God's family is important. We need to make sure none are lost. And when they wander, or lose their way, as that duckling did, we're to urge them to return and welcome them in to the family."

The parade of ducks ended at a patch of ground on the side of the church. They spread out, foraging for food as traffic resumed on the street. Though Pastor Steele didn't mention the unwed mothers, for Callie his meaning was clear. Folks remained motionless, staring at those ducklings milling around on the carpet of grass.

"Looks like they enjoy a fellowship dinner as much as I do," Pastor Steele said with a grin.

"Pastor, what if that duckling was rebelling? Left his family on purpose?" someone called from the back.

"We don't know why that duckling fell behind. Perhaps he was slower. Perhaps he was rebellious. Or maybe only distracted, but the mother duck's decision to wait wasn't based on the duckling's behavior. Her decision was based on love, wanting none of her family to be lost."

No one said anything for a moment, not even the naysayer. But within minutes, people started coming up to Callie, offering to help.

Hal removed his hat and put in the first dollars. "Reckon you could use some money to make a go of the place, Callie." Loretta joined her husband and they passed the hat through the crowd until it all but overflowed with money.

Off to the side, Commodore stared at those ducks. How long had he been standing there? He moved toward the church steps with slow, measured steps.

Hal stopped his progress. "Commodore, Jake didn't take the money. Here's what was missing." He pulled the bills from his pocket and handed them to Commodore.

Like it burned his fingers, Commodore dropped the money in the hat. "These young women need it way more than I do."

Her mouth gaping, Callie whirled toward Jacob. She couldn't remember the last time she'd been speechless.

Commodore stepped past the sheriff and stopped in front of his wife. "A man can live his life with regrets. Regrets that eat him up inside. It's rare when that man gets a chance to make things right."

What was this about? The wobble in Commodore's voice alarmed Callie.

"But I have that chance today. At least, I hope I do." He took his wife's hand. "Long before I knew you, Dorothy, I fell in love with a young woman. And she fell in love with me. I hope it doesn't hurt you to hear that."

Dorothy never took her eyes off her husband. "No, that was a long time ago."

"The girl's father refused to let us marry. He said I wasn't good enough for his daughter." His eyes turned soft. "She saw it differently." He gave a sad smile. "I'm not sure what she saw in me. But she'd be disappointed in the man I've become. I've not been a good husband to you. I apologize for that."

Tears welled in Dorothy's eyes but she didn't speak. Or couldn't.

"This young girl and I... We, ah, well. We got in a family way. Her name was Irene Squier."

Commodore's words, words Jake could barely comprehend, bombarded his brain, turning it to mush. He tightened his grip on Callie's hand. She leaned into him, holding him steady.

Around him, people gasped and whispered.

Commodore looked at his wife, then swept his gaze over the bystanders. "Jake's name isn't Smith. His real name's Jacob Mitchell."

Dorothy grabbed her husband's arm. "Jake's your son?"

Commodore nodded then turned to Jake. "You resented my attitude toward that house of Callie's. It's a constant reminder of heartache. Losing Martin. Failing Irene. Failing our boy all these years." Tears welled in his eyes. "I'm ashamed of my spinelessness."

Dorothy wept openly. "Why didn't you tell me? We could've talked about it. Worked it out."

"Guess that would be fear. Fear you'd hate me for what I'd done. I'm sorry. So sorry about all of it."

Jake fought the resentment flaring up inside him. This man who had hounded him from the first moment he'd arrived in town, was his father? "You've known who I was all this time?"

"I had no idea who you were—until I found those

postcards in the lean-to." Commodore shook his head. "They weren't from your mother, Jake."

Jake closed his eyes and prayed for strength as an image of a petite young woman with dark hair filled his mind.

"I'm sorry, so very sorry about…your mom, about everything. I—" Commodore looked away, as if unable to meet Jake's gaze. "I wrote and mailed those postcards, signed them 'Your mother.'" He scrubbed a hand over his brimming eyes. "I thought that's what she'd want me to do."

Jake snorted. Why not admit that he'd sent them to ease his guilt?

Sheriff Frederick handed Callie his money-filled hat. "If you sent those postcards, Commodore, why didn't you recognize Jake's name?"

Wasn't that just like a lawman, always investigating? "He sent those postcards to Jacob, in care of the orphanage. No last name," Jake ground out.

"But surely other boys named Jacob resided in that home."

Jake sighed. "Not with that same birthdate."

Her eyes laden with sympathy, Loretta put an arm around him and Callie. "I knew your mother, Jake, and I see her in you. She'd be proud of the man you are."

Those simple words brought Jake comfort. "I'd like to talk to you about her."

"I'd like that, too."

Loretta faced Callie. "I'm sorry. Sorry for fighting the unwed mothers' home when underneath I knew what you wanted to do was right." She sighed. "I let fear control me. Well, no more. I've got some talking to do to Tillie Sunderland, too. It's time to heal wounds, to start anew." She lifted a hand. "I hope you will forgive me."

Tears flooding her eyes, Callie drew Loretta into a hug. "Of course I forgive you. Thank you."

Smiling, Loretta headed off, no doubt in search of Mrs. Sunderland.

On shaky legs, Commodore moved closer. He appeared to have aged overnight. "Irene loved you, Jake. The minute she knew…she wanted you. We planned to get married." Tears filled his eyes. "But her father moved her out of town the night we told them about the baby. I didn't know where they took her."

"That's terrible," someone said.

And it was. Jake looked at Elise, surrounded by her parents, holding little Katie Marie, then on to Grace and Joanna, all of them with tears running down their faces.

A couple of women came up and gathered Joanna and Grace in their arms. Jake's heart stuttered in his chest. One of those ladies was Mrs. Sunderland. Maybe something good had come from this after all.

Commodore grabbed a handkerchief from his pocket and handed it to Dorothy, then tucked her in his arms. "In early May, I got a letter from Irene, telling me she loved me. How much she loved our baby, who was soon to be born. She promised that once she turned eighteen, we'd be together.

"I held on to that. I'd make something of myself, show her father I wasn't some riffraff from the wrong side of the tracks." His voice broke. "A few weeks later, I got another letter, this one from the senator. Irene died in childbirth, he said. He'd put the baby, a boy she'd planned to name Jacob, in an orphanage. He told me where I could find him if I wanted to claim the baby"

Like a knife wound to his gut, it stabbed at Jake that his mother's parents hadn't wanted him, most likely blamed him for their daughter's death. Now they were gone, too.

His face contorted with emotion, Commodore turned to Jake. "I went to that orphanage. Saw you lying in that bed, so tiny and helpless. You frightened me. I didn't have money, any means of caring for you. So I walked away." He sobbed. "By the time I opened the store and had the means to care for a child, I'd met Dorothy." He turned to face his wife. "I wasn't sure how the scandal would impact our marriage. I couldn't bear to lose another woman I loved… so I went on denying my son's existence." A sob. "I've wondered if Martin's fall from the roof of that house was my punishment for not claiming my firstborn."

Pastor Steele shook his head. "God wouldn't kill your son to punish you."

Dorothy put her arm around Commodore. "You've made some big mistakes. Mistakes that have shaped our lives. At least now I understand that wall between us, a wall I could never penetrate, but I never stopped loving you."

"I love you, dear wife." Commodore's face crumpled as he turned to Jake. "I know you despise me and I don't blame you." He turned to walk away. "I don't deserve your forgiveness."

All eyes turned on Jake. He glanced at Elise. Her father, a stubborn man, had hurt her time and again. Yet, Elise had forgiven him. And because of that forgiveness, look what they had.

A family.

Jake knew he should be angry, but he couldn't find any other emotion except one. Forgiveness.

The crowd had grown silent. People stood with heads hanging, eyes downcast, several were crying.

Jake lifted a hand and stopped Commodore as he and Dorothy started to walk away, looking deep into his father's eyes. "I forgive you."

His expression blank, as if Jake's words hadn't sunk in, Commodore sputtered something garbled that Jake couldn't make out. Then, weeping, he swayed and fell into Jake's arms.

Something frozen, inside Jake since he was a boy of seven, softened, then melted then slipped away. He had a father. Not a perfect man, but then who was? In each other's arms, they wept for lost time and for Irene who somehow seemed to be part of the wonder of that moment.

Dorothy patted her husband's back. "We lost one son, but God granted you another chance with Jake."

Swiping at his tears, Commodore straightened. "Will you stay in town, Jake, and give me time to know you?"

"I'll stay if I can spend it with Callie." He took her hands in his. "The house is yours. I have no intention of taking it. I know I've hurt you. For that I'm sorry." Though the prospect of losing Callie slashed at his heart, he forced out the words he had to say, "I'll move on if that's what you want. All you have to do is say the word."

Looking into those green eyes filled with such hope but also with dread, Callie's eyes glistened. Why had she ever believed Jacob was capable of treachery?

The answer came, not an easy one. She'd let her marriage to Martin color her view of Jacob. Unable to bear another disappointment, unable to handle more hurt piled on the pain of her past, for surely another loss would destroy her, she'd refused to see Jacob with unbiased eyes.

She'd refused to trust the steps toward God she'd seen him take. She'd refused to trust his love, yet his actions made that love unmistakable. Her lack of trust made it easy to believe that he'd rip the home she loved from under her.

Her faith might've kept her strong, but she hadn't forgiven, not really. She'd held on to her anger at Martin, at Commodore, and let that determine who she was, the

actions she took, and the things she believed. Fear of failing in another marriage had kept her heart closed.

Yet Jacob, a brand-new believer, just taught her what
genuine forgiveness looked like when he'd taken the man
who'd denied his fatherhood and badgered Jacob at every
turn into his arms and wept with him.

"Oh, Jacob, I'm sorry. I'm the one who hurt you. I
didn't trust who you were when you were exactly as you
appeared—a man I can respect." She raised a palm to his
jaw. "If you'll forgive me, I'm ready to take a chance on
love again."

He wrapped Callie in those strong arms of his. "You're
the woman I want to be my wife." Then he opened his arms
wider to include Commodore and Dorothy—his parents—
and Grace and Joanna as they stepped close and joined an
ever-widening circle of love, of family. Clearly showing by
his actions that he would not only love her, he'd share her
mission to care for unwed mothers.

Mrs. Sunderland came forward. "If folks weren't so fast
to judge, perhaps Commodore would've stepped up and
raised his son." She glanced over at Pastor Steele. "I've
learned a lesson today. A lesson I won't forget."

Glancing at Callie, eyes wet and apologetic, Loretta
patted Mrs. Sunderland's back. "We'll show these young
women God's love."

Mildred wiggled into the circle. "And to show Jake how
much I respect his skills, what he's made of himself, I want
him to remodel my home, shed its years and purpose, turn
it into Peaceful's Historical Museum. I've got enough stuff
to fill it," she said with a laugh, then offered her hand. "I'm
your first client in that business you plan to start."

Jake took her hand. "It's a deal. If you'll keep us stocked
in gingerbread boy cookies."

Mildred chuckled. "I'll save the smiles till last."

"I don't need any smile but Callie's." Jake squeezed Callie's hand and gazed into her eyes with such intensity that the crowd faded, and all she could see was the man. A man who cherished family and commitment, a man of faith and integrity, a man she could trust.

"I've repaired your home, but I want more than a business arrangement with you, more than three meals a day and a roof over my head. I love you, Callie Mitchell."

At his declaration, the lonely shell surrounding her spirit shattered, releasing her from the pain of her past. "Jacob Squier Mitchell, I love you. You've repaired more than my home." Tears stung her eyes. "You've repaired my heart."

"As you have mine. I've wanted a family all my life. I love that baby you're carrying. I want to be more than an uncle to him. I want to be a father. We'll start that family with three. Add Commodore and Dorothy, Mildred here and the ladies of Redeeming Love and their babies—" He laughed. "I'm losing count. But we've got plenty of love and that big old Victorian."

Jacob shared her dream, wanted it as much as she did. He would be a wonderful father, a considerate husband. What had she ever done to deserve this man?

He dropped to one knee. "Callie, will you be my wife?"

With her heart overflowing with peace and love, knowing God had brought exactly the right man into her life that day when a drifter had shown up on her porch, and now took residence in her heart, Callie smiled down at him. "My answer is yes. I want to marry you, Jacob, have a family with you." He rose and tugged her into his arms, arms that felt like home. "No other man will do."

* * * * *

Dear Reader,

Thank you for choosing *Wanted: A Family*. I hope you enjoyed Callie and Jake's story. This book means a great deal to me personally. One glance in the mirror of my soul confirms how often I fail in my Christian walk. I'm thankful every day for God's perfect grace in the person of Jesus Christ and what He did for me. Sadly, we know people have hurt or been hurt by judgment. When we extend grace to others, as Callie and Jake did in this story, we're not condoning the sin. We're forgiving the sinner as God's Word commands.

I love to hear from readers. Write me at Steeple Hill Books, 233 Broadway, Suite 1001, New York, New York 10279. Or email me through my website, www.janetdean.net. Visit my blog at www.janetdean.blogspot.com and my group blog www.seekerville.blogspot.com.

God bless you,

Janet Dean

QUESTIONS FOR DISCUSSION

1. Callie felt responsible for her husband's death. Did you understand her guilt? Was her view logical?

2. Commodore Mitchell, Callie's father-in-law, carried a heavy burden of guilt. How did he handle his mistakes? What impact did his past have on others?

3. Did you understand Callie's passion for unwed mothers as well as the town's resistance? What did Callie's friends and church members fear? Were those fears justified? Should we allow fear to guide our decisions?

4. Jake's experiences in his past shut him off from others, including God. He trusted no one, relying only on himself. Did you understand his reasoning? How did his self-imposed isolation impact his relationship with Callie?

5. In Callie, Jake sees a woman who doesn't let hardships in her past dictate her choices today. How is she able to overcome those hardships?

6. Callie senses that Jake is hiding something. Why is she especially sensitive about his lack of openness?

7. When opposition to the unwed mothers' home escalates, who and what does Callie turn to for wisdom?

8. How do the unwed mothers in the story affect Jake and his attitude about his birth mother?

9. Why does Callie believe Jake schemed to bring about ownership of her house? What is behind her suspicion?

10. Is it believable to you that Pastor Steele was able to teach an important biblical truth by using God's creatures? Why?

11. When Commodore reveals Jake's parentage, how is Jake able to forgive his father for denying him? What has Jake learned? How did his newfound faith in God enable Jake to love and be loved by Callie?

HISTORICAL

TITLES AVAILABLE NEXT MONTH

Available April 12, 2011

YUKON WEDDING
Alaskan Brides
Allie Pleiter

THE LAWMAN CLAIMS HIS BRIDE
Charity House
Renee Ryan

AT THE CAPTAIN'S COMMAND
Louise M. Gouge

THE SHERIFF'S SWEETHEART
Brides of Simpson Creek
Laurie Kingery

REQUEST YOUR FREE BOOKS!

2 FREE INSPIRATIONAL NOVELS
PLUS 2
FREE
MYSTERY GIFTS

Love Inspired

HISTORICAL
INSPIRATIONAL HISTORICAL ROMANCE

YES! Please send me 2 FREE Love Inspired® Historical novels and my 2 FREE mystery gifts (gifts are worth about $10). After receiving them, if I don't wish to receive any more books, I can return the shipping statement marked "cancel". If I don't cancel, I will receive 4 brand-new novels every month and be billed just $4.24 per book in the U.S. or $4.74 per book in Canada. That's a saving of at least 23% off the cover price. It's quite a bargain! Shipping and handling is just 50¢ per book in the U.S. and 75¢ per book in Canada.* I understand that accepting the 2 free books and gifts places me under no obligation to buy anything. I can always return a shipment and cancel at any time. Even if I never buy another book, the two free books and gifts are mine to keep forever.

102/302 IDN FDCH

Name	(PLEASE PRINT)

Address	Apt. #

City	State/Prov.	Zip/Postal Code

Signature (if under 18, a parent or guardian must sign)

Mail to the **Reader Service:**
IN U.S.A.: P.O. Box 1867, Buffalo, NY 14240-1867
IN CANADA: P.O. Box 609, Fort Erie, Ontario L2A 5X3

Not valid for current subscribers to Love Inspired Historical books.

Want to try two free books from another series?
Call 1-800-873-8635 or visit www.ReaderService.com.

* Terms and prices subject to change without notice. Prices do not include applicable taxes. Sales tax applicable in N.Y. Canadian residents will be charged applicable taxes. Offer not valid in Quebec. This offer is limited to one order per household. All orders subject to credit approval. Credit or debit balances in a customer's account(s) may be offset by any other outstanding balance owed by or to the customer. Please allow 4 to 6 weeks for delivery. Offer available while quantities last.

Your Privacy—The Reader Service is committed to protecting your privacy. Our Privacy Policy is available online at www.ReaderService.com or upon request from the Reader Service.

We make a portion of our mailing list available to reputable third parties that offer products we believe may interest you. If you prefer that we not exchange your name with third parties, or if you wish to clarify or modify your communication preferences, please visit us at www.ReaderService.com/consumerschoice or write to us at Reader Service Preference Service, P.O. Box 9062, Buffalo, NY 14269. Include your complete name and address.

*When David Foster comes across an unconscious woman
on his friends' doorstep, she evokes his natural born
instinct to take care of her.*

*Read on for a sneak peek of A BABY BY EASTER
by Lois Richer, available April, only from Love Inspired.*

"You could marry Davy, Susannah. He would look after
you. He looks after me." Darla's bright voice dropped. "He
had a girlfriend. They were going to get married, but she
didn't want me. She wanted Davy to send me away."

David almost groaned. How had his sister found out?
He'd been so careful—

"I'm sure your brother is very nice, Darla. And I'm glad
he's taking care of you. But I don't want to marry him. I
don't want to marry anyone," Susannah said. "I only came
to Connie's to see if I could stay here for a while."

"But Davy needs someone to love him. Somebody else
but me." Darla's face crumpled, the way it always did before she lost her temper. David was about to step forward
when Susannah reached out and hugged his sister.

"Thank you for offering, Darla. You're very generous. I
think your brother is lucky to have you love him." Susannah
brushed the bangs from Darla's sad face. "If I end up staying with Connie, I promise I'll see you lots. We could go to
that playground you talked about."

Susannah's foster sister Connie breezed into the room.
"I'm so glad to see you, Suze. But you're ill." She leaned
back to study the circles of red now dotting Susannah's
cheeks. "You're very pale. I think you need to see a doctor."

"I'm pregnant." The words burst out of Susannah in a
rush. Then she lifted her head and looked David straight in
the eye, as if awaiting his condemnation.

But it wasn't condemnation David felt. It was hurt. He'd prayed so long, so hard, for a family, a wife, a child. And he'd lost all chance of that—not once, but twice.

How could God deny him the longing of his heart, yet give this ill woman a child she was in no way prepared to care for?

Although David has given up on his dream of having a family, will he offer to help Susannah in her time of need? Find out in A BABY BY EASTER, available April, only from Love Inspired.

SHLIEXP0411R

Love Inspired
SUSPENSE
RIVETING INSPIRATIONAL ROMANCE

TEXAS RANGER JUSTICE

Keeping the Lone Star State safe

Follow the men and women of the Texas Rangers,
as they risk their lives to help save others, with

DAUGHTER OF TEXAS
by **Terri Reed**
January 2011

BODY OF EVIDENCE
by **Lenora Worth**
February 2011

FACE OF DANGER
by **Valerie Hansen**
March 2011

TRAIL OF LIES
by **Margaret Daley**
April 2011

THREAT OF EXPOSURE
by **Lynette Eason**
May 2011

OUT OF TIME
by **Shirlee McCoy**
June 2011

*Available wherever
books are sold.*

Steeple
Hill®

www.SteepleHill.com

LISCONT11IBC

ISBN-13:978-0-373-82862-3

Shelter Of Hope

The ramshackle Victorian house is all that widowed mother-to-be Callie Mitchell has left. But she's *going* to make that house into a true home—a home where she and her baby will be safe and happy…and where women in need can find refuge. And if that means trusting stranger Jacob Smith to help with the repairs, then so be it.

Jacob came to town with a handful of old postcards and one goal in mind—to find the mother who'd abandoned him years before. He never planned to stay…and he certainly never planned to care for Callie. Yet as they rebuild the house together, Jacob and Callie also build the *family* they've always wanted.

$5.50 U.S./$6.50 CAN.

ISBN-13:978-0-373-82862-3

50550

9 780373 828623

EAN

INSPIRATIONAL

a LOVE INSPIRED®
HISTORICAL book from

HARLEQUIN

www.eHarlequin.com